deadly
DECEIT

NEW YORK CITY SYNDICATE
BOOK 1

Settle Myer (signature)

SETTLE MYER

Book Cover by Y'all That Graphic

Edited by Owl Eyes Proofs & Edits

Formatted by Settle Myer using Atticus & Canva

Table of Contents

Author's Note

Deadly Deceit is the first book in a standalone duet. It's a dark cozy romance meaning the romance is sweet... but the story includes dark themes.

In this book you will find killing for pay, murder, the death of a parent, violence (stabbing, shooting, physical violence), mentions of child abuse, mentions of rape, mentions of human trafficking, suicidal thoughts, minor drug use, stalking, torture (not between main characters), blood play, profanity, graphic sex including pegging, anal play, degradation, slapping (during sex), praise, voyeurism, and a MFM scene.

If you have a specific trigger, please reach out to the author.

Please also be aware: this story is set in New York City and includes both real and made up locations. One more thing: I'm an 80s baby and the nickname Rainbow Bright mentioned in this book is play off the popular television series Rainbow Brite. So, yes, I know it's not spelled the same way. I did that on purpose.

Dedication

To the people tired of always putting on a mask of happiness when life is kicking your ass: save your smiles. Embrace your darkness

PLAYLIST

CAN YOU FEEL MY HEART – BRING ME THE HORIZON

CHOKEHOLD – SLEEP TOKEN

BLEED ME DRY – MEMPHIS MAY FIRE

WICKED WAYS – HALESTORM

THE DEATH OF PEACE OF MIND – BAD OMENS

UNBREAKABLE – NEW YEARS DAY

LEARNING TO SURVIVE – WE CAME AS ROMANS

THE SUMMONING – SLEEP TOKEN

SILENCE – MARSHMALLOW, KHALID

LOLLIPOP – FRAMING HANLEY

HEADS WILL ROLL – YEAH YEAH YEAHS

UNTIL THE DAY I DIE – STORY OF THE YEAR

I'M NOT OKAY (I PROMISE) – MY CHEMICAL ROMANCE

I STAND ALONE – GODSMACK

GREAT FAIRY FOUNTAIN (FROM "THE
LEGEND OF ZELDA") [PIANO ETUDE] – ERIK CORRELL

SCAN TO LISTEN

Chapter 1

Delancy

The kills become easier.

Every death by my hands adds a layer of numbness, sending me deeper into a pit where humanity can't survive.

I was twelve years old when I took my first life. I was ordered to kill or be killed. It was a lie. I was going to die no matter what.

When I woke up from a coma a week later, hooked up to machines and pain ricocheting throughout my body from being stabbed and left for dead, I shut down.

No words. No emotions. Nothing.

I was asked about what happened. About the men responsible. Paper was shoved in my face trying to get me to write it down since I refused to speak. My father tried to beat the answers out of me, leaving me with bruises and a busted lip that never healed properly.

Still, I did nothing.

Specialists were brought in, one after another, until I was finally diagnosed with traumatic mutism. My father sent me away to a youth psychiatric hospital because he didn't want to deal with a *useless child*; something he said to my face before backhanding me across the cheek.

The ring he wore on his middle finger cut my skin deep, resulting in another scar to remember him by.

I spent the first year in that hospital wishing I were dead. I'd lay in bed for hours—the nightmares keeping me awake—thinking about all the ways I could kill myself. Not that I would have been able to follow through in that fucking place where cameras watched your every move and nurses checked in on you every fifteen minutes.

With no options to leave this world, I turned my dark thoughts on the men who forced me to kill. On my father who blamed me for my mother's death. On what he did to my brother who tried to protect me from his abuse but got similar bruises and scars.

Suddenly I had something to live for: Vengeance.

I took my medications and went to my therapy sessions. After a few years, I started speaking again. I was the perfect patient up until my eighteenth birthday when I was released.

My brother picked me up. On the drive home, he told me our father had fallen ill and went to die in some hospice in Upstate New York.

Not even a goodbye.

Good riddance.

It's not like he would have asked me about that night again. He eventually found out after beating it out of my brother—the only person I told before shutting down.

What happened to me twenty years ago was the catalyst to who I am today.

A hitman.

I kill to feed my demons. I kill to rid the world of monsters like me.

I'm one of the best in the industry aside from the one called Colpa Sicario. A person I've been trying to track down since they suddenly entered the game five years ago. I don't even know if they're a man or woman or nonbinary. But one thing is clear: I need to find them. I want to *kill* them. Or maybe we'll hate fuck each other before fighting to the death.

I'm known as the Marionette because I pull my strings and control the murder scene. I frame the dead as if they're dolls... my puppets... staging them to make the death appear accidental. If I'm lucky, I can pin the kill on another person.

The Marionette.

I hate that fucking name.

I hate the label because I was never meant to play God.

When I was ten, I wanted to be a musician because my mother taught me how to play the piano. I was good at it too.

At age eleven, I wanted to be a firefighter because the house across the street went up in flames and the firefighters let me climb on their truck.

On my twelfth birthday, I wanted a baseball themed party. My mother hung decorations around the house: streamers with baseball gloves on them, cut-out paper baseball bats, and banners with baseballs. We had concession inspired snacks like Cracker Jacks, nachos, and hot dogs.

When I was twelve, I wanted to be a professional baseball player.

By the end of the night, whatever dreams I had of a normal future had turned into nightmares. I suppose I never would have had a normal life because of the family I was born into.

Instead, I became a monster. The darkness followed me, haunted me, and begged me to seek vengeance.

It's been twenty years, and my body count has reached triple digits. I'm not quitting until I kill the man responsible for the day I nearly died.

The day my mother was murdered.

I'm not picky when it comes to the type of hit jobs I take. I couldn't care less why someone wants another person dead. But my favorite kills are the liars, cheaters, abusers, and rapists.

The man on the bed who I'm currently straddling is many of those things.

The knife sinks into his chest and his hazel eyes widen. He frantically scratches at my gloved hands as blood pours from the wound and out of his mouth. I watch the life drain from his panicked face, his hands weakening and dropping to his sides.

Finally.

This assignment was bloodier than I'd like. I prefer poisons. They're effective and can sometimes be blamed on an undiagnosed medical condition. But I do what the job entails, and the client wanted this man to die a humiliating death.

It took me months to plan it all out.

Howard Marks, fifty-five years old, accused fraudster who swindled millions out of the rich and famous. The person who hired me was desperate. He tripled his offer, more than I'd ever been paid to kill, because no one would take the job. Howard is a powerful man. He's famous. His face is always on some news program talking about who the fuck cares. No one wanted the job because high-profile killings are the hardest to do discreetly. His death will be plastered across the media.

Not only did Howard Marks scam my client out of five million dollars, but the creep also fucked my client's twenty-year-old daughter... who's now pregnant.

Which is why I have Howard's dick in a jar.

It's not the first time a client wanted a souvenir. It's also not the first time I've cut off a dick. Howard's cock is a bonus that I'm getting paid extra to retrieve.

The dick was the first to go. All three inches of it. How this twenty-year-old woman was wooed by this schmuck, I'll never know. It wasn't about the money. Her father has enough of it. Maybe she fucked Howard to spite dear old daddy.

While Howard slowly bled out from the cut off appendage, I played a video message from my client. I didn't pay much attention. I never do. It's usually the same. "You wronged me. You must die." My client also managed to get Howard's will amended to leave part of his fortune to the young woman he got pregnant and her unborn child.

I can't even think about the legal shit storm this presents. Surely this will be contested by his two adult children. Instead of wondering about this asshole's family drama, I begin the setup.

The Marionette at work.

I grab Howard's passed out wife from the closet and set her on the floor, leaning her against the wall across from the bed. Next, I place the gun—which I found in Howard's safe—in her hand and raise the barrel to her head. I squeeze the trigger and blood splatters on the wall and across a copy of the will I put on the bedside table.

When police arrive, they'll find the wife's fingerprints on the knife in his chest, a cut off dick in her hand—one from a John Doe, given to me by my contact at the morgue since the client wants Howard's dick—and text messages on Howard's phone from his wife, accusing him of cheating and writing her out of the will.

They'll assume she took her own life after killing Howard for having an affair.

The wife is just as vile. She knew what her husband was doing. She spent the money he stole. The couple also owns dozens of nightclubs across the country that are hubs for sex trafficking. Something the police will uncover while investigating this murder/suicide.

Once the scene is set, I triple check to make sure I don't leave any evidence behind. I change out of my blood splattered clothes, stuffing the soiled ones in my backpack before slipping out of the penthouse. I take the stairwell down to a back entrance to stay out of sight. I'd hate to get caught after all that work. Not to mention I have a dick in a jar inside my backpack. That one would be hard to explain.

Surveillance cameras are installed on every floor, including the stairwell. I don't know shit about technology. I hate texting and using the Internet. Social media confuses the fuck out of me, and I only use burner phones to communicate with my brother and to accept hit jobs. Which is why I hired my hacker buddy to take care of the camera situation.

He accessed the building's security system and looped the camera feeds for a few hours while I completed the assignment.

I pause just outside the building to scan the area. During the day, the sidewalks would be crowded with people rushing to their jobs, cars would be bumper to bumper on the street, and horns would be honking for no fucking reason. But it's four in the morning and the night is quiet. Only the drumming of my heart, racing with adrenaline and paranoia, can be heard.

Killing? That's easy. Avoiding getting caught during the getaway is what racks my nerves.

I walk down the block, turn right, then left and right again before coming up on the street where I parked my motorcycle. Retrieving my helmet from the case, I put it on and start up the roaring engine to get the fuck out of here.

The assignment was on Billionaires' Row on the southern end of Central Park in Manhattan. That's another thing. Assignments on the island are always riskier. Manhattan has too many people. Too many eyes. Too many chances to get caught, which is why I plan my kills late at night.

I weave in and out of traffic and cross the Queensboro Bridge into Astoria.

Despite having millions of dollars to my name—saved in an offshore, untraceable account—I rent cheap apartments in all five boroughs that I use as safe houses where I can hide in plain sight. Living a flashy lifestyle would make it easier for my enemies to find me.

The apartment I leased in Astoria is small, which is fine because I'm rarely there. Or, at least, that was the plan. Up until two months ago, I only used it for sleep, showers, and occasionally to fuck. I don't have sex often. Only when my hand is no longer enough to satiate my needs.

I take out my keys to unlock my door and pause at my neighbor's muffled giggles.

Fuck me.

Noah is entertaining again.

Noah McAllister. Thirty-one years old. Five foot ten. Brown eyes. Hair color unknown because it's always dyed various shades of the rainbow.

This month, it's purple.

She's insufferable. She's a bartender at some bar on the east side of Manhattan, which means she comes home at five in the morning after her shift, making noise in her kitchen, or fucking whoever she picked up at work.

The walls between our apartments are paper thin. I hear *everything*. Every cough, every laugh, every godforsaken moan.

She's a faker. I know they can't please her because the moment they leave, the sound of her vibrator pierces through the wall and overtakes the quiet of my apartment.

Her toys make her come and a part of me wants to barge into her place and show her what good sex can be like.

I shake the thought from my head. I cannot get involved with my neighbor. Besides, we can't stand each other. In fact, I've considered killing her. I've broken into her apartment a few times and held a knife to her neck while she slept. Then my eyes would wander over her full body—she sleeps naked quite often—and my dick would convince me to keep her alive.

I've been suffering since the day she moved in.

She stays up late, and I wake up early. She bangs on her wall, yelling at me to turn down the music I blast while cleaning or working out or fucking my hand because I can't stop thinking about Noah's plump ass and plentiful curves. Her pouty lips, soft stomach, and melon sized tits that she pushes out every time she sees me.

I remember the first time we met not long after she moved in two months ago. I'd woken her up hours after she returned home from what must have been a busy shift. She beat on my door, and I opened it to find Noah with her pink hair piled in a messy bun on the top of her head. She wore short shorts, a tight tank, and a sleep mask pushed up onto her forehead.

She was so pissed with the way her chest heaved with heavy, frustrated breaths.

I wasn't sure if it was because of her anger or her attraction to me. The way her pupils dilated as her eyes raked over my bare chest, down my abs, and to my gray sweats. Her nipples hardened in the thin tank the moment she saw the outline of my cock. I almost grabbed her right then and shoved my tongue into her mouth.

She might have let me.

I'm too exhausted tonight to mess with Noah and her latest conquest, so I hop in the shower and wash the blood and sweat off me. I put my soiled clothes in a trash bag to take to the incinerator at the funeral home down the block when I wake up.

It's nearly six in the morning when I finally lie down. Before falling asleep, I hear Noah moan and call out another man's name.

Jealousy burns in my chest. The only name she should be screaming is mine. The thought haunts my waking hours because I've never had such a visceral reaction to anyone. I don't let myself feel any emotion other than anger to fuel the kills. Noah gets under my skin because she's one of the few people who stands up to me and looks me in the eye.

Most people sense the evil woven within my DNA. Noah is oblivious to the dangerous man she constantly taunts. It's as if she feeds off my reactions like a vampire draining their victim of blood.

I've become obsessed with her. There's something about her that draws me in.

It's why I've been staying at the Astoria safe house more often.

My heavy eyelids fail to stay open, and the last thought before slipping into my nightmares is how beautiful Noah McAllister must look on the cusp of orgasm.

Chapter 2

Noah

Music blares from the other side of my bedroom wall, jolting me awake.

Fucking Delancy.

I groan and reach for my phone on the bedside table, squinting open an eye to check the time.

Nine a.m. Oh, great. He let me sleep in. Usually, he plays music at seven. Why the hell is he even up this early? I heard him come home at five this morning, stomping around as if that would have stopped me and my one-night stand from keeping quiet.

I glance over at the man next to me. His mouth hangs open, and he's snoring exceptionally loud. Maybe Del turned up the music to drown out Adam's chainsaw melodies.

Adam was a decent lover. He's a big man, plus-size like me. A tall teddy bear who I enjoyed cuddling with more than the actual sex, which is saying something since I hate cuddling.

I only cuddle when I'm drunk. Adam managed to catch me in a rare drunken state. I can hold my liquor, but last night I went overboard after my dad texted me saying he wanted to meet me for lunch this week. My fantastic night turned sour the minute I confirmed I'd be there.

He'd have sent his cronies and dragged me out of this damn apartment, kicking and screaming, if I had said no.

The music next door ends and a door slams shut—great, maybe Del left—and Adam wakes with one final, raucous snore. He sucks in a never-ending breath and stretches, letting out his best porn star moan before he turns his head to look at me.

A sleepy smile spreads across his face.

"Good morning, sexy."

A wave of cringyness washes over me. I never liked being called sexy. Pet names in general aren't my thing: baby, honey, sweetheart.

No. Ick.

I'm nobody's sweetheart.

"Good morning," I say.

No pet name for him.

Before Adam gets any ideas about kissing me with his morning breath or initiating morning sex, I sit up and get out of bed. I find a pair of shorts and a tank on my clean clothes chair and slip them on.

"I'd offer you coffee, but I ran out yesterday. Out of food too. I really need to go grocery shopping. Plus, I'm a horrible cook. I'd burn the eggs and toast, or you'd end up with food poisoning. So..."

My back is to him, but I can hear him moving around behind me.

"Yeah. No worries. I need to head out anyway. I'm meeting friends for brunch and after last night with all the sweating we did, I could really use a shower."

Cringe.

"Unless..." Crap. "I shower here, and you join me. Maybe we go for round two?"

Ugh. No. I hate shower sex. Not to mention my apartment's shower is too small to fit two big bodies inside.

"Tempting, but I also have brunch plans with my bestie in SoHo, so I need to get ready and head out."

I should feel bad. Aside from the pet name and the mention of sweaty sex, Adam's a sweet guy. Super sexy with potential to be a great fuck if I cared or had the time to instruct him.

But Adam's not *him.*

The golden retriever man shrugs and keeps getting dressed while I head to the bathroom to relieve myself. I brush my teeth and wash my face, removing the make-up I forgot to take off before bed. Once I pile my purple hair into a heap on the top of my head, I return to the living area of my large studio apartment where Adam stands in front of my bookcase looking at my photos.

"A traveler, huh?" He asks over his shoulder. He's holding a picture of me standing in front of the Eiffel Tower sparkling at night.

"I travel for work a lot."

He frowns and sets the frame down. "Aren't you a bartender?"

"It's for my other job."

He turns around to face me, rubbing the back of his neck. "What do you do for your other job?"

"I kill people," I say with a grin.

Adam barks out a laugh. "That's funny. Are you a comedian?"

"I get stage fright." I wink, which makes his puffy cheeks blush.

"So, uh, do you want to do this again sometime?"

"Sure!" I say and head towards the door. "I'll text you."

"Let me give you my number."

"You already did. Last night."

He didn't.

I open my door wide, giving Adam space to walk by.

He pauses before passing and leans down for a kiss. I allow a quick peck on the lips and stifle the urge to shove him out of my apartment.

I should really stop bringing one-night stands back to my place.

Of course, before I can close my door, my annoying neighbor emerges from the pits of hell to taunt me.

Damn. I really thought he left.

Delancy leans against the doorframe to his apartment, arms crossed. He tsks while watching Adam descend the stairs. I hate it when he does that. His silent, judging stares are so loud. And he stares a lot. He wasn't much of a talker when we met, but now he talks too much... and I can't get him to shut up.

Once Adam is out of sight and hearing range, Delancy huffs a laugh.

"You little liar."

"Stalk much?"

"Why'd you lie? Is it because you faked it, Rainbow Bright?"

"I didn't fake it!"

He raises a brow at me.

"Fuck off, Del."

"I'm not a computer, Noe."

"My name is Noah, not Noe. Stop calling me a word you never hear."

"No."

The last thing I see before slamming the door in Del's face is his narrowed eyes.

I hate him and his stupid nicknames for me.

Noe. Rainbow Bright. Skittles. Crayon. Kevin.

Kevin took me a while to figure out. It wasn't until I saw a commercial promoting *Home Alone* airing on one of those channels that show Christmas movies the entire month of December that I realized he nicknamed me after the main character, Kevin McCallister.

He's an idiot. My last name is spelled differently.

I moved in two months ago, and I've hated Del since day one. His snarky comment about my pink hair, which prompted me to dye it purple the next day. His gorgeous face that's always stuck in a scowl. His dumb black hair that falls in a perfect mess.

I hate how much I love that he's taller than me because not a lot of dudes are taller than me.

I hate his mesmerizing blue eyes and how fucking hot he looked just now in his gray sweats and no shirt because he's about to go for run even though it's forty degrees outside. His body is packed with muscles, and my eyes greedily devour him every time he returns from his workout, glistening with sweat.

I hate how good he always smells. Like sweat and the sun and expensive cologne; tangerines mixed with nature—the woods after a fresh rain.

And I hate how mysterious he is with all the scars littering his body, including one on his upper left lip and another along his left cheek.

The alphahole personality kills any attraction I have for Delancy "last name unknown" because he refuses to tell me and it's not on his mailbox—I've checked.

I could find out if I cared. I have my resources. But I don't care. I *don't*. Not about Del or his hot body.

Ok fine. That's a lie. I want to fuck him more than I want the coffee I'm about to brew—sorry, Adam, I lied. I need the fuel to wake me up because there's no way I'm going back to sleep now. Del always knows exactly what to say to piss me off. Like, how did he know Adam couldn't make me come? My fake orgasms are Oscar-worthy. Besides, this time I *did* come... but it wasn't because of Adam. If I told Delancy I was thinking about him while fucking someone else, he'd never let me live it down.

I flip off the door as if Del was still there and head back to my kitchen to start the coffeemaker. While it brews, I climb back into bed, retrieving my bullet vibrator from the bedside table drawer. I need to relieve my built-up tension before I start the day.

"About time, bitch," my best friend grumbles as I stumble into Boqueria, our favorite restaurant in SoHo. The trendy, modern Spanish restaurant touts the best Barcelona-style tapas in America. I give her a hug, and she pulls back with a wrinkled nose. "Girl, you smell like sex."

After getting off—and screaming Del's name into my pillow—I fell asleep in orgasmic bliss and woke up just in time to catch a train here. No shower. So, I don't doubt how pleasant I smell.

"Jealous?" I tease.

My bestie is stunning. Her long, dirty-blonde hair is French braided with the tail hanging over her shoulder. She's wearing a purple turtleneck sweater tucked into black jeans, showcasing her plump body.

Sage Manilow, no relation to Barry, is a big girl like me. We both don't give a fuck what the world has to say about our bodies. We dress how we want, fuck who we want, and do whatever we want. We're happy and that pisses off the miserable fatphobes, which only encourages us to keep living our happy little lives.

Well, happy on the outside, I suppose.

My life has been one clusterfuck of misery.

It began when I was eleven, and I witnessed my mother's murder. I was inside my room reading when I heard her scream. I ran out and hid at the top of the stairs after seeing two large men in the living room. They had my mom on her knees with her hands tied behind her back. She was crying... sobbing...

Then one of the masked men held a gun to her head.

He pulled the trigger, and I screamed and ran off, locking myself inside my bedroom. The men banged on the door, kicked it, and splintered the wood. I thought they were going to get in, but something must have spooked them, because suddenly they were gone. I was found hiding in my room ten minutes later.

I emerged to strangers downstairs, mostly men in ill-fitted suits and a few police officers, talking to my father. The moment he saw me, he scooped me up into his arms. He held me for several minutes while I sobbed into his neck. I refused to let go until he forced me to sit on the couch and left me there to go talk to a new suited stranger who just walked in the door.

I watched them just stand around talking, doing nothing except for the one person going around the apartment collecting evidence. No one walked up to me and asked me what I saw. I at least expected them to take me to the hospital to be checked out. Physically and mentally. I'd just seen my mother get murdered for fuck's sake.

They did nothing.

That was the night I learned my father is the Don of the Empire Mafia—a crime organization that's been around for decades and has power over law enforcement, New York City politicians, and other important people in this godforsaken city.

Up until that night, I barely knew my father. He was in my life, but he was hardly around. Always busy with work, my mother would say.

Losing her meant losing my sanctuary. She was my best friend.

The week following her death, I woke up every night screaming in terror. Nightmares haunted me. Seeing her getting shot replayed not only while I slept, but while awake. I'd stopped eating, stopped smiling. I was scared of everything and everyone.

My father didn't have time to deal with my mental breakdown. He had a mafia to run after all. So, he changed my name and let people believe I had died too. He said it was to protect me from his enemies. Then he sent me away to live with a distant aunt on the opposite side of the country where I was ordered to go to therapy for the horrors I saw that night.

It was only supposed to be temporary because my father wanted me to return home when I turned eighteen.

He had plans for me.

But on my eighteenth birthday, I wasn't ready to go back to the home where my mother took her last breath. Therapy may have dulled the nightmares and allowed me to turn my fear into rage, but I will never forget.

I tried to live a normal life. I went to college in Northern California. I traveled the world. But the rage never went away.

Now I'm thirty-one, and I returned to New York City two months ago. Not because my father wanted me to come home. And it's not because he wants me to learn the business.

How could he ask me to do such a thing after his 'business' is the reason my mother is dead?

I'm back because I'm determined to find out who's responsible for her murder.

I'm back because I plan to dismantle the Empire.

My father won't be the first powerful man I've destroyed.

"Um, hello!" Sage waves her hand in front of my face. "You just spaced out. Was the sex that good you just went through a replay? Tell me there were multiple orgasms. Hand necklaces? Bite marks? Does your kitty cat hurt, at least?"

"I wish."

I sip the mimosa she ordered for me and chase it down with water. I'm way too dehydrated after last night.

"Aww. Was it bad? What happened? Is it because you still have the hots for your grumpy neighbor?"

I pick up the menu, avoiding my best friend's eyes. "I don't know what you're talking about."

"Just fuck him already. Put me out of my misery."

Sage and I met at the bar we work at. We clicked instantly and now, two months later, we're inseparable. We talk about everything. Well, not everything. She doesn't know about my family. She doesn't know I'm a mafia princess and my father wants me to take over some day. I can't let her get involved in this part of my life.

Just like I can't tell her I have blood on my hands.

"Oh, shit," Sage whispers. "An unbelievably hot man just walked in."

I glance over my shoulder to see this hottie who has her speechless, which never happens.

Oh hell no.

It's as if speaking about him conjured his presence.

Speak of the devil and he shall appear.

I quickly turn back around and hide behind my menu. "That's grumpy neighbor!"

"What? Holy shit, Noey. He's hot as fuck."

"Did he see me? Please say he didn't see me."

"Oh, I saw you, Kevin," Delancy says, his deep voice vibrating throughout my body and awakening my thirsty cunt.

I sit up straight in my chair and glance up at the man. He's dressed immaculately: black pants, shirt, and suit jacket. His hair is brushed back, revealing his gorgeous blue eyes.

"Are you stalking me?"

He leans down, planting a hand on the back of my chair. He smells fantastic, as usual. His mouth is right next to my ear as he says, "What if I am?"

I ignore the thought of how hot it would be if Del was, in fact, stalking me.

What is wrong with me?

Stalking fantasies have never been my thing, especially with what I went through as a kid. Scary men breaking in and murdering my mother?

No thank you.

My next-door neighbor breaking in and ravishing me? *Please.*

"Hi, I'm Sage." My best friend's interruption saves me from the whimper that was creeping up my throat.

Del stares at me for a few seconds in that silent, sexy way of his, then finally averts his eyes to Sage. He plasters on a smile.

"Delancy." He doesn't take her offered hand, which I find rude, and gives Sage a nod before turning his attention back to me. "I'm meeting someone here."

"Congratulations."

The door to the restaurant opens at that moment, and we turn our heads to watch a curvy redhead walk in and scan the room. She spots Del and waves.

"Ah, there's my date." He makes a point to look at me when saying 'date,' adding his cockiest smirk.

The fucker.

"Good for you. I'm sure it's been hard all these nights alone with your hand. Have fun, Laptop."

I might have heard him growl when I turn my attention back to my best friend, refusing to give him a second glance.

"A date?" Sage asks once Del and the woman walk off to sit at a table on the opposite side of the restaurant. "Ouch."

"No. No ouch. This is good. This is fine."

"Is it?"

"Yeah. Maybe this means he'll stop bothering me. Besides, we're just neighbors. He's allowed to date or fuck whoever he wants. I know I do. Like last night."

Sage picks up her menu.

"Okay," she says, drawing out the word and trying to hold back a smile.

Thankfully, our server arrives at that moment, so I don't have to kick my best friend's ass.

After we order, I allow myself a glimpse over my shoulder and find Del staring back at me with a heated intensity. I quickly turn away, feeling my cheeks warm.

What's he up to? There's no way it's a coincidence that he showed up at mine and my bestie's favorite restaurant.

Maybe he *is* stalking me.

Chapter 3

Delancy

I've been stalking Noah for weeks now.

This morning, I overheard her telling that asshole, Adam, that she was meeting her bestie in SoHo for brunch. I know there's only one spot in SoHo where the women like to meet. Boqueria is their favorite restaurant, so I told a past hookup to meet me here.

I wanted to make Noah jealous, but I don't think it worked.

I need her to desire me, obsess over me, so I can fuck her and get her out of my system.

Instead, I'm the one desiring her, obsessing over her. She's beginning to get in the way of my plans.

She's distracting me.

It's been ten minutes since Noah and her friend left and the redhead across the table—Vickie—is talking about God knows what.

I take out my phone and text my brother who heads the Queensboro Mob.

Got a job for me?

I started my killing career taking hits for the QBM. When that wasn't enough, I expanded and became the Marionette.

I check the kill order message board, but nothing piques my interest: either because the jobs don't pay enough or it's too complicated of a hit.

Typically, I wait a few days before accepting my next assignment. Taking jobs back-to-back opens the door for errors. I like to plan and scope out the target before making my move.

But I'm desperate to murder someone. I need to relieve this tension that builds every time I see *her*.

I could just give in and end her life.

The thought makes my heart ache and my stomach twist with panic.

I tuck my phone away because I know Elias won't respond anytime soon. He's horrible at communication, especially texting.

So, that means my urge for violence will just need to be satisfied some other way.

Maybe I'll find an underground fighting match and beat the shit out of some cocky amateur.

Or maybe I'll go snoop around Noah's place.

Yeah. That idea *excites* me more than spilling blood.

I stand and take my wallet out of my suit jacket's pocket and extract a hundred-dollar bill to toss on the table. That'll cover our meal and fifty percent of the tip.

"I have to go," I say and storm out of the restaurant.

Outside, I flag down a cab. Before I get inside, Vickie places her hand on my arm.

"You need me to help with whatever's bothering you?"

No. I can't.

She's not *her*.

But maybe Vickie can help me forget, even if it's for a few minutes.

I step back for her to get in and she tells the driver her address. The moment the cabbie takes off, her hands reach for my pants. She gives me a sly smile as she undoes my belt and glances to the front, but the man is on the phone, not paying attention.

She pulls out my cock and licks her lips, breathing heavily. Her nipples harden in her skintight top. Vickie is an exhibitionist. The two other times we've met to fuck have always been in public. She loves being watched... the thrill of potentially being caught.

Her lips close over the head, and I sigh when her tongue laps up the pre-cum. She fists me up and down a few times, then stops and frowns.

"You're not into this, baby?"

I glance down at my semi-hard dick. Apparently, it only wants to be buried in one mouth. One pussy.

And that would be Noah's.

"Keep going," I say and close my eyes, thinking about how fantastic Noah looked today in her pink crop top sweater, black skirt, and black stockings.

"That's better," Vickie says.

I shove her head down on my cock, making her gag as the tip hits the back of her throat.

The driver's eyes dart to the rear-view mirror and widen. I place my index finger over my mouth and smile. He shakes his head but does nothing to stop us.

The only way I can get off with Vickie's mouth on my dick is thinking about Noah. Her plump lips. Her soft stomach that she loves to show off. Her thick thighs that need to be around my head.

Does Noah think about me when she's fucking her one-night stands?

I want nothing more than to punish my rainbow bright. Spank her for making me feel this way. She isn't part of my plan.

My balls tighten, preparing for release.

"Swallow," I grunt, holding Vickie's head in place as I pour cum down her throat.

"Better?" Vickie asks after removing herself from my cock and wiping spit and cum off her chin.

I nod, zipping up my pants and latching my belt in place.

Before she can question me further, because I know she didn't believe the lie, the cab pulls up to her apartment building. Vickie gets out, leaving the door open for me. When I don't follow, she leans down to look inside the car.

"You're not coming?"

I hold up my phone as if I just got a text or call. "Something came up. Rain check?"

She frowns then smiles faintly. I should feel bad for using her to get off, but to be fair, she offered. I never promised I'd reciprocate.

Maybe that makes me an asshole.

"I'll hold you to that rain check, baby."

She shuts the door, and I roll my eyes.

I hate it when she calls me baby.

I instruct the driver to take me back to Astoria and hand him two hundred dollars for the trouble.

Noah doesn't appear to be home so after I set my keys on the table, I walk through the living room to the set of windows along the far back wall to access the fire escape. I make my way across the metal landing to Noah's living room window and peer inside, listening.

Yep. Not home.

I put on my gloves that I keep in my pocket in case of emergency—not that breaking into Noah's apartment is an emergency—and test the window, which is locked. That's fine. I'll get it open. This is an older building and the locks on the windows are shit. They're loose and rusted and with a little jiggling, the latch shimmies open, and I slip inside.

She should really get these locks reinforced.

It smells like sex in here. My jealousy rears its ugly head, and I have no right to be jealous, especially after the stunt I just pulled at the restaurant and in the cab ride after.

I walk to Noah's bookcase, which has one shelf full of photos. She's traveled a lot. Places I've never been to like Brazil, Costa Rica, and South Africa. I pick out my favorite picture of her and take it out of the frame, then tuck it in my pocket. I return the frame to the shelf with the stock photo still inside, thankful that Noah didn't toss it out. It'll take her longer to realize her photo is missing.

I don't usually break in during the daytime, only at night when she's asleep, but I've been needing to go through her belongings to see if I can find anything out of the ordinary. I ran a background check on her, but it was too perfect. Too... boring.

Noah is far from boring.

The moment I saw her moving in, I wanted her. I learned her work schedule. Who she's friends with. She just moved back to New York City, but from where? Despite stalking her, there's a lot I still don't know. I'm not able to follow her around twenty-four seven. Sometimes she disappears for days before returning home.

Something tells me she's not who she says she is. She has secrets, and I'm determined to find them out. Even if that means straying from my plans for revenge.

It's infuriating because I don't have time to stray.

Noah's spacious studio apartment is chaotic. Her bed is unmade, and the condom wrapper Adam used is strewn on the floor with a bunch of dirty clothes. She has stacks of books on the floor along the wall, in addition to the ones stuffed in her bookcase. Curious about what she likes to read, I select a romance with a bare-chested man on the cover. I make myself at home and stretch out on her red couch to flip through the pages.

Whoa.

Noah, you *naughty* little vixen. This book is porn on pages.

I didn't know that was a thing.

Okay, I'm keeping this too.

I stand, tucking the book in the back of my pants before moving on to her bedside table. The top drawer is full of sex toys: vibrators, dildos, nipple clamps, butt plugs, lube, condoms... a strap on?

Fuck.

My cock jumps at the thought of Noah using it on me.

I'm tempted to take everything. If she can't get off without her toys, maybe she'll knock on my door and beg me for help.

I behave myself and choose only one, pocketing her bullet vibrator.

The kitchen is at least clean. Inside the cabinets, I find a box of Pop Tarts and take out a packet, leaving the last one for her. I finish perusing her place while eating the sweet treat. It's been years since I've had one. My mother used to buy them for me and my brother all the time.

Her bathroom is also clean, but full of products. All kinds of shampoos and conditioners, body washes, lotions, perfumes, and other things that I have no idea what they're used for.

God, it smells wonderful in here.

After leaving the bathroom, I continue along the back wall and crouch down next to a laundry basket in a corner full of small photo albums. I grab the top one and flip through it. There are more photos of her traveling. I've yet to see one of her traveling *with* someone. A solo traveler, I'm assuming?

I'd love to travel the world with her.

I shake the thought from my head and keep flipping the pages. At the back are pictures of Noah when she was younger. I'd say around ten or eleven. There are photos of her at ballet, playing the piano, the violin, the flute. Photos of her holding a bunny, a kitten, a puppy, riding a camel in the deserts of Egypt.

There are several of her as a child posing with a woman who is clearly her mother. She has dark brown hair, the same brown eyes, and a cheeky chipmunk smile that Noah has shown me out of spite too many times to count.

I take one of the photos of this woman out of the plastic sleeve and flip it around.

No name on the back.

I don't find any pictures of Noah beyond this young age with the woman. Is she dead? I wonder what happened to her.

My gut is sounding the alarm, so I steal a few of these photos too.

The closer I get to Noah, the more mysterious she becomes.

I've tried to keep my distance since she moved in (stalking from afar counts, right?), but now I'm intrigued. I have a job to do. I can't get distracted, but I've already decided to make an exception for this one.

Chapter 4

Noah

It's been a few days since I've seen Del, and I'm both relieved and pissed.

Him showing up at mine and Sage's favorite restaurant was all too suspicious, and I'd planned to question him about it.

But, of course, he's been MIA.

Now, I'm heading to meet my father for lunch, and I'm having the worst day.

After I nearly sat in pee on the subway, then missed my stop and had to take a train back, but that train went express and skipped my stop—I'm ready to murder the next person who looks at me the wrong way.

"You're late," a disappointed voice grumbles as I sit my ass on the cushioned chair of Lenetti's.

Dad's pride and joy.

It's the first restaurant he opened in New York City two years after moving here from Italy when he was twenty-one years old. Now he owns a dozen restaurants and other various businesses around Manhattan and the Bronx.

"Why do you smell like piss?"

Ugh. Maybe I did sit in that pee.

"Good to see you too, Babbo." *Dad.*

He stands, walks to where I sit, and kisses the top of my head.

This is only the second time I've seen him since returning two months ago. I told him I was busy settling in, and he was busy doing his criminal thing, and we never found the right time to meet more than that.

I wasn't busy. I'm just not at that level of relationship with him.

Even though I refused to move back when I turned eighteen, I'd still visit him once a year for the holidays and attend his annual Christmas party. That all changed five years ago when I started looking into my mother's death. He refused to talk to me about it, saying the police and his team of private investigators were handling it. I was so mad at him. It seemed like he didn't care, like he had moved on.

So, I stopped visiting. I claimed my life was too busy, which was technically true. Freelance work kept me occupied. Babbo kept my bank account fed, allowing me to live my life the way I wanted, but I never used his blood money and donated it to charity instead.

Now he's trying to make up for all the years he missed out on. Except, he's being overbearing and protective, and it makes me regret moving back.

I scowl at the old man, his wrinkles growing deeper the longer I'm in his presence.

"Why are you late? You know I worry about you."

"Train delays."

"Why do you insist on taking that filthy transportation?" he growls, his anger making his Italian accent thicker. "How many times have I told you to allow my driver to escort you around the city?"

I lean back in the chair, crossing my arms because I've managed to stay alive for thirty-one years without his help. Doesn't he know that the last time I lived with him, I nearly died?

"I'm an adult, Babbo. I don't need a babysitter. Besides, it's New York City. You know driving takes longer."

"I'd rather you late because of traffic than to not show up because you're dead."

"Well, I'm here now. Late and alive."

"Enough, Noah." He slams a fist on the table, knocking over my empty glass. A worker rushes over, tips it upright, and fills it with wine. I give the man a thankful nod and take a long draw of the bitter liquid.

Gio Lenetti is the scariest man I know. He always has been. He's a big guy, 400 pounds. Fatness and tallness run in our family. He's six foot six. I'm five ten and 280 pounds. His temper, however, is shorter than my patience with Del.

"You know I have enemies. You know every day I worry they'll find you now that you're back. They could take you away from me just as they did your mother."

His voice breaks, and I sigh, softening my defiant demeanor.

"I'm sorry." I cover my father's fisted hand with my palm. "I know you worry, but I swear I'm careful."

He takes a puff of his cigar and says nothing until he composes himself.

"I want two of my men to escort you."

My eyes widen. "No, absolutely not."

"I want you to stop working at that vile bar."

"What? No. I like working there."

"I will give you all the money you need."

I stifle a groan.

"You will learn how to shoot—"

"Babbo, stop!"

The restaurant goes silent. It's just us and the workers, but it's obvious they've never heard anyone raise their voice to their boss.

Probably because that person would end up with a bullet in their head.

"Look... I didn't move back so you could reign over my life. I won't stop working because I need my independence. It's a fun job, and that's what I need right now. As for having two of your soldiers following me around... Fine. If it makes you feel better, they can escort me when I go out. Only when I go out. They will NOT show up at my job."

He thinks about my demands, petting his clean-shaven chin. "They go to your bar and sit nearby but out of the way. Observing. Ready to step in when needed."

I pinch the bridge of my nose. He won't give up no matter how hard I fight. "Okay, sure, but they better not boss me around. I won't hesitate to stab them."

My father laughs as if I'm joking.

I'm not.

"Don't underestimate me, Babbo. I'll kick their asses. I told you I learned self-defense while I visited Brazil."

He shakes his head, still chuckling. Then his smile fades. He takes hold of my hand from across the table. "A punch or a kick is no match for a bullet."

I wouldn't put it past my father to make me start wearing a bulletproof vest.

"I'm serious about you learning how to shoot."

I *hate* guns. It's not because when I was ten and tried shooting one of the long ones at my father's gun range and the kickback left a killer bruise. No. I hate guns because it's the weapon used to kill my mom.

I'd much rather hold a knife in my hand.

"Mio angelo," *my angel,* "listen to me. I received word that another hit has been put on me."

I rip my hand out of his.

"What? By whom?"

He takes a sip of his whiskey. "I don't know, but I'll find out."

See? This is why I want nothing to do with his mob life. Someone always wants to kill the boss or his family.

New York City has three crime syndicates: the Empire Mafia, the Queensboro Mob, and the Lords of Staten Island. I always wondered if it was a rival mob responsible for my mother's death but neither the QBM nor the Lords ever took claim.

I later learned that twenty years ago, the night after my mother was murdered, *all* the mafia wives, and some of their children, were targeted and killed.

That's another reason I'm back. I need to figure out how to get in touch with a QBM member, or someone with the Lords, so we can compare notes. But the moment I tell them I'm Lenetti's daughter, I'm dead.

I hate this world.

I hate being heir to the Empire Mafia—a job I've told my father several times that I don't want—but he will do whatever it takes to make sure his legacy lives on.

But if his enemies know I'm back, I have no doubt they'll kill me to end his bloodline.

"I want you to head out to the gun range this week," my father says, his deep voice making me jump. "Ryan and Bryan will go with you."

Ryan and Bryan? Really?

He stands and buttons his suit jacket. "No more subways either."

And with that, he walks away.

Chapter 5

Delancy

It's the middle of November and my least favorite month is on the horizon.

I haven't seen Noah in a few days, even though I've heard her through the walls plenty of times. I'm not avoiding her on purpose. I've been busy helping my brother with a QBM task. He rarely needs my help, so I forced myself to answer his call.

My demons are restless.

I need to kill again.

But it's still too soon after my last assignment. Fucking Vickie's mouth did nothing to ease my urge for violence. In fact, I think it made it worse because I felt *guilty* afterwards.

Guilty that it wasn't Noah.

Maybe the shooting range can help. Guns aren't my favorite weapon to kill with, but they're useful for sniper hits when I'm unable to get close to a target. I rarely accept sniper hits since I'm unable to pose the kill as an accident. It opens me up to the vulnerability of a job being traced back to me. Still, I like to keep my shooting skills sharp.

The biting cold slices through my leather jacket as I weave in and out of morning rush hour traffic on my black and orange KTM 990 Duke motorcycle. My fingers are already numb despite the gloves I wear. I hate winter. The cold reminds me of my childhood—being left to die outside in the snow. I tried to run. I made it out the front door of our house before a pair of large, strong arms caught me and plunged a knife into my stomach. When I was found, frostbite was beginning to kick in, and I was minutes from dying.

I was told I was lucky to be alive. Everyone said my guardian angel was protecting me that night.

No.

This was no divine intervention. God wouldn't let me live just so I could spend the rest of my years killing and seeking revenge for my mother's death.

Perhaps it was the devil who saved me.

I've already killed the men who forced me to slit her throat. For years, I stalked them. Played games with them to ignite fear in their every waking moment. I put them on edge for months before making my move.

The man who tied my mother down to the chair was first. I kept him in the basement of an abandoned home, deep in the mountains of the Catskills. No one could hear his screams as I left him there for days to piss himself, starve, and lose his mind. Before his organs failed, I returned. I gave him water and food, just enough to survive while I carved small, but deep cuts all over his body.

A slow, agonizing death.

The man who put the knife in my hand was next. I cut off *his* hands and applied a tourniquet so he wouldn't bleed out. I strung him up to a wall and played a game of knife-throwing. I left him there with knives embedded in his legs, stomach, chest, and arms until the life slowly drained from him.

I saved the man who chased after me and stabbed me for last. I dumped him out in the woods in the middle of a big snowstorm and hunted him. Just when he thought he'd lost me, I'd fire a shot his way. It took him nearly five hours before he ran out of steam and collapsed into the snow. His skin was blue and frost bitten when I approached him. I stabbed him in the same spot he did me and left him there to die.

The bobcats and cougars ate well that night, leaving me barely any remains to dispose of the next day.

His blood is still warm on my hands. It's been eight months since I finally ended his year-long torture.

The moment I turned eighteen, I've been on this path of vengeance and there's one more name on my list—the man who ordered her death. Killing him will shift power within the New York City mafia scene.

My shoulders ache, and my body desperately needs sleep. I tried to catch up last night, but Skittles spent hours watching some ridiculous reality TV show. My banging on the wall did nothing but prompt her to turn up the volume at full blast.

I want to strangle her.

The thought quickly turns sexual as I imagine my hands giving her a lovely necklace while I fuck her into the mattress.

Get a grip, Delancy. Stop thinking about fucking your neighbor.

The thoughts are becoming too frequent. The more I see her, stalk her, hear her moans from the other side of the wall, the more I crave to be near her. Or perhaps it's the way we banter because I've never met someone who is as fast with the quips as her. I've met my match, and it's exhilarating.

This is a sign to move out and retire the Astoria safe house, but for some reason, my stomach turns at the thought of leaving.

"You gotta be fucking kidding me," a familiar silky voice sounds from behind me.

I'm at a stall, preparing my weapon, and slowly turn to find my lovely rainbow bright. As if thinking about her summoned the woman who haunts my thoughts, twenty-four seven.

"Kevin, you look like a disaster this morning." My eyes travel up and down her body. A *beautiful* disaster. She's wearing leggings and an oversized t-shirt that hangs off her shoulder, revealing a purple sports bra to match the purple mess of hair piled on top of her head.

"Stop calling me Kevin!"

"Did someone kidnap you from bed?" I sniff the air between us and ignore my cock jerking at her jasmine and citrus scent. It's an expensive perfume. Her favorite. "No time for a shower, Smelly Cat?"

"Fuck off with that. I smell fantastic!"

She reaches for my gun, her fingertips skimming over the metal, but I snatch her by the wrist before she's able to grab it.

"Whoa there, Killer. Keep those slutty paws off my baby."

Surely, she wasn't trying to grab my gun to shoot me.

"Slut shaming?" She tugs her arm from my grip. "How sexist of you, Laptop."

This little brat.

"What are you doing here? Are you stalking me?" I ask, secretly hoping she *is* stalking me.

We're all the way in the Morrisania section of the Bronx. This city is massive, and I run into her here?

I'm not a fan of coincidences.

Not to mention she walked into the gun range owned by New York City's most notorious mobster. Does she know the danger that surrounds her?

"Why would I stalk you, Del? We literally live next to each other."

Fair.

"I'm here to learn how to shoot a gun, dumbass."

Interesting. Why would a bartender need to learn how to shoot? Is she planning to carry? Gun laws in the Big Apple are strict. Though, she doesn't seems like one to abide by the laws.

"Guns are dangerous," I say as if she's a child. "They go bang bang real loud."

She growls, and it's rather adorable. It's why I enjoy messing with her.

Her anger is intoxicating.

"Who's teaching you how to use a gun, anyway?" I look around and see a couple of big guys standing behind her. They're regarding me as if I'm about to strike out and murder Noah.

Wait... are they her bodyguards? Those men sure are acting like they're protecting her.

"It's none of your business who's teaching me or why I want to learn, you nosey motherfucker."

The snark catches me off guard and a laugh slips past my lips.

"What's so funny?"

I quickly recover, shaking off the shock of finding another human amusing, and say, "You're letting one of these yahoos teach you?"

"What? Can you do it better?"

I offer her the cockiest smile, which seems to piss her off based on the red in her cheeks deepening and return to my stall to pick up my gun. Pointing at the target on the far end, I fire five shots, then hit the button to bring the paper to me. I tear it off and hand it to Noe.

Her mouth drops open.

"Who the hell are you?"

The corner of my mouth turns up and that funny feeling of amusement returns. Fuck, why do I like it?

"Teach me," Noah says, her eyes lighting up with... lust. She's... turned on?

My gaze drops to her tits, and I wonder if her nipples are hard underneath that top.

"Stop ogling me and teach me how to shoot, Del."

If she were mine, I'd punish her for being such a brat. A bossy little brat. I take a step back, waving my hand at the stall for her to step in. I attach a new shooting target paper to the hook before sending it to the back and reload the magazine as Noah gets into position. She eagerly reaches for the gun when I set it down.

I tsk and slap her hand, garnering a frown from her. I grab the supplied shooting earmuffs and plastic eyewear.

"Always wear protection."

I smirk, placing the glasses on her face. Her mouth forms an 'o' as if understanding the double innuendo. I try to put the earmuffs on her too, but she snarls and snatches it from my hands to do it herself.

"Treat all guns as if they're loaded, never point it at another person, and keep it aimed at the floor, your finger off the trigger until you're ready to shoot."

She rolls her eyes at my safety lecture and fidgets on her feet. She may be putting on a strong front, but I can tell she's nervous.

I place my hands on her shoulders and turn her to face the target, tapping my toe on the instep of her feet.

"Spread these and bend slightly. Toes should align."

She follows my instructions and once comfortable in her stance, she leans back.

"Lean forward, not back," I whisper, my breath brushing her ear. She shudders at the sensation. I smooth my hands over her arms, adjusting them to line up with the target. "Hold the gun with both hands. Cup this hand over the other."

Her breathing picks up, and she's leaning into me again. I don't immediately correct her posture, instead enjoying how amazing her body feels against mine.

"Index finger goes along here hovering the trigger guard until you're ready to shoot." I trace the pad of my finger along hers and she shivers again. "Close one eye and line the target with the notch at the end of the gun. Once you have it in view, fire."

I step back and wait for her to adjust. After a few seconds, she closes her eyes and pulls the trigger.

She winces at the recoil, which she likely felt in her wrists.

"Did I hit it?"

"Not even close. Try again and this time, keep your eyes open."

She sighs, frustrated, which makes me want to smile again. Who even am I?

"How many are in here?" she asks, manhandling the gun, pointing it at me while trying to figure out how to eject the magazine.

"Eleven more. And didn't I say to never point a loaded gun at someone?" I growl, pushing the barrel away from my chest.

"Unless I want to kill them?" She smiles and winks.

I ignore my cock hardening as I picture Noah standing in front of someone, the barrel of a gun to their head, and shooting them point blank. Blood splattering over her face and chest. Better yet... I imagine her straddling a man with her thick thighs, holding a knife over her head before plunging the blade deep into his chest.

I shake the images. Noah may be chaotic and feisty, but she's no killer.

"Focus, Skittles." She flips me off. "Think about what makes you angry—"

"*You* make me angry."

"Take that hatred and anger and divert it to the gun and the target. Vengeance is a powerful state of mind."

The smile on her face drops at my words. Shit. What did I say? What memory did I just trigger?

An array of emotions passes over her beautiful face. Ones I'm quite familiar with: sadness, rage, retribution.

She positions herself in the stall—correctly this time—and lifts both arms. After stretching her neck side to side, her shoulders relax. She's focusing on the target, following my instructions to the tee, and a strange swell of pride takes over me.

The gun fires once... twice... three times. Noah giggles and fires five more bullets.

"Okay, Scarface, calm down," I say, snatching the gun from her trigger-happy hands.

I prompt the target to return and tear the paper from the holder.

"Well, would you look at that? You actually got some shots on the target this time."

She yanks it out of my hand, her eyes going wide the moment she spots a bullet hole smack dab in the paper man's groin.

"Holy shit! I did it!" she squeals and throws her arms around my neck.

I stiffen and hold my breath, not sure what to do.

It's been decades since anyone's properly hugged me. It's different from the physical touch that comes with fucking. Hugging is so... personal.

My hands hover at Noah's sides, not daring to touch her. Because once I start, I won't be able to stop, and that thought terrifies me.

Noah must sense my unease and releases me. She steps back and glances over her shoulder at the two goons. They've got their palms on their guns, ready to shoot as if I'm about to attack Noah when she was the one who launched herself at me.

"Sorry," Noah whispers. She holds her head down, ashamed. It's strange because I've never seen this woman ashamed of anything. She always radiates confidence when around me. I want to lift her chin and tell her she did nothing wrong. That it's me. I'm the one too fucked up to hug her back.

I hastily grab my gun and secure it in my holster, then collect my ammunition and leather jacket. Without saying a word, I leave.

"Delancy, wait!"

Noah's voice trails after me, but I'm already halfway to the door.

Fuck!

I let her get to me. I let her distract me. This is why I can't get attached to anyone. I lose focus, and I'm too close to finally killing the man who ordered my mother's death, and I can't let a woman fuck it all up.

Even if that woman ignites the very spark of life that's been dead for twenty years.

She's making me want to live again.

And I hate her for it.

Chapter 6

Noah

I haven't seen Delancy in a week. He's been avoiding me since that day at the shooting range when I hugged him.

My hugs aren't that horrible. I mean, I get that we've only known each other a couple months, and it's purely a hate/hate relationship, but he's the one who was being all sexy. Hovering behind me (I could have sworn I felt his cock getting hard), smoothing his hands over my arms like he was staking his claim over me, tracing his fingertips over my fingers and whispering in my ear, his hot breath against my skin making me shiver.

I was seconds away from dropping my pants and bending over, begging him to call me his dirty little slut while taking me from behind.

Hearing Del say 'slutty paws' awakened my degradation kink, hitting me at full force.

But the more I think about his reaction and sudden departure, the angrier I get. I can't wait to see him again and give him a piece of my mind.

No, that'd be too nice.

I'm going to kick his ass.

He may be taller than me, and packed with more muscle, but I doubt that pretty boy knows Jiu-Jitsu. I spent six months in Brazil learning the martial art form. My professor was surprised by how well I did despite my size. Rude, but the comment filled me with pride.

Still, Del surprised me by knowing how to fire a gun. I bet he *can* fight too. How else would he have gotten those scars?

Ugh. Who is this man!?

Work tonight was brutal. I check my phone for the time, then scan the space, making sure everything is spotless. Once satisfied, I lock up and walk toward the subway.

When I get home, I'm drawing myself the hottest fucking bath. Then I'll pour myself the biggest glass of wine and soak in the tub while reading a smutty book until my fingers and toes are pruned. I'll end the night with my bullet vibrator, coming so loud that fucker next door will be forced to tug on his dick, wishing his hand was me.

I pause at Del's door and listen but all I hear is my fast-beating heart, still revved up from work tonight. Or is it beating so frantically because of how anxious I am, hoping to run into him?

He's got to show his face at some point.

After entering my apartment, I make all the loud noises, just in case Del really is home and asleep.

Slamming doors and cabinets.

Blasting music and singing at the top of my lungs (I'm a wonderful singer).

Vacuuming (I have hardwood floors, but the living area rug needed a good cleaning.)

I only stopped with the noise because it's midnight and Del's not my only neighbor.

When I finally make it to the bathroom to start my bath, disappointment sets in.

He really isn't home. He really is avoiding me.

I hate him.

While letting the tub fill with water, I select a new book to read.

Huh. That's weird. I'm missing one. Did Sage take a book without asking? I can't remember the title. I just know it had a bare-chested man on the cover. It's too late to text her so I make a mental note to do it tomorrow. I choose a spicy enemies to lovers romance.

I turn to my bedside table next and open my toy drawer.

What the hell?

Where is my bullet vibrator? I sigh. It's my favorite toy and I've lost it before in the sheets of my bed. I'm too tired to search for it.

Giving up on getting off tonight, I head into the bathroom.

I hiss as I sink into the water, the heat soaking my sore muscles. Leaning my head back, I inhale the jasmine and white tea bubble bath.

It takes all of one minute for me to doze off, only waking when my head goes under water. I didn't get to read my smutty romance book, but my fingers and toes are most definitely pruned.

I drain the tub and rinse off in the shower, scrubbing the day away. I always feel like there's a layer of grime on my body after doing this job.

Before burying underneath the covers of my bed, I chug the rest of my wine. The second my head hits the pillow, I fall asleep.

My body protests waking up. Muscles I didn't even know I had throb with pain. Work last night did a number on me and it probably wasn't the best idea to drink a full glass of wine right before falling asleep. I should have rehydrated with water.

I groan as I crawl out of bed and rush to the bathroom to relieve myself. Before heading into the kitchen, I pull up a music app on my TV and blast the Top 100 pop hits channel. A song I've never heard of plays and it's catchy and fun enough that I dance around the kitchen while making coffee. As it brews, I stare into the fridge as if that will magically produce food. My stomach grumbles at the thought of an omelet.

I should just order food.

Ooo, wait. I have Pop Tarts. I grab the box from the cabinet and frown when I only find one pouch left.

I know I had two.

Maybe Sage took one too. Though she never takes anything of mine before asking. Unless... have we reached that level of friendship? What's hers is mine? Butterflies dance in my stomach at the thought. I've never had a best friend before her, always too hesitant to bring other people into my life because of who I am. Sage is different because even when I tried pushing her away, she never let me. She's always been accepting of me.

I'll tell her everything eventually. I'll give her the option to dip out if my life is too terrifying for her.

Especially when I tell her my biggest, darkest secret.

The coffee machine beeps, letting me know it's done, and I shimmy my way over to grab the coffee pot. When I turn around, I scream and the coffee pot slips out of my hand, shattering on the hardwood floor. The hot liquid splatters on my bare feet and legs.

"Jesus fucking Christ!"

"Nope. Just me," Delancy says.

I limp to the counter to grab paper towels, but Del is already handing them to me.

"I'm surprised how well of a dancer you are since you sing like a cat in heat."

I flip him the bird while I wipe the coffee off my legs.

Del disappears for a minute while I sweep up the broken glass and mop the floor. He returns with a first aid kit.

"How the hell did you get inside my apartment?"

He sets the kit on the counter and searches the contents.

"Your door was unlocked."

"No, it wasn't."

"It was. You should really lock your door. This city is full of psychopaths. There could be a killer living in this very building."

He leads me to my tiny kitchen table and chair and sits me down.

"You're not going to gaslight me, Laptop. I know I locked the door last night. I checked it right before I went to sleep like I always do and... what are you doing?"

He's setting ointment packets and bandages out on the table as if he's about to perform surgery on me.

"You got cut by the shattering glass and burned by the hot coffee."

Before I can respond, he has my right foot in his lap and smooths what I assume to be burn relief on my skin. Next, he applies an ointment for the cuts on my shin.

He's taking care of me?

He's so gentle and attentive and looks sexy as hell.

Who is this man?

"Where have you been?" I ask as he wraps my foot with a bandage. He glances up at me through his black locks falling into his blue eyes.

"I had to work."

"Bullshit."

He ignores me and takes hold of my other foot.

"I had to work," he repeats, softer this time. More sincere.

Fine. I guess I believe him.

"What do you do for a living, Delancy? And don't lie to me. Don't avoid the question like you always do."

He pauses momentarily as if gathering his thoughts.

"I'm a... private investigator," he says cautiously. "I was called away on a job."

He sets my foot on the floor, deciding it doesn't need medicine or bandages.

I want to ask him about this job that took him away from me for a week. So, he's a private investigator? That might explain why he knows how to shoot a gun. Is he former law enforcement? A part of me feels like he's not telling me the whole truth.

He holds my wrist and lifts the sleeve of my robe, checking my arm for injuries since some of the coffee splattered the sleeve.

Wait. No. Shit. I try to pull my arm back, but he holds on to me tighter.

"What happened, Noe?" Del's voice is low and laced with anger. "Who did this to you?"

"No one."

I quickly tug the sleeve down to hide the cuts and bruises along my forearm. Del releases me and I stand, leaving him at the table. But he follows me into the living room where I pace.

"It happened at work. There was a fight and—"

He grabs me by the arm and pulls me against his body. His heavy breaths mix with mine and for a second, I wonder if he's going to kiss me.

Instead, he tilts my head to the side and spots a bruise on my neck. He brushes the pad of his thumb over it, making me shudder.

"And this?"

His fingers spread over my neck and skim down to my shoulder. He pushes the fabric of my robe back, tracing the inch long cut there.

"This?"

When I refuse to answer again, he tugs on the robe's belt, pausing to give me time to protest. I don't and it falls off my body. His enraged eyes scan my breasts, my nipples hardening under his heated stare. The tips of his fingers graze the bruises along my chest before moving to the cuts and scars on my stomach and sides.

New cuts and bruises from last night and old ones from past jobs.

"Who gave these to you? Answer me, Noah."

The way he says my name—livid and full of demand—lights a fire in my stomach. I whimper.

His eyes dart back up to mine at the sound.

"Give me a name. I just want to talk to them."

"I take self-defense classes," I say, hoping he believes me. "Sometimes I get my ass kicked."

He waits for me to continue, staring into my eyes as if he'll find the truth there.

"Why did you leave so suddenly at the gun range?" I blurt before he can ask more questions.

My words seem to snap him out of this protective demeanor—a side of him I wouldn't mind seeing more.

It's sexy as fuck.

Del steps away from me, and I scramble to put my robe back on, suddenly feeling vulnerable and embarrassed about what had just happened.

He points at a takeout box on the counter. "I brought you breakfast. A ham and cheese omelet and hash browns."

He backs away towards the door.

"What are you doing? Are you leaving?"

"Yes. I have to... I can't... I'm sorry... I..."

He stumbles over his words, and I've never heard him so flustered.

"I swear to God if you don't stop so we can talk about what just happened... Delancy—fuck I wish I knew your last name so I can properly curse you!"

He's out my door and down the hall as I continue yelling at him. Seconds later, I hear his motorcycle rev up and he takes off.

Chapter 7

Delancy

She's lying to me.

She didn't get those cuts and bruises from her job bartending or from a self-defense class.

Who is this woman?

Two months ago, when she moved in next door, I asked my hacker contact to run a background check on her. I do it with every tenant of every building I use as a safe house. Noah McAllister has basic social media pages (she likes to party and travel), no outstanding debts. Her mother, Sasha, died in a car accident when she was eleven and her father, Barry, is—huh.

I don't remember what her father does. A mechanic maybe? In fact, I'd glanced over her background check and found it so vapid, with nothing standing out, that I didn't even care to look into her father's history.

Now I'm wondering if it's all fake. Someone who doesn't want to be found will either make sure any evidence of their true existence has been erased or they'll create a false life to hide the real one. Even my friend didn't notice anything out of the ordinary to require further digging.

What if she's in danger?

Her injuries... needing to learn how to shoot a gun... the goons who escorted her...

Is she running away from an abusive relationship?

I could protect her.

The thought surprises me enough that I nearly crash into a box truck on the highway.

I've zoned out for the last fifteen minutes, speeding through morning rush hour traffic. Muscle memory takes me to the only place in the world where I'm at peace. Where I can clear my head from this woman who quickly became an obsession.

Grapevines snake up the brick entrance to St. Orion's Cemetery in Fresh Meadows, Queens. Weeds tower around the base of the arch and along the black iron fence. The cemetery has been neglected due to lack of funding or some bullshit. Most of the headstones are covered in filth: dirt, bird shit, moss, and mildew. The few families that still pay their respects here manage to upkeep their loved one's plot.

My mother was one of the last people buried here before the land was declared at capacity. Her final resting place sits near the back of the cemetery where I keep the grass cut down and the gray marble tombstone clean of grime. I smooth my hand over the engraved letters.

Imogen Carter

A Loving Mother & Wife

She was more than a wife and a mother. She was my best friend. She supported me in all my dreams, even if they seemed unattainable. When my older brother decided he was too cool to hang out with me, my mom was there to build forts in the living room or be the princess the knight in shining armor saved.

"I don't have flowers to give you this time, Ma."

I pick up the dead arrangement from the last time I visited and set it aside, reminding myself to toss it in the trash when I leave. I reach into my pants pocket and take out the photo of Noah I stole after breaking into her apartment the other day.

I still don't know why I find her so fascinating. I typically only stalk the people I intend to kill. With Noah, being near her puts me at ease in a way I can't explain. Far too many times, when my nightmares kept me awake, I'd sneak into her apartment and watch her sleep.

Maybe it's because she has nightmares too. I watch her toss and turn and call out for help.

Or maybe it's because she's chaotic while I'm more laid back. She keeps me guessing.

There's something else about her that she's hiding from me.

I'll figure it out.

She draws out my possessive side anytime she brings home a lover... and I've learned Noah is attracted to all genders. I've been tempted to kill whoever she fucks, jealous that they get to touch her, kiss her, *taste* her. Then I realize she might be blamed and thrown in jail. Instead, I rifle through their wallet or purse, get their info, and hand it over to Jed. I encourage him to dig up all their dirty secrets—if they have any—and reveal them to the world.

Cruel, sure, but I kill people for a living, so I feel it's rather nice of me.

"So, there's this woman..." I stare at the photo of Noe attempting to hold up the leaning Tower of Pisa. Cliché, but I'd expect nothing less from her. A smile spreads across my face, unwillingly. She looks happy here. Beautiful. Her dark black hair is styled in curls around her round face. She's wearing a black leather jacket and a body-hugging purple dress. Her soft stomach, wide hips, and thick thighs are outlined in the most delicious ways.

A twig snaps behind me and within seconds I tuck the photo away and stand, pointing a gun at whoever dared sneak up on me.

I stare down the barrel of a Beretta.

"How did I know I'd find you here, little brother?" Elias says and cocks the gun, pressing it into my forehead.

"I come here once a week. Sometimes more. Doesn't exactly take a genius to figure that out."

"Yet you're still alive. Certainly, if your enemies knew where to find you, you'd be dead by now."

"Then why haven't you pulled the trigger, Elly?"

He grinds the cold end of the barrel into my forehead. He hates the nickname I gave him as a kid.

I no longer recognize my brother, and it has nothing to do with his appearance. He's still as handsome as ever. His hair is dark like mine. His light blue eyes are weighed down with fury. Even after twenty years, he's never forgiven me.

He pulls the trigger but nothing happens.

It wasn't loaded.

He did that to let me know he's in control. Or maybe it was to scare me, but he should know it takes a lot to garner a reaction from me. At least when it comes to him. I've become numb to my brother's antics.

He's never said he blames me for our mother's death, but I know he does. Yet he won't do anything about it. He won't kill me. He won't even kick my ass. He just stays angry. It's almost as if his hatred for me is the only thing he lives for.

He needs me, though. I'm the only close family he has left besides our insignificant uncles, aunts, and cousins.

Elias drops his arm and secures his gun in the holster hidden in the jacket of his designer suit.

"Give me an update," he demands and runs a hand over his stubbled chin, then through his black wavy hair.

We may have similar features, including hair and eye color, and we're both tall, but Elias is a hefty man. Big with equal parts muscle and fat, like the wrestlers we used to watch on TV as kids. Elias could have gone into the WWE and crushed every competitor.

I light a joint before sitting down on top of mom's grave, leaning against the headstone. Elias turns his head at the sound of the spark wheel and glares at me. I give him the cockiest grin because he hates when I do this, saying I'm disrespecting Mom. I know she'd be right next to me, asking me to pass the joint.

She was a cool mom like that.

"I have to go back to the gun range. I wasn't able to stay long."

"Why? What happened?"

I shrug. "I got distracted."

He clenches and unclenches his fists at his sides.

"Stop fucking around, Lance."

I scoff. "Me? What about you? What are you doing to help? I've done everything. I killed and tortured those men. I'm crossing into enemy territory, digging for information. I'm the one doing the dirty work."

"I'm running the QBM. That's what I'm doing. I'm cleaning up your mistakes and keeping your ass out of prison," he growls, his hands on his hips. "Honestly, Delancy, you're getting sloppy. A strand of your hair was found inside Howard Marks's apartment."

"Don't know him."

"And don't get me started on the cock found in that woman's hand."

I shrug. "My client wanted a trophy."

"Well, investigators wanted to run tests to make sure it was a match. You're lucky I know the district attorney and stopped that from happening."

"Lucky," I snort. "Maybe I should go buy a lottery ticket."

"Fuck off, would you? Listen, little brother. I covered for you like I always do, but what happens if I can't get a hold of my contacts in time to destroy evidence? I'll tell you: we'd both be fucked. Stop. Making. Mistakes."

I don't respond to that because he's right. And I fucking hate that he's right.

Elias was sixteen when I was forced to kill our mother. He returned home that night after hanging out with his friends and found her lying in a pool of her blood. He took her into his arms, begging her to wake up. He sat there for half an hour crying, helpless and scared.

Elias eventually called our father, who rushed home from his office at QBM headquarters and found me nearly dead in the snow on our front lawn.

He didn't take me to the hospital or call the cops. Instead, he took me to the doctor on his payroll who had medical supplies in his home. I was stitched up in a makeshift hospital room where I stayed, recovering, until waking up a week later.

Elias was there by my side the moment I opened my eyes.

"They made me do it," I whisper.

Elias's head jerks up at the scratchy sound of my voice.

"Do what, Lance-a-lot?"

"The men. They made me kill her."

My brother's face pales, his nostrils flare, and pure anger and disgust washes over his face.

"I didn't want to—"

"I know."

"I'm sorry–"

"So am I."

I thought he'd understand. I thought he'd comfort me and tell me everything was okay. Instead, he could barely look at me.

He told me not to tell our father. He said Percy Carter would have killed me for what I'd done.

I believed him because when I refused to speak, Percy was furious. He demanded I tell him everything. What the men looked like, sounded like, names, anything to help find them.

It was too late. My humanity was gone.

When Percy died shortly after my eighteenth birthday, Elias took over the Queensboro Mafia. He was only twenty-two, but he had no choice. Our father didn't include me in the will and was very clear that Elias was the one to lead the organization. My brother is fucking smart too. He shadowed my father and learned the business. He was more than ready to lead.

I'm glad because I wanted nothing to do with the Q BM... until Elias suggested I be their hitman and allowed me to have an outlet for the rage festering inside me. I was nineteen when he gave me my first assignment. I was twenty when I branched out to take other hit jobs. I was twenty-five when people began calling me the Marionette.

Now I'm almost thirty-two and considered one of the best in the country, maybe even the world, despite rarely traveling for my hits.

Unlike Colpa Sicario, who thrives on international assignments.

Elias spent his life hating me for what I did, but he still kept me close. Together, we uncovered our father's secrets. Secrets Percy kept from us, and even his underboss, Martin, our uncle.

Elias and I spent hours in his office, sorting through our father's paperwork. He had files on the men who barged into our home and kept them hidden in his safe. He had their names, addresses, and pictures. Seeing their faces as an adult when I no longer feared them instilled rage throughout my body.

We can only assume he never took action because the files didn't include information that linked these men to our rivals. He didn't want to accuse the other Dons of murder and start a mafia war. The city was different twenty years ago. The QBM was newer and not as powerful as the other two crime organizations that run the city.

Or maybe it took him years to gather the information in the files, and he died before he could seek his revenge.

So, Elias and I decided to do it for him. For *us*. One by one, I tracked down the men. They lied about being affiliated with either rival mob. They refused to give me information about their boss.

Until the last man who broke after weeks of torture. He gave me a name.

After taking a deep inhale of the joint, I stamp it out on my shoe and stand.

"I have to go."

Elias grabs my arm when I attempt to pass him.

"Stop taking extra hits and focus on this." He waits for a response, but I don't know what to say. I need to kill to stay sane. Killing corrupt and evil assholes keeps my demons away. "Please, Lance."

My brother's pleading voice manages to pierce through this emotionless wall I've erected. It's the first time since we were kids that he's looked at me with something other than animosity. Perhaps our relationship isn't a lost cause after all.

"Okay, Elly. I'll stop." At least, I'll stop after I complete my next kill—which I accepted long before big bro spurred this request of me.

Elias gives me a single nod and lets go of my arm. I don't look back as I leave the cemetery.

If I'm going to put a pause on taking jobs, I'll need another outlet. Something to take my mind off the memories that never seem to fade. Something to tame the resentment for the rich and powerful and the life I was born into.

I take the highway back to the Morrisania section of the Bronx. Back to the gun range owned by Gio Lenetti: the leader of the Empire Mafia and the man responsible for placing a hit on my mother.

He's the most powerful man in the city. He has high-ranking city officials on his payroll. Killing him won't be easy, which is why I'm taking my time. It's why I need to worm my way into his organization.

Once he's gone, the QBM can take claim as the most powerful mob in New York City.

We're prepared to fight for the spot.

Even though my rainbow bright distracted me while at the gun range, I did notice how secure the place is. Huge guards wearing suits and earpieces, packing heat, stationed at doors.

Time to let my charm do the work. I rarely use it because I have no need to make friends. But now I do. I need to get access.

It might take a few weeks, but this is how I get close to Lenetti.

It's going to take patience… which is why I need that new outlet more than ever.

Chapter 8

Noah

Fucking Delancy.

I can't stand him.

He left suddenly... *again.*

I waited all day and night for him to return only to fall asleep on the couch because he never came back to his apartment.

It's Saturday, and I don't have plans tonight. Maybe I should go back out to the gun range. I've owned guns before, but I just never understood the appeal. They're so... impersonal. Messy. The easy way out. Give me a knife any day.

The last time I even used one was a few years ago and my aim was shit. So, yeah, I need to practice.

Del's re-direct approach helped me understand. It got me *excited* because when I find the men responsible for my mother's death, I won't hesitate to shoot the motherfuckers in the middle of the head.

I've been blankly staring at the shelves of my living room bookcase, trying to figure out what's wrong with it. Something's off, but I can't quite pinpoint what exactly. I dusted the other day. I cleaned my entire apartment top to bottom out of frustration over the asshole next door. Maybe the cleanliness is what's so jarring.

My phone chirps with a text.

Bestie

Hey! I'm feeling sexy and want to go out tonight. Come with!

I laugh because Sage is always sexy.

Me

I'm down. Let's go to Club 99 SoHo. 9pm?

Bestie

See you then, babe

She adds a kissy face emoji.

I'm *not* in the mood to fake laugh and flirt tonight, but Del is driving me crazy, and I need to blow off some steam. What better way than to find someone to fuck?

Wait a damn minute...

Now that I think about it, I used to have the best sex life. Then I met *him*. Delancy ruined sex for me.

It wasn't until Adam that I finally accepted how desperately I want to fuck Del. He's been making a home at the depths of my subconscious, slowly chipping his way out to the forefront. I need to get him out of my system. Especially if he's going to be weird every time he sees me because of that malicious hug at the gun range.

He's hot and cold. One minute he's caring for my wounds and the next he's running away.

Fucking men.

I need this night out. Maybe I'll bring someone home and let Del listen through the wall to what he's missing out on. I mean, I know he already does that, but the thought of him sitting alone in his apartment, dick hard in his hands while listening to my moans, turns me on.

Or I could invite him to join.

The buzzer to my apartment sounds. I called my hair stylist, Jenny, to book an in-home appointment because it's time for a change.

My stomach twists with excitement at how Del will react to the new look. My hair gives him ammunition. He loves poking fun but what I have planned will hopefully garner an entirely new reaction. One that includes him taking me by the throat and fucking me against a wall. Or the floor.

Or anywhere, for fuck's sake!

It takes a couple hours for Jenny to complete the transformation. I tip her generously and tell her I'll text her when I'm ready for a new color.

I'm about to start the beautification process for tonight when there's a knock on the door that's so unnecessarily loud, I swear a SWAT team is on the other side.

I grab my knife, hiding it behind my back before answering... only for Bryan and Ryan, two of my father's goons, to stroll in. They're twins in their late twenties who have permanent scowls on their tanned and handsome faces.

"Crap. I forgot I asked you two to do this. You didn't tell my dad, did you?"

They look at each other, then back at me with a mask of guilt.

"Seriously? Fine, I'll deal with him later." That must have been what the text was about telling me to come by the restaurant tomorrow. "I need to get ready, but you boys have at it."

They're changing my locks and adding additional ones. I don't trust Del. He claims I left my door unlocked, but I know for a fact I didn't. He totally picked the lock, and I bet he learned that useful skill as a "private investigator."

I still don't believe that's his real job.

Abercrombie and Fitch get to work while I head into the bathroom to shower and shave. By the time I walk out, the guys are done and sitting at my tiny kitchen table, eating the ham and cheese Hot Pockets I'd been saving for a lazy day.

"Thanks for the new locks. You may go now."

"Not if you're going out," Bryan, the one with short buzzed blond hair, says. "You know you're supposed to call us when you leave this apartment, which you've been doing a lot. How do you keep getting past us, anyway?"

"I have no idea what you're talking about."

My father has them stationed on the street in front of my apartment. Not that that's stopped me from ditching them whenever I want.

"Listen, Bry Guy," I begin, dropping my robe to get dressed. He's not even phased by my naked body. His brother Ryan, however, stares at me, eyes as big as saucers with his mouth hanging open. "There's no way I'm letting you two follow me around all night, cock blocking me. Now, if you'd kindly fuck off..."

I slip on my red laced panties and strapless bra. Bryan rolls his eyes while Ryan adjusts himself and squirms in his seat.

"Your father will kill us if we disobey his orders," Ryan says, gulping.

"I won't let him."

Bryan chuckles, knowing I can't do shit to stop my father when he has his mind set on killing someone.

I sigh and angrily snatch my dress off the hanger. "Fine, get the fuck out so I can finish dressing. I'll meet you out in the car."

"Nice try, Princess," Bryan says. "We'll wait outside your door."

I flip them off the moment the door shuts.

They can't tell me what to do. I'm a grown ass adult. A little immature sometimes, sure, but being responsible gets depressing so sometimes, I have to keep things... feisty.

I shimmy on the strapless black dress, the skin-tight fabric stretching over my rolls fantastically and makes my tits look luscious. My hair falls over my shoulders in thick, dark red curls, and my makeup is light except for the maroon lipstick to match my hair.

If only Del could see how fucking hot I look right now...

Not that I'll see him tonight. I doubt he knows how to have fun. Has he ever been to a club? I can't imagine him dancing.

Shrugging on my red leather jacket, I grab my clutch and red stilettos then crawl out my window bare foot. I climb down the fire escape and onto the ladder that leads to the ground of the trash area behind my apartment building.

I'm lucky the super keeps it clean back here, so I don't step on a broken piece of glass or a mouse. More than often, I'm climbing up not down because I locked myself out of my apartment. At least the locks on the windows of this building are shit—

Wait.

Is that how Del got in?

I glance up at the fire escape and sure enough, his unit connects with mine.

Guess it's time to reinforce those windows.

Unless I want *Del to keep sneaking into my apartment.*

I creep around the corner of the building to make sure one of the guys didn't come out here to wait. That would have been smart: one waits at my door, the other in the car. But neither twin is outside, so I rush down the sidewalk to the corner bodega where I called my Uber.

My dad is going to be pissed that I ditched my protection again, especially since I agreed to let them escort me out in public.

Oops. I lied.

After a forty-minute ride from Astoria, the Uber pulls up to the front of Club 99 SoHo. It's one of those upscale spots that's frequented by the rich and famous. Which means it's discreet. No security cameras inside or out. That's why I drag Sage here. My father doesn't have spies at this club. At least, none that I've seen because I certainly would have heard about it.

Aside from the gun range and his restaurants, Gio Lenetti also owns about a dozen bars and clubs around Manhattan and the Bronx. Too many times over the past two months after a night of partying, I'd wake up to an angry text from my father yelling at me to only go to the clubs owned by him so he can keep an eye on me.

My phone buzzes and Bryan's name flashes across the screen again. That's the tenth time he's called now. I have about twenty text messages from Ryan too. They've probably tried to trace my phone's location, but I made sure that wasn't possible a long time ago.

A long line wraps around the corner of the club, packed full of people dressed in their sleekest attire. Sage is waiting at the entrance, flirting with the bouncer, Marco. He's a huge guy with an equal amount of muscle and fat. He's not too tall, about my height, and he has long curly hair that he keeps up in a man bun on the top of his head. His brown eyes light up when speaking to Sage.

She's hooked up with him a few times, which helps get us a fast pass inside. It's very clear he's in love with her, but my best friend is like me. She's not looking for commitment. At least, for Sage, she has reasons. She's a divorcee who's about to turn thirty-three. Her asshole ex stole her identity and racked up thousands of dollars in debt. He went to jail, but his sentence was only a year.

I keep telling Sage I can get rid of him, but she dismisses the idea as if I'm joking. I'm not. I will kill him if she says the word. Or maybe she knows I'm serious and doesn't want me to get in trouble and that's why she also refuses to tell me about the other horrible things he's done to her.

"Noey!" she sings once spotting me.

"Damn, woman," I praise, giving her a once over. She's wearing a body-hugging red midi dress with a sweetheart neckline and built-in corset to give her breasts a bouncy boost. Her blonde hair is up in a high ponytail. All she needs is a whip to complete the dominatrix look.

Sage poses like a pinup model, one hand on her hip, the other up in the air.

"Do you like? I'm feeling really demanding right now and want to find a good boy to boss around."

"I think I'm in love with you," I laugh, hooking my hand through her arm.

"Do you want to watch? I'll let you give orders." Her eyes light up in excitement at the prospect.

"Maybe. We'll see how the night goes."

Marco unhooks the red velvet rope and lets us inside. We ignore the boos from the people waiting in line, throwing back our heads and cackling like the evil bitches we are.

Heat greets us the moment we step into the coat check, a welcome to the harsh winter air outside. We hand over our jackets and walk down a long hallway where flashing lights are synced to whatever song is playing over the speakers.

Passing through a velvet curtain, we enter the main space.

Club 99 SoHo used to be a theater in the eighties. It's four stories tall with balconies on each level, allowing people to stand around and chat or observe the dance floor below. A DJ is set up on a small stage at the back and four cages hang on either side where hired dancers are gyrating.

Bodies already crowd the massive dance floor. We squeeze our way through, heading to the bar lining the left side of the massive space.

Sage flags down the bartender. Harry gives us a wave and a wink, letting us know he saw us. He already knows our orders since we're somewhat regulars here now.

While waiting, I turn and scan the crowd, hoping to find someone to take home. I barely get a good look at the beautiful people when I'm suddenly jolted to the side by a massive body bumping into me.

"What the fuck?" I bark.

I whip around to see who the clumsy asshole is and nearly choke on my next words. "Oh, well, hello there."

A gorgeous man stands before me, his green eyes wide and face growing red from embarrassment. He's tall and slim with chiseled cheeks and a well-defined jaw.

A God, perhaps?

"I am so sorry." He runs his fingers through dirty blond hair. "I didn't mean to run into you like that. Someone knocked into me, and it was a domino effect."

I wave him off, blushing. "It's okay. It happens."

He looks behind me.

"Are you here with a boyfriend?"

I raise my brow at him. Real smooth.

"No, just my girlfriend." I point my chin back at Sage who gives him a little wave and blows him a kiss.

A sly smile spreads across his face that might have been creepy if my horniness and his beauty weren't currently clouding my judgment.

"Let me buy you a drink." He holds up his hands at whatever look I just gave him. "As an apology for accidentally bumping into you."

"Was it an accident? Bumping into me?"

"Cross my heart," he says, followed by the motion. He winks and gives me another mischievous smile to tell me he, in fact, meant to bump into me.

He does some finger wagging to get Harry's attention, then points to himself and me and mimes taking a drink. Harry nods, but I catch the eye roll before he turns away.

Blondie doesn't notice the shade because he's now leaning his arm on the bar, crowding my personal space. I don't mind. He smells fantastic: rose, amber, sandalwood, and other scents I couldn't name. Expensive for sure.

I glance over his shoulder at Sage, and she mouths 'oh my god.'

"You know... I've seen you in here before," he says.

"Oh yeah? And why haven't you introduced yourself until now? Do I intimidate you?"

"A little, yeah."

Good. He should fear me. I have plans for him.

Harry arrives with our drinks. A vodka soda with a splash of cranberry for me and whiskey for my target. He holds up his glass.

"What should we toast?" I ask.

He smirks. "How about to 'Cillian O'Connor, finally working up the courage to speak to the beautiful woman who will surely want to dance with him.'"

I snort as we clank glasses. "Just dance? You don't want to fuck me?"

He chokes on the booze, and I hide my humor by taking a sip of my own drink.

I set down my glass and grab Cillian's hand.

"Dance with me, Cilly Boy." *Killy Boy.* I'm so clever.

"I think it's only fair you tell me your name since you now know mine," he says while following my lead.

"Is it?" I laugh. "Fine. You can call me Rio."

"Rio? That's an interesting name."

"It's short for Sicario."

Chapter 9

Delancy

Fuck fuck fuck.

Noah just walked onto the dance floor, dragging my mark along with her.

Why the hell is she holding hands and flirting with Cillian O'Connor? I should warn her. Tell her the asshole is a rapist who covers up his crimes with money and blackmailing. I should tell her that the last woman he fucked got pregnant and was found dead at the bottom of the stairs to her apartment building.

Cillian is the son of Finn O'Connor, boss of the Lords of Staten Island. I've been wanting to kill him for years. He's had a hit on his head for as long as I can remember but no one has dared take the job.

Contract killers don't like getting involved with the mob, and New York City currently has three powerful ones.

But I'm not your typical contract killer. I'm a mafia hitman who doesn't give two fucks about the retaliation that will follow by killing Cillian. He's fucked around with the wrong people. He's killed, or ordered to be killed, too many people with ties to rival mobs, including the QBM.

The woman he murdered after getting her pregnant was my cousin.

I stand in the shadows of the balcony on the second level, watching my beautiful rainbow bright below. She looks sexier than ever. That black dress clinging to her voluptuous body. Her tits round and pushed up. Her long legs in those fuck me heels.

She dyed her hair dark red to match her plush burgundy lips.

She's no longer a bright kaleidoscope of colors but a fiery fox... a vixen luring unsuspecting lovers.

No wonder my target is on the dance floor with her, grinding his dick into her plump ass. Cillian loves shiny, pretty things, and Noah McAllister is certainly his next conquest.

Jealousy ricochets throughout my body. The urge to protect her, to claim her as mine and keep her safe, overwhelms me.

It's a sensation I've never experienced before.

Cillian's hands roam over my vixen's wide hips, his fingers splayed on her soft stomach as he kisses her neck. Noah laughs and reaches her arm up to fist his hair.

I want to kill him more than ever.

I scan the crowd for the two goons who accompanied Noah at the shooting range, but they're nowhere to be found. I've seen them lurking around our apartment building a lot more lately. She's definitely being protected but why and from whom?

And why aren't they here stopping this dickwad from fondling her?

It takes everything within my body not to go down there and rip him off her, throw him to the ground and bash his head on the concrete dance floor until his skull cracks, splattering brain matter everywhere.

It's been ages since I've wanted to violently murder someone. I don't like my kills to be bloody unless the job specifically states to do so.

I would make an exception for him.

But I can't go down there. I can't take Noah in my arms and kiss her to claim her as mine. I can't blow my cover.

Instead, I'm forced to watch her kiss him.

They make out for what has to be five minutes before coming up for air. She glances up into the balcony where I stand, and my heart forgets to beat. I step further into the shadows.

Did she see me? Recognize me? Certainly not.

She smirks in my direction—there's no way she saw me. Right? RIGHT?—then whispers in Cillian's ear. He nods excitedly and takes hold of her hand, leading her through the crowd and off the dance floor.

They stop next to a thick blonde woman, and Noah speaks with her briefly before leading Cillian to the exit.

Fuck. They're leaving.

My stomach sours, and my chest aches with how fast my heart is beating.

I'm... panicking.

I'm... worried about her.

I can't think about these strange emotions. How human they make me feel. I'm rushing down the long balcony walkway and descend the stairs. When I get to the lobby, I stay hidden behind a corner wall, waiting for them to get their coats. Every time I peek around, his hands are somewhere new: her ass, her lower back, in her dark red hair so he can pull back her head and kiss her neck.

I hate PDA. It's too sweet... too happy and loving.

Yet if Noah were mine, I'd make sure everyone knew. I wouldn't be able to keep my hands and lips off her in public either.

After an excruciating two minutes, they have their coats and the horny couple leaves. I rush up to the window and toss the worker a hundred-dollar bill and my ticket.

"I'm in a hurry," I seethe.

The pixie girl's eyes widen before she disappears to search for my leather jacket. She returns in record time, and I rush outside to my bike.

My hands shake as I unlock the helmet case, my fingers fumbling with my keys while trying to insert them into the ignition.

Get it together, Delancy.

Noah and Cillian are long gone, but I know where he's taking her. It's where he always takes all the women he picks up at clubs.

The high-rise in the Financial District disappears into the cloudy night. The streets are busy except for the side road where I need to enter to get to my vixen. He takes women down this dead end because it's dark and there are no cameras around.

I park my bike at the end of the street and walk a block to the building. There's a code to get in, one I know from my surveillance of Cillian over the last few months. The green light flashes and a beep sounds after I enter the four digits.

I slip inside, passing through a long hallway. This part of the building is lacking in security. Cillian has made sure of it. He doesn't want any trace of who he brings to his secret penthouse. A place where he feels he can do anything he wants without the consequences.

Down at the end of the hallway on the left is a pair of double doors, which I assume are for laundry service. What I need is on the right. I press the up button for the freight elevator and wait. It takes a few minutes for it to arrive, and my anxiety rises with each ticking second.

While Cillian has made sure not to have security in this area, there's still a chance I'll run into someone.

When the doors finally open, I slip in and push the button to the Penthouse. It requires a keycard to ascend, so I pull out the one I stole from a grounds worker this morning, hoping it hasn't been deactivated yet. The elevator begins moving, and I exhale a long breath of relief.

I scan the corners of the box and find no cameras, unless there are some hidden in the panel, which I doubt Cillian would allow. Not to mention, if security was watching, they'd stop the elevator on the next floor and detain me.

After less than a minute, the elevator slows and comes to a stop on the top floor. The doors open to a foyer of white swirled marble, walls decorated with expensive artwork, and two large abstract sculptures. There's another door that leads into the actual penthouse. I turn the knob and it unlatches.

Idiot didn't lock this door.

My footsteps are silent as I walk across the sitting room's floor. The cream furniture matches the cream walls, which are decorated with more expensive paintings by artists I couldn't begin to name. I pass a bathroom, the kitchen, and the dining room before the soft notes of music playing from a room deep within the penthouse hits my ears.

Damn, they're already in the bedroom?

That was fast.

Beyond the living area—which should have a fantastic view of downtown New York City if it weren't for the cloudy night—is a hallway. Framed photos hang on the walls and there's a long and thin table with a vase of flowers and a stack of books on top. The dull music gets louder the longer I walk, passing closed doors left and right.

I know the bedroom at the very back is Cillian's room. I broke in a month ago and planted surveillance cameras in there and a few others throughout the penthouse to watch and record his crimes. He's brought women here to violently fuck—some who were into it, many who weren't. He shot a man in the head in the living room after he refused to pay up for who the hell knows what. And he's sat at his kitchen island conspiring with men—who I recognize as Lords members—to kill a whole list of people; names I didn't get because they never said them out loud, but I'm guessing they're victims of his father's strict loan shark operations or maybe even rival mob members.

Now my rainbow bright is in there with him. My *vixen*. The woman who somehow managed to warm the frozen organ that sits in my chest.

What's his plan for her?

She seemed into him at the club. Could this just be a hookup? What if I'm overreacting?

I need to be sure she's in danger before barging into this room to save her.

The music is loud so if they're talking or fucking, I can't tell.

Wait...

Was that a whimper?

Fury ignites within my chest. Images of Noah, spread out before Cillian while he fucks her, dance across my vision. My hand reaches for the knob of the door and I'm seconds from bursting into the room.

Then I hear a humph and a thud.

The song ends.

"I've been wanting to do this for weeks, Cilly Boy," Noah says.

What the hell?

There's a groan and another whimper. Then a sound I'm all too familiar with; a knife plunging into flesh.

I twist the doorknob and enter the room.

Noah is straddling Cillian on the ground, the knife protruding from his chest. She's nearly naked except for a red bra and panties—a fantastic see through lace set. Blood is splattered across her frontside, and her chest rises and falls with heavy breaths.

Haven't I fantasized about this very thing?

No. This can't be right. My rainbow bright's no killer.

Unless... is she?

"Noah?"

The sound of my voice startles her, and she jumps up to stand.

"Delancy? What the hell? Did you follow me? I thought that was you at the club." She looks down at her bloody frontside, to Cillian's lifeless body, to her open, soiled hands. "I can explain."

"No need to explain, Vixen. I came here to do just that."

Chapter 10

Noah

"You what?"

Did he just say he came here to kill Cillian? I think I misheard him.

"I'm here to kill Cillian."

Oh... um. "Okay... what do you mean by that?"

"What do you think I mean, Vixen?"

Vixen? What happened to Rainbow Bright? Oh... my hair. I dyed it. That clever fucker.

"Who are you?" I ask.

"I'm a hitman."

"What?"

He's not. He can't be. He's been living next to me for two months. I'd know if he was a contract killer. Right? I mean, what are the odds that two contract killers move in next to each other?

Something's not adding up here.

"This was my mark." He points at Cillian, still dead on the floor.

"That's insane," I say and slowly back away. I need a weapon. The knife I killed Cillian with is still in his chest. My other knife is in my clutch, which is discarded on the floor at the side of the bed with my dress. If Del's telling the truth, and he's a contract killer, then he might try to kill me for claiming his mark and cashing out on the hefty pay day.

"Why are you backing away from me, Noah?" he asks, holding a hand behind his back, surely ready to grab a weapon.

Fuck. He knows. He's figured it out.

"Tell me why you killed Cillian. What did he do to you?"

I say nothing, and he narrows his eyes at me.

"Are you in trouble? Is that why..." His thoughts are moving a mile a minute. I can see him silently working through everything. He suspects what I am, yet his brain won't let him accept it. "I can help you clean this up. I'll make it look like an accident."

His eyes search the room as if taking stock of every drop of blood and all the things I touched.

An accident? He can make a knife in the chest look like an accident? The only person I know who can do that is...

I gasp. "Marionette?"

His head jerks up to mine. "What did you just say?"

"You're the Marionette."

"How do you know about that?"

Wait. He's not just any contract killer. He's my *rival*?

He stalks toward me, his eyes darkening with something that should terrify me, but it's turning me on instead. Which confuses me because I should hate him. He's the one threatening my title as best contract killer in the country—maybe even the world, but who's keeping track?

No, I don't hate him. I've been dreaming about this moment. Will he want to play with me?

His large hand clutches my chin. "Tell me, Kevin. How do you know who I am?"

I'm back to Kevin? It's my least favorite of his nicknames. I was starting to love Rainbow Bright. Even Skittles was cute. And Vixen? Fuck, I'm wet just thinking about him calling me that a few seconds ago.

I slam my elbow against his arm, forcing him to release his hold. He stumbles back, his eyes wide. When he starts for me again, I kick him in the stomach and send him crashing into Cillian's wall of mirrors. Shards of broken glass fall to the ground on top of him.

While he's down for the count, I run to the side of the bed and lift my discarded dress, finding my clutch underneath. By the time my knife is in my hand, and I turn around, Del is in front of me. I slice him across the forearm before he knocks the weapon out of my hold and grasps my hair at the nape. Tugging my head back, he digs the tip of his own knife into the side of my neck.

"Who are you?" he snarls.

I whimper as the sharp blade breaks skin, causing blood to trickle out. He's not being gentle and instead of scaring me, I'm so fucking aroused, my panties are getting soaked.

"I'm Noah," I whisper. He hasn't secured my hands, so I rub them over his muscular chest, then slide them down his stomach.

He pushes the knife's tip deeper before I reach his cock and tightens his hold on my hair. He narrows his eyes when I moan.

"Tell me. Who. Are. You?"

I arch my body, brushing my front against his. He loosens his grip on my hair enough that I'm able to lean in.

"I think you know who I am."

He shakes his head and lowers the knife.

"No," he says and takes a step back.

"Colpa Sicario."

"No!" His voice booms in the quiet room.

"What's wrong? Too scared to kill me now?" His shoulders hunch in defeat and when his blue eyes meet mine, they're full of confusion... of betrayal. My heart responds to this side of Delancy because I've only known him to be grumpy and void of all other emotions.

Now? He almost seems heartbroken.

Because he was planning to kill Colpa Sicario. He just didn't know it would be me.

He slowly walks back to where I stand, dragging his feet like a zombie.

Once there's only a few inches between us, he lifts his hand and caresses my cheek. He runs his thumb over my lips, and I stop myself from snatching it between my teeth.

Such compassion from a man who kills for a living.

I breathe in deeply, consuming his sweaty, woodsy scent: cedar wood with hints of tangerines.

His fingertips skim along my jaw and down my neck before snaking around to grip my hair again.

Then he crashes his lips into mine.

I open my mouth to let his tongue lash my own. I groan and the sound only intensifies this kiss. My hands fist his shirt as I pull him closer to me.

I need more.

He's devouring me with his magical mouth, and my hands are frantically working to remove his shirt when a pain rips through my right side.

I break the kiss and look down.

"You stabbed me?"

He pushes the knife in deeper.

"You asshole!"

His mouth twists into a wicked smile, proud of himself.

"You missed some vital organs, Marionette."

He pulls out the knife, and I grunt at the stinging, biting ache. I hold the wound as blood begins pouring down my hip and leg.

"I know exactly where the vital organs are, Vixen," he says, stabbing me *again* in my upper left arm. He wipes my blood from the blade on his black cargo pants. "Maybe I want you alive so I can play with you. Torture you."

His eyes roam my body as if picking out another spot to impale, and it's enough of a distraction to make my move. I head butt him; blood immediately starts gushing out of his nose, then I hook my foot around his leg, knocking his feet from underneath him. He falls to the ground on his back—still clutching the knife.

"Joke's on you," I say, straddling him. "I get off on pain. Stab me again. Make me come."

He doesn't hesitate and sinks the knife into the meat of my right thigh.

Fuck that hurts. I love pain, but not this shit. Still, I put on a show, mewling and closing my eyes as I grind my hips on his crotch. His cock grows hard underneath me.

"Yes, Delancy," I moan, then slap him hard enough his head ricochets to the side.

He growls and slices the knife across my stomach. The wound isn't deep enough to cause internal damage, but blood starts leaking from the cut.

My palms flatten on Del's chest as I continue to move my hips in a circular motion. He leans his head back on the floor, closing his eyes.

"Does that feel good?"

He nods and drops the knife so he can smooth his hands up and down my thighs, spreading blood in streaks. I'm not sure if it's my blood or his. Probably both.

I slap Del again, harder than last time, forcing his lip to break open.

"Noah!" he roars and flips us around until my back hits the ground.

I kick out my leg, hitting him in the nuts. He falls off me, grabbing his injured jewels.

I scoop up his knife and fall to my knees. With the cuts he gave me on my stomach, arm, and thigh, I'm close to passing out.

Not until I fuck him up some more.

I slam the blade into his thigh, and he cries out in agonizing pain.

"Here we are," I say, swaying. My vision is starting to blur. "Number one and number two."

After composing himself from the nut kick, Del rips the knife out of his thigh. He doesn't even flinch as blood spurts out and onto the floor. My aim must have been shit, and I didn't cause enough damage.

That's a shame.

The cut I made on his forearm, however, will definitely leave a scar. Blood continues to trickle out down to his knuckles.

He matches my stance, on his knees before me as he takes in my body. I'm still covered in splatter from killing Cillian and now my own... I'm sure I look like a horror show. A murder victim. Or a murder suspect. Still, heat and desire stare back at me.

"Finish the job. Kill me, Delancy."

Before he can respond, dizziness claims me. There's a sensation of falling before I'm delved into blackness.

I wake up in an unfamiliar bed, sore and barely able to move.

"Careful, Vixen, you don't want to tear your stitches."

I swat my arm towards the voice, attempting to smack the man, only for his warm hand to stop me from making contact. When my eyes finally focus, I see Del smiling back at me.

"Good morning, sweetheart."

"Don't fucking call me sweetheart, asshole." I rip my arm out of his grip. I hate pet names and even though him calling me sweetheart makes that organ in my chest flutter ever so slightly, I'd never tell him that. If he knew I *liked* being called all his silly nicknames (minus Kevin), he'd never do it again. "Where am I?"

"Cillian's guest bedroom."

I glance around the space and sit up, wincing at the throbbing pain.

"How did I get here?"

"I carried you."

"How? I'm nearly 300 pounds."

"And?"

My eyes move to his arms. Fine. I suppose he is fucking ripped. He smiles, the cocky bastard, seeing me checking him out.

"How long was I asleep?"

"About three hours. It's three a.m."

"You stabbed me. Four times."

"You told me to."

"It was the blood loss. I wasn't in my right mind."

"Oh yeah?" he chuckles and pinches my nipple through the fabric of my bra. I gasp and try to hit him again. "Is that why these are hard right now? I can basically smell how wet you are."

"Nice bruises," I say, admiring the half-moons under his eyes from when I head-butted him. "Is your nose broken?"

"Nope."

"Damn."

I toss the covers off my body.

"What are you doing? You probably shouldn't get up."
The panic in Del's voice—because I doubt he's cared for
many injured women in his life—makes me huff a laugh...
which hurt like a bitch.

"I have to pee. Help me or get out of the way."

He rolls his eyes but offers his hand. I take it, ignoring
the thrill that shoots up my arm and spills in my stomach,
awakening the butterflies.

It's been a long time since a single touch has made my
stomach flutter.

Del cautiously leads me to the bathroom across the hallway. He's careful and patient as I hiss and groan with every
step. He's also limping, and I'm quite proud of myself for
giving him that hole in his thigh.

By the time we make it to the toilet, I stand there, staring
at the porcelain throne as I try to figure out how I'm going
to do this.

"Do you need help here?"

I frown and nod.

If he's in pain from the wounds I gave him, he doesn't
show it as he kneels and slips the tips of his fingers behind
the bands of my panties.

He slowly slides them down and not once does he look
at my pussy just inches from his face. Instead, he locks his
blue eyes with mine.

"Use me as an anchor to sit down."

I grip his shoulders and when my ass hits the toilet seat, I let out a long breath of relief.

"Thank you. You can leave now."

He pauses as if considering staying but gives me an unsure smile before leaving.

I'm surprised I hadn't pissed the bed with how much pee I release. Once finished—and feeling a million times better—I manage to pull my panties back up. I carefully and slowly wash my hands, then use the sink's counter as a crutch to raid the medicine cabinet. I find a bottle of pain meds—the good stuff that Cillian probably smuggled—and pop one in my mouth, washing it down by using my hand as a cup.

I tuck the bottle in my bra and wipe the surfaces down to remove my fingerprints from everything I touched. By the time that's done, I'm sweating and exhausted as I inch my way out of the restroom. I pray to whatever god will listen that the painkillers work fast.

I pass the guest bedroom to check out Cillian's room and find the place wrecked. Cillian's body is on the floor, lying in a pool of his blood, in front of the shattered glass mirror that broke when I kicked Del into it.

I spot my reflection in the rest of the wall-o-mirrors.

Del kicked my ass. What's crazy is I'm not even mad at him. I *did* tell him to stab me.

My dark red hair is frizzy beyond control, my eyeliner resembles a raccoon. I'm still in nothing but my bra and panties. The blood splatter was at least cleaned off my skin.

My face heats with the thought of Del sweeping a wet cloth over my stomach, chest, and neck.

"Damn, Vixen, how do you make murder look so good?"

The reflection shows him checking me out from behind. I turn and cross my arms and Del's eyes fall to my cleavage.

"What's your plan with Cillian?"

"Deadly home invasion. You should see the living room. I destroyed everything. His office too. I broke into his safe and stole everything inside: money, jewelry, gold." He opens his hands. "His enemy list is long. No one will ever suspect anything out of the ordinary."

"What about our blood?"

"I have a law enforcement source who destroys evidence. I already gave him the heads up."

Of course he did.

Del stalks toward me, and I step back until my ass bumps into a dresser.

"Why didn't you kill me?" I ask, my voice a near whisper. It's stolen by this man who's now in front of me, his hard front flush with my softness. He pushes a piece of my hair back behind my ear and glances down at my lips, then back to my eyes.

"Who says I'm not going to kill you?"

I snort and the corner of his mouth turns up, stretching the faint scar on his lip. I want to touch it. I want to ask him how he got it. Same with the matching scar on his cheek. Something tells me those injuries aren't from his work as a contract killer.

What about the scars on his chest and stomach? Were they from fights like ours? I gave him two new scars. Almost as if I've staked my claim over him.

He staked claim over me too.

"Who stitched me up?"

He has yet to step back. I might be panting, my voice breathy, because I can't function when he's this close to me. Despite me being five-ten, he towers over me by a few inches. He makes me feel small, which never happens.

Del traces his fingertips over the bandage on my arm, then to the one on my side. I shiver and goosebumps prickle my skin.

"I did."

"Did you stitch yourself up too?"

"Yes."

God, why is he so perfect?

Never mind that he tried to kill me. He's still sexy and perfect and devours me with every sweep of his eyes.

"Tell me why you followed me in the club."

His eyes move back to mine. "I was following Cillian. I was planning to kill him tonight. Then when he bumped into you... I thought he was going to take you home and rape you. Or harm you. Cillian was a horrible man."

"I know. That's why I accepted the hit on him a couple weeks ago. Guess whoever wanted him dead had assurances put in place."

Del clenches his jaw and turns his back to me.

"Does that make you angry, Puppet? That I'm the one who took him out?"

He swings around, his fists balled at his sides. He's breathing hard, clenching and unclenching his fists over and over. Then his tense shoulders sag.

"How did you become... how, dammit?!"

I shouldn't want to explain myself. I shouldn't want his validation. But I do.

I push off the dresser and walk to him.

"I'll tell you everything." Well, not *everything*. "But maybe we shouldn't be hanging out at a crime scene. We've been here too long. And I need a shower."

Del nods and points his hand at the door.

"Lead the way, Vixen."

Chapter 11

Delancy

"Hell yeah! I've been dying to take a ride on your motorcycle!" Noah says as we approach my bike parked down the block. "KTM 990 Duke, right?"

"You know bikes?"

"Not at all, but I looked yours up online."

"Stalker," I say with a laugh.

But my laugh fades as I see her wince with every big move she makes. Her pain has lessened, thanks to some pills she told me she stole from Cillian. But I know she's still hurting. She'd never admit to it though.

"Actually, I think I need to call us a car."

"What? Why!" Noah whines.

"Your injuries..."

My motorcycle is a smooth ride but what if I hit a bump and her wounds open back up?

She scoffs. "Fuck that. I'll be fine! I always wanted to be someone's pretty little backpack."

Pretty is such an insignificant word when it comes to Noah McAllister. She's beautiful. Gorgeous. She's a word that has yet to be invented to describe how exquisite she is.

Before we left Cillian's penthouse, she slipped on the dress she wore to the club and braided her hair, letting the tail fall over her shoulder. She put herself back together, but I'd love nothing more than to destroy her again with a night of sex and worshiping.

This new obsession of mine is both terrifying and exhilarating. I want to run from these feelings but at the same time, embrace them... embrace her... and never let go.

"Okay, my pretty little backpack." I hand her my helmet to put on. "I'll take you for a ride."

She giggles at the innuendo while securing the helmet's straps underneath her chin.

"Wait," Noah says as I climb on. "I can't go back to my apartment." Before I can ask why, she continues. "I'll explain later. Just... take me to one of your safe houses."

"How do you know I have—"

"Safe house, *Marionette*."

Of course she knows I have safe houses.

What about her?

She just moved back not too long ago. Maybe she hasn't secured any safe houses yet.

Or she doesn't want me to know where they are.

Noah's arms slide around my torso, and she squeezes hard enough that I almost can't breathe. Her front smashes against my back, and I close my eyes at how intimate this is.

Not as intimate as our kiss.

How she whined as if begging for my taste. How she melted into me as the kiss deepened.

Then I stabbed her.

I had to. Payback for the loud sex. For being Colpa Sicario.

For driving me mad.

When she begged me to do it again, that might have been the moment I knew I could never let this woman go.

Once I'm certain Noah is secure, we take off. She yelps and squeezes me tighter.

I take us across the Brooklyn Bridge, heading to Flatbush. The ride is quick since traffic in the middle of the night is scarce.

At some point, Noah gets comfortable. She loosens her hold around me, and her balled up hands flatten on my stomach. My cock jerks as she smooths her palms up and down my abs. As if she can't get enough of me.

I can't get enough of *her*. I remember how devastatingly deadly she looked nearly naked and covered in blood while straddling Cillian. Her small hands wrapped around the knife's handle with the blade embedded in his chest. How wonderful she smelled when I cleaned and stitched her up: jasmine and hints of citrus.

It felt wrong to touch her, clean her, while she was passed out, but I couldn't risk bringing anyone in to mend her injuries.

My eyes are heavy. I've been awake for nearly twenty-four hours. It was worth it to see Noah in action. I'm not even pissed anymore that she's Colpa Sicario. Which means Guilt Killer or Sin Killer in Italian. How could I be angry? She's perfect. I want to ask her what her plan was after she killed Cillian. How was she going to frame it?

Her kills are passionate. She's not concerned about making a mess or posing it as an accident. But at the same time, she's careful enough not to leave evidence behind.

I pull up to a two-story building where I rent a loft above a pizza place.

"Are you hungry?" I ask, locking up my bike in a narrow alleyway.

"God yeah. I want a slice of pineapple and ham. And cheese sticks."

"I should kill you right now. Pineapple does not belong on pizza."

"Wrong, Puppet. Just for that, I want *two* slices of pineapple and ham."

I wince at the nickname. "Seriously? Puppet?"

"It's cute! Come on!" She laughs, then blanches from pain.

"Fine. I'll grab the slices." I toss her my keys. "You go upstairs... behave yourself."

"I hope you have wine," she yells as I turn and walk inside the pizza shop.

"**Y**our place is amazing," Noah says the moment I return.

She's changed into one of my tank tops and a pair of my sweats. They're both too small for her, but I quite like how the fabric clings to her body, allowing me to see all her wonderful curves.

She walks around the massive living room, snooping through my stuff. I have a line of bookshelves along one of the brick walls, and she's reading the spines of every book. I don't have many. Maybe three dozen. Once in a while, she scrunches her nose, letting me know she found a genre she's not a fan of.

I read a little bit of everything: mystery, thrillers, horror, non-fiction, and now romance after stealing Noah's smut book.

She reaches a corner where I store my instruments. Her fingers pluck at the strings of the acoustic guitar then press down on the white keys of the keyboard I have leaned up against the wall.

"You play?"

"Not like I used to."

She frowns but doesn't ask me to explain, and I exhale a little bit because I don't want to talk about that part of my life. At least, not right now.

On the right side of the living area is a white couch and matching oversized chair set up in front of the flatscreen television hanging on the wall. Tall windows line the third wall, which I always keep shuttered with blackout curtains.

The loft expands into a dining and kitchen space with small storage space overhead. Previous tenants might have used it as a bedroom, but I hide my weapons up there.

The living area was big enough to build walls for a bedroom since I'm not a fan of open concept, mostly when it comes to sleeping. I'd much rather have a door to close so I can have somewhat of a warning in case an intruder or an enemy finds me.

"Here," I say, placing Noah's pizza on a paper plate, adding fake gags.

She flips me off, then grabs the plate and the glass of wine she poured before I returned home, and curls up on my couch, her legs underneath her.

She's definitely made herself at home, turning on the TV and finding a rom-com to watch.

A sexual groan erupts from the woman at her first bite of warm Hawaiian pizza, and she does a little happy dance in her seat. I toss an accent pillow at her head, but her reflexes kick in and she bats it away just in time. She sticks her tongue out at me.

The brat.

Noah washes down her food with a sip of sweet Riesling that I've had on my shelf for years. I'm not much of a wine drinker, but I kept that bottle around for some reason.

"This is heaven." She sighs and takes another bite. "Can we stay here forever and forget about our jobs as contract killers?"

Yes. I think, refusing to voice my desperation to have her in my life.

She laughs at whatever the actor in the movie just said. I haven't been paying attention, instead, I've been watching *her*. She laughs a lot, and I never realized how addictive that laugh is. It's hearty, not quiet in the least. I've heard her giggles through the walls of our apartments on many occasions, but to be in the same room as her when she's s o... happy... it's all too consuming. I'm becoming a glutton for her presence.

"Are you going to stare at me all night?"

I immediately look away, blushing from being caught.

I rarely blush, yet this woman constantly has me flustered.

"The cuts and bruises you had that morning I snuck into your apartment... was that from a hit job?"

She scoffs. "You *broke* into my apartment."

"Is it breaking in when you leave your window unlocked?"

"I left it unlocked one time. Besides, those flimsy window latches wouldn't have kept you out."

"They didn't."

"How many times did you break into my apartment?"

I shrug and she narrows her warm brown eyes. "A few."

"Did you do it while I was home? Did you watch me sleep?"

"Would that turn you on?"

"I sleep naked."

"I know."

Her mouth drops open, her cheeks coloring a lovely red.

Yep. She's turned on.

"The cuts and bruises, Noe."

She rolls her eyes but smiles.

"Yes, I got them during a hit. The man wasn't going to die quietly. He grabbed a kitchen knife and nicked me a few times and got a few good punches in too."

"What was his crime? How did you kill him?"

"He beat the fuck out of his girlfriend and put her in a coma. She's brain dead and now her family has to make the tough decision to end her life. I met her sister at the bar where I work. She stopped in to get a drink, to try and escape her life just for a few minutes. We started talking and at the end of my shift, I offered to help. I really enjoyed stabbing the fuck out of that asshole."

I wonder if she'd let me tag along on one of her jobs. I'd love to watch her work.

"And you just left him there to be found?"

"I ransacked the place and made it look like a deadly home invasion."

Just like I did Cillian. I guess we're more alike than I imagined.

"Don't worry, I made sure to clean up any evidence that could be traced back to me."

She's perfect. I can't believe I've been living next to my rival for two months. No wonder I've been so drawn to her.

I hate coincidences, but if Noah knew I was the Marionette when she moved in, she would have tried to kill me by now.

Was it fate?

"Tell me how you became Colpa Sicario."

"Do we really have to talk about this?"

"Yes," I say, standing to pour myself more wine. I grab another slice of supreme pizza and smile remembering Noah's nose scrunching at the sight of the olives and mushrooms.

She sighs, preparing herself for difficult memories.

"My mother was murdered when I was eleven."

"Mine too. Well, I was twelve, but still…"

She pauses and gives me an empathetic glance.

"Keep going," I urge, not meaning to distract her by blurting out my trauma.

"I heard her yelling when two men broke in, so I came out of my room and hid at the top of the stairs. Then I saw one of the fuckers shoot her point blank. I screamed. They ran after me, but I made it back to my room in time to lock them out.

"They tried to get in. They almost did, but one minute they were kicking and punching the door and the next there was nothing but silence."

She takes another drink of her wine to compose the rest of her thoughts.

"I had nightmares every night that first week after. I'd wake up screaming and covered in sweat. My father didn't have time to deal with a traumatized child, so he sent me away. He also claimed it was to protect me, worried the men would come back for me.

"I spent years in therapy for what I saw, and when I turned eighteen, my father begged me to return home. He promised the threat was over, but I wasn't ready. I enrolled in college, attempting to live a normal life. I even got my degree in business management."

This would explain her fake background report. A new life was created to protect her from the men she witnessed killing her mother. My question now is what's her real name? Why was her mother targeted? Who is her father? Was he someone important and her mother became collateral damage?

We'll get to those questions eventually. I don't want to scare her away right now by interrogating her.

"After graduation, I traveled. I took self-defense classes because I never wanted to be put in the same situation as my mother. I wanted to be able to fight back and taking these classes did more to help me heal than therapy ever could. Don't get me wrong, I needed therapy, but I needed to fight more. I started out with karate, then over the years advanced to Jiu Jitsu. I spent months in Brazil—"

"That explains how you were able to kick my ass—"

"And I was going easy on you."

I smile and take a bite of my pizza.

"About five or so years ago, I started looking into my mother's death... the circumstances of that night. The men were never caught—at least, that's what my father claimed—and when I asked him about it, he dismissed me as if I didn't have a right to know. It pissed me off, so I took things in my own hands.

"I stayed busy because I didn't have many clues, and I ran into a lot of dead ends, but as I investigated, I came across other horrible people. People who did similar things to what happened to my mother. So, I started killing them."

She shrugs as if she just confessed to enjoying iced coffee over hot coffee.

"That's when people started calling me Colpa Sicario. The Guilt Killer. It's funny because I never meant to make contract killing a career. I go about it in an unorthodox way. I'm all over the place, so I'm surprised I haven't been arrested or killed yet."

She underestimates herself.

She's badass.

Surely, she knows this?

My stomach flutters at the thought of Noah out there kicking ass and killing monsters. My dick also takes notice. If it weren't for her injuries, I'd ravish her right there on the couch. Fuck her until her pussy's pleasantly sore. Choke her while she orgasms to heighten her release. How wonderful my hands would look around her neck.

"What about you? How did... how did your mother die?"

I flinch. I knew she was going to ask. I didn't mean to let that slip out. Talking about that night is not something I do. Ever. With anyone. Not even my brother.

I swallow hard and exhale a long stream of air before answering. "Her throat was slit."

"I'm so sorry, Delancy." She moves as if she's about to come over and comfort me. I want that more than anything, but I hold up my hand to stop her.

"By me. I was the one who killed her."

She sucks in a sharp breath.

"They made me," I whisper, my voice cracking. "It was three men. They showed up at our home, it was around ten at night. Mom and I were watching a game show on television—she loved game shows—I can't even remember which one. I think my memory blocked it out. I remember everything else. They shot down the door. She rushed me into a closet to hide but the door didn't shut. I watched them tie her up... I watched them..."

I shake my head, not wanting to voice the unspeakable things they did to her against her will.

"I was crying so loud that they found me. After dragging me out, they ordered me to kill her, or they'd kill *me.* They laughed and laughed when I begged them not to make me do it, tears streaking down my cheeks. One of the men pulled out his knife and sliced it over my arm. It stung. I'd never felt such pain up until that moment. Not even when I fell out of a tree and broke my arm when I was six."

I trace over the scar. Something I do every day to keep my mission for revenge in check.

"It scared me and suddenly, I didn't want to die. I took the knife from them and held it to my mother's neck. My hands shook violently.

"Do it, baby," she said. *"Mommy loves you but do this so you can live."*

"So, I did it. I slit her throat. I remembered the way she regarded me as her life faded. Not with fear or disappointment, but with all the love a mother can have for her child. I never understood that, and I never believed I deserved that look from her. I'd failed her. I *killed* her."

I pause to swallow down the tears burning my throat.

"One of the men snatched the knife from me. He told me I was next. I ran outside into the cold winter night. It had snowed that morning. My mom and I built a snowman in the front yard, which I knocked over trying to escape. I wasn't fast enough. The man caught me, stabbed me, and left me to die."

My eyes are closed, but the cushion next to me dips, letting me know Noah is there. She takes my glass of wine and empty plate and sets it on the end table.

"Lay your head in my lap."

I open my eyes and gulp.

"What?"

"I don't think you've ever been coddled, and I want to coddle you. Lay your head in my lap so I can run my fingers through your hair."

The tears lingering in my throat beg to be released. I want to suppress this vulnerable feeling like I always do, but she's right. I don't allow other people to take care of me. Not since my mother was killed. Even when I turned eighteen, Elias told me to learn how to take care of myself, as if I hadn't been holed up in a psychiatric hospital since the age of twelve with no clue how to be human.

I lie down on my side, wincing at the bruises Noah gave me during our fight. My forearm, thigh, and nose still throb with pain. She buries her fingers into my hair and combs them over and over—more like she's petting a sick puppy than a dangerous killer. Her nails rake over my scalp, and I can't help the soft moan that escapes.

We stay like this for several minutes, neither of us speaking. Only the sound of the rom-com playing in the background.

I'm grateful we didn't get to the part about *why* my mother was targeted. Because then I'd have to confess that I'm part of the QBM. But what about her? What are her secrets? While I've stalked her, I can't follow her around all the time. I'm eager to uncover what else she's hiding from me.

Chapter 12

Noah

The next day, I wake up to do damage control. Del destroyed my phone after I killed Cillian, then went into a ten-minute rant about burner phones. I tried to explain that my personal phone is hella secure, encrypted or some shit, and I never have anything incriminating on it. But, whatever, I already ordered a new encrypted phone that I have to pick up tomorrow.

I use one of his burner phones to call my father to spin my story. I explain that I told his twin goons to meet me at the club—certain my father will believe me over them—but lost my phone while dancing. I got really drunk and went home with Sage and have been holed up at her place ever since.

He demanded I give him the address so he could send his men over to retrieve me. I gave him a decoy address to buy myself enough time to return home and grab some clothes. Del and I plan to lie low for the next week or so, anticipating the fallout from Cillian's murder.

Not that we'll get caught.

We were both careful about avoiding security and street cameras and Del said his law enforcement contact will take care of whatever evidence we left behind. Besides, everyone knows Cillian was an asshole who had a lot of enemies. Investigators will be focusing on that list for months.

"You know you don't have to go with me," I say, following Del to his motorcycle. "I can just call an Uber. Oh, wait. I can't. *Somebody* destroyed my phone."

"I can't believe you're leaving a digital trail by using that car service app. And don't even get me started on all those strangers you brought home to fuck. *Never* bring people to your personal space. It makes you vulnerable, susceptible to an attack."

Fine. He got me there. But is it a crime?

"Maybe I like living dangerously."

"It wasn't fucking smart, Skittles."

I'm going to kick his ass again. Even though my heart danced with joy at the nickname. One he doesn't use often.

"Like I said, I don't need a babysitter. I can go by myself. Can I take your bike?"

"I'm going," he begins, sassy and mad at me. He also ignores the bike comment. "I want to get some things from my apartment too."

He grabs the helmet and puts it on me. My heart flutters at the sweet move. He's so focused as he brushes my hair back and secures the strap underneath my chin.

God, he's beautiful. I'm not used to seeing him this close, and I can't get enough. His long eyelashes, dark blue eyes, thick black eyebrows, and long strands of midnight hair on his head. His scars that make me want to kiss the raised skin.

Even though he's busted all to hell from our fight, he's still perfect.

I clear the lust from my throat and distract my desire by pestering him some more. "You have everything in your loft. What else could you need?"

He finishes with the helmet, taps the top, and smiles. No... he grins like he's up to something. "I've been reading this book, and I'm dying to finish it. It's called... *Her Indecent Desire* or something like that. Man chest on the cover. It's quite good."

I gasp. "You fucker! That's my book. I knew you stole something from me! What else did you take?"

He winks, puts on his helmet—I notice he has two now, one for me and one for him—and swings his leg over the bike. He pats the seat behind him.

"Get on, Vixen."

I consider rebelling or pouting, but he looks too fucking hot in his black leather jacket, jeans, and t-shirt, so I get on like a good girl.

We weave through traffic, which isn't too bad since it's after the evening rush. It's a cold late November night, and my bare hands are freezing. I slowly move them down Del's stomach and underneath the bottom of his shirt. His abs constrict underneath my icy skin.

"Noah," Del warns, his voice barely audible over the bike's engine.

"My hands are cold and you're warm," I whine, smoothing the palms up and down the sculpted muscles.

It's not long before they're toasty, but I keep going, loving the way Del reacts to my touch. I skim my palms down until I reach the buttons of his jeans. I snap one open, then another before he realizes what I'm doing and grabs my hand.

"You're going to make me crash," he growls.

"Then you better hold on tight," I yell back.

I slip my hand into his pants and rub my palm over his hardening cock. He moans at the contact, and I squeeze around the shaft. It's straining to break free from his boxers, but it's not possible with the way he's seated on the bike. I start stroking him, gently at first, then rougher. He swerves at one point, so I pause until he's able to compose himself.

We're almost to our street. I'm working him pretty well at this point, and I know he's approaching the edge. Right when he parks in front of our building and shuts off the engine, I extract my hand and jump off the bike.

"What the fuck, Noah!"

"That's for destroying my phone."

"I'm going to kill you."

"You won't."

Del gets out his keys to unlock the building's front door when the smell of gasoline and rotten eggs hits me.

A gas leak?

"Shit. Del, run."

We bolt off the building's steps and get halfway down the sidewalk when the explosion hurls us forward. I land on a pile of trash at the curb, forcing the air out of my lungs.

"Delancy?" I wheeze and attempt to get up off the ground.

My ears ring, my body protesting the sudden movement after the hard landing. A series of sharp pains rip through my side, across my stomach, on my arm and then my thigh. I look down to see all my stitches have opened. The exposed skin on my hands and face singes with first-degree burns. Thankfully, my clothes and heavy jacket protected the rest of my body.

My legs don't want to work, so I crawl on the ground. Debris digs into my palms and knees as I make my way through the yard, determined to find Del.

Thick smoke and flames fill the air, making it hard to see. It's been a few minutes of searching and calling Del's name. I hear police and fire sirens in the distance, growing louder by the second. Panic builds in my stomach, racing through my veins that I'm not going to find him. That he's dead and the only person to ever understand my trauma and my need for vengeance is gone.

A muffled groan sounds from underneath a detached door.

"Noah," the gruff voice says.

"Delancy?" I manage to get on my feet and rush over to the blown down fence that separates our building from the neighbors.

The door isn't too heavy, and I'm able to push it off him.

"Are you okay? Are you hurt?" I ask and frantically move my hands over his body, searching for injuries. His stitches from our fight have opened. His hands and face also have slight burns. Something wet clings to my palm after passing over his side. He has a piece of wood sticking out of his skin.

He immediately rips it out.

"Del, no!"

"It was a surface wound. I wouldn't be awake and talking if it had hit vital organs. Don't worry."

He holds out his hand, and I help him stand. He winces the moment he takes a step. "I think my ankle is sprained."

The sirens are nearly upon us. A block or two away.

"Can you walk on it?"

"Yeah, we need to get the fuck out of here."

Del uses me as a crutch as I lead him back to the bike.

"I'll drive," I offer, despite me never driving a motorcycle and being a bit terrified about driving Del's baby.

"No, I'm okay."

He hands me the helmet, and I shake my head. "No time."

"Put it on," he growls. I scowl but do as he says. I swear I hear him say brat underneath his breath.

We're on his bike and seconds after turning on a street away from the inferno, police and fire arrive. I can't even think about cell phone video or home security footage that captured our escape.

Del takes us back to his safe house in Brooklyn. By the time we're ascending his stairs, I'm struggling. The loss of blood from all my stab wounds reopening has me dizzy and nauseous.

My eyes flutter, and I sway on my feet.

"Stay with me, sweetheart," Del says, patting my cheek.

"Don't call me sweetheart, asshole," I mumble, making him smile.

Inside the loft, Del leads me into the bathroom and sits me on the closed lid of the toilet. He disappears and returns with a bottle of one of those sports drinks, which he shoves in my hand.

"Electrolytes," he says, and I chug the drink while he grabs a suture kit from his bathroom closet. "This is going to hurt, okay?"

I nod and he pierces my skin, stitching up the first of my reopened wounds.

The ones he gave me.

He must realize this as I watch regret wash over his face.

"What are you thinking about?" I ask, trying to distract myself from the pain.

He shakes his head. "If I hadn't stabbed you four times..."

"I told you to. I egged you on."

The corner of his mouth turns up. "So, you admit it wasn't the blood loss?"

I huff out a laugh. "It wasn't the blood loss. Besides, I stabbed you too. I get two more jabs at you and we're even."

"I think we're already even if you count the head butting and kicking me in the balls."

I laugh, then wince. Okay, no being funny while injured.

Del finishes repairing the stitch on my side and moves on to my arm. God, I love how focused he is on doing a good job... on taking care of me. I find it hard to believe he's the hardened contract killer with a body count in the triple digits.

"Tell me about a happy moment with your mom," I say.

He sucks in a sharp breath, not expecting the change of topic. His brows furrow, and his lips form a fine line. It's clear he doesn't like recalling memories of his childhood.

I don't blame him.

"One time, she took me to the Brooklyn Botanic Garden. It was summer, and I was eleven. My brother didn't want to go. He never wanted to do anything fun like that. I think it's because my father expected a lot from him. He was the oldest, and he was expected to take over—"

He pauses and glances up at me. Had he almost revealed something to me?

"—the family business one day, so he was always shadowing my father. Because of that, I mostly hung out with my mother. She loved everything about nature. Sometimes we'd go to Central Park and just hang out there all day. She'd bring a picnic basket and a book, and I'd run around and chase bugs or some shit.

"The day at the Botanic Garden was different because she'd told me it was her birthday. I had no idea. I was just a kid. I didn't know about adult things like my parents' birthday or their ages.

"We celebrated with lunch and a piece of cake, then we went to the Gardens. She wanted to sit on a bench and wait for a butterfly to land on her. She said when a butterfly lands on you, it signifies joy or indicates a huge change is coming to your life."

He exhales a shuddering breath.

"It took five minutes before the first one flew over to us, but it landed on me, not her. Then another and another. After a few minutes, I was covered in them. My mom was laughing so hard; she could barely snap a picture with her

Polaroid camera. I still have that picture too. I look at it anytime I'm—"

He stops talking and clenches his jaw. I want him to finish what he was saying, but I won't push him, because I know how hard it is remembering the ones who are no longer here.

"That was six months before she died."

It's clear he's done sharing this memory with me and starts working on my burns in silence, applying a gel from his first aid kit.

"Can I see it? The photo?"

He smooths the medicine over my jaw, then on my knuckles, considering my request. Once done, he extracts his wallet from his jeans pocket and flips through the contents until finding the photo.

He hands it to me, and I smile as wide as my face will allow. He still has the same dark hair and blue eyes, but as a kid, his cheeks were puffy. I notice no scars either, so he must have gotten them after age eleven.

Tears gather at the back of my throat, and I swallow them down, not wanting to cry about the time before when we were both innocent... before darkness claimed us.

I hand the photo back and stand. "My turn to fix you up."

"Are you feeling okay? You were trying to pass out on me earlier," Del says.

My heart flutters because he's always thinking about me, concerned about me, protecting me. I'm not sure what I did to deserve him. "I'm good now. Come on, let me operate."

"Do you know how to stitch?"

"Not in the least, but how hard can it be?"

He opens his mouth to argue, but I place my finger over his lips.

"Just trust me. I'll be gentle with you, Puppet."

He nips at the pad, and I yelp, pulling it back. He laughs, proud of himself.

Slowly and carefully, Del takes off his t-shirt, then his jeans, and sits down.

I do my best not to ogle his body and focus on the injury on his side from the wood. It's still bleeding, and I don't know how he hasn't passed out by now. He *does* look a little pale. I pierce into his skin, and he doesn't make a sound. He doesn't make a move. His tolerance for pain and all his scars tell me he's become numb from all his suffering. I want to murder every single person who's harmed him... even though I'm one of them.

While I stitch up Del's thigh, he applies the gel for his burns. I'm between his legs as I work and the way he stares down at me in this... intimate position makes my cheeks heat.

He's looking at me as if he's ready to throw me on the ground and fuck me until the only name I can remember is his.

I don't know how I was able to focus, but I finish the stitch, proud of how clean it looks.

The slice on his arm isn't as bad, only needing two stitches.

"Tell me about your scars."

I say, trying to distract myself from his searing stares.

I expect him to refuse to talk about them, so I'm surprised when he points to the one on his right forearm first, then to the one on his left stomach. "From the men who forced me to kill my mother."

He taps three other scars: two on his chest and one on his shoulder. "All of these were from hit jobs. From marks who fought back. I have a couple on my back too."

I finish the stitches on his forearm then wrap his sprained ankle.

Once done, I stand before him and reach out my hand to graze the scar on his cheek with my fingertips. My thumb skims over the raised skin on his mouth.

"And these?"

He swallows hard, his eyes filling with pain.

This time he doesn't answer me. That's when I know they're from someone who was supposed to love him. Someone who was supposed to protect him.

I have no doubt it was his father.

I cup his head in my hands and lean in because I need to kiss him. I need to let him know he doesn't have to be alone again, but the sound of a phone ringing interrupts us. Probably my father calling on the burner phone.

Del closes his eyes, and I rest my forehead on his.

"Back to reality," I whisper.

Fuck. I'm falling in love with this man. I tried to resist him the moment I moved in next to him two months ago. I could never figure out why I was so drawn to him. Now I'm sure that it was his darkness calling to mine.

Chapter 13

Delancy

I leave Noah to handle her overbearing father and hop back on my bike to return to our destroyed apartment building.

What the fuck happened?

Was it really a gas leak or is someone trying to kill us?

Or me.

Or her.

She talked about her mother's murder and how her father hid her from the men responsible. Have they found her?

I pass a staging area for the media, and the reporters yell at me, microphones pointed my way to lure me over for an interview, but I ignore those leeches and walk under police tape. The officer stationed there nods, recognizing me because he's a QBM soldier.

I spot my brother standing in the debris littered yard talking to a police sergeant.

"What are you doing here, Elly?" Astoria is neutral territory.

I must have been hallucinating when relief passes over his face the moment he sees me.

"Lance. What the fuck happened?"

"No fucking clue. But why are *you* here?"

He sighs and grabs me by the elbow to pull me aside. "I know where all your safe houses are, brother."

Rage builds in my spine but instead of causing a scene by fighting with my brother, I rip my arm out of his grip.

He leads a mob organization. I'm his enforcer. Of course, he has eyes on me.

"Tell me what you know," I say, and turn away from him to survey the damage.

"There are traces of gasoline in the unit next to yours."

"But no traces in mine?" I ask when I walk back to where the sergeant stands.

My brother's source, who always gets me out of trouble, frowns. "Most of the gasoline-soaked furniture and belongings appear to be a woman's. Unless those burned up romance books are yours?"

He chuckles, and I consider punching him so hard, his nose caves in. Sexist asshole.

"Pull up your camera feed," Elias says, not even asking if I have security cameras because he knows I'm a paranoid fuck. Since I don't know shit about technology, my hacker/tech guy Jed had initially set everything up and showed me how to securely log in to view the videos.

I find the time of the explosion on my feed and a few minutes before, there are two masked men carrying gasoline containers letting themselves inside Noah's apartment. What the hell? Did they have a key? I didn't install cameras inside her apartment, so I fast forward until they exit her place without the red plastic containers, obviously leaving them inside.

One man pauses just outside the unit and lights a cigarette. He takes a puff, then flicks it inside and closes the door.

A few minutes pass by before Noah and I are seen walking up to the building.

"I know they're wearing masks, but do they look familiar?" Elias asks.

"No. I'll show Noah and see if she recognizes them."

"What have you gotten yourself into with that woman, Lance? What do you know about her?"

I shake my head.

Nothing, apparently.

"Any deaths? Injuries?" I ask, avoiding my brother's question.

"An older woman in her seventies died."

Mrs. Crowley. That's a shame. She always smiled and waved at me. She didn't seem to fear me. Not like the other residents who avoided eye contact with me anytime we passed by each other.

"About a dozen others were injured."

I pull out a joint from my jacket pocket and light it, taking a huge drag and letting the pot soothe my frayed nerves. I manage to get one more puff in before Elias snatches it from me and stomps it into the ground.

"There was a gas explosion here, you idiot."

I shrug and nod my chin at the apartment building. "Can I go in and salvage some stuff?"

"Check with the fire chief," the sergeant says. "My guys are done in there."

I don't bother finding the fire chief because he'll likely tell me no. I do, however, grab my fake badge from my jeans pocket in case someone tries to stop me.

At least two walls of my unit still stand. I grab an empty duffle bag and load it up with a few clothes and weapons. I rarely keep personal items in my safe houses. Any photos or knickknacks owned by my mother are in a storage unit out in Fresh Meadows.

In the bedside table drawer, I remove the book I stole from Noah, a few of her photos I snagged, and her bullet vibrator, and add them to the bag.

Noah's apartment is nearly leveled, and the flooring is unstable, so I go back outside to sift through the debris on the ground. I find a few of her clothes that aren't burnt to shreds. I also find almost all the framed photos she had on her bookcase. I add them to my duffle and keep searching. It takes nearly an hour before coming across her photo albums scattered underneath a piece of metal door.

"Hey," Elias says after I stuff the albums in my bag, zip it up, and stand. "One of the firefighters found this."

He holds up a necklace with a cross. I'd seen Noah wear it a couple times. It has the initials SL on the back.

"Seems important."

I take the chain and pendant from Elias and nod.

"Did the police get video from neighbors? Ring footage, anything like that?"

"Not yet. I'll send someone around and make sure everything with your ugly face on it is deleted."

Was that... a joke? A tease? My brother being... funny?

I turn to leave, but Elias calls my name, stopping me. "I'm glad you're okay, brother."

If he sees the shock on my face, he doesn't react.

What the hell is wrong with him? I know he's still not over his latest breakup, but he's been incredibly... emotional lately.

He's almost acting like a real brother.

I obsess over that thought on the ride home and come to the conclusion that Elias huffed too much gasoline and smoke at the fire scene.

When I walk into the loft, Noah is asleep on the couch. Her mouth hangs open, and she's snoring. She's also drooling. I notice an empty bottle of wine on the table and the pain pills she stole from Cillian next to it.

Oh, okay. She's wasted as fuck.

I cover her up with a blanket and kiss her forehead. She stirs but stays asleep. I set out the clothes I salvaged, but store the book, vibrator, and photos in my safe. I have plans for those.

After showering and crawling into bed, I struggle to fall asleep. I remember Noah's hand on my cock while on my motorcycle and how badly I wanted to punish her for giving me blue balls. I fist my cock, attempting to relieve this tension she's caused—that she always causes—and within minutes, I'm coming all over my hand.

I wash off my release and finally feel rested enough to doze off. Tomorrow, I'll meet with my tech guy and go over the surveillance video again. I'll see if he can track these men on street cameras.

Why the fuck would someone want to kill Noah?

I have a suspicion this has something to do with her mother's murder.

I still need to question her about why she was targeted.

But would revealing the truth change everything between us?

That's what I'm scared of finding out.

Chapter 14

Noah

Someone was trying to kill me.

The explosion was all over the news. I watched the reports, and I was waiting for one of the reporters to show videos of Del and me riding away on his motorcycle.

Thankfully, Del had already returned to the scene—or maybe he said he'd called someone, I can't remember—and collected all the footage recorded on cell phones or surveillance. I don't know what he—or whoever helped him —did while he was there, but not long after, the blast was deemed an accident: Mrs. Crowley's gas oven was broken and leaking, and it blew up when she lit a cigarette.

Now it's been a little over a week hiding out in Del's safe house in Brooklyn.

He hasn't been around much. Despite the men wearing masks in the surveillance video, Del was determined to identify them. He'd be gone all day, then return late at night after I'd already fallen asleep on the couch or in his bed—I'd hoped he'd join me, but he never did. I wondered if he was avoiding me again because of how... personal we've become with each other.

After I picked up my new encrypted phone, I made the necessary calls. First, I contacted the bar where I work to let them know I'm taking an emergency leave of absence. I don't financially need the job, but I love the excitement that comes with the bar scene, making drinks, and fucking strangers.

Sometimes I find my marks at the bar.

Next, I texted Sage to let her know I was alive and that I'd be recovering at my father's townhouse on the Lower East Side. I knew she wouldn't want to visit because she's not a fan of Gio Lenetti based on the things I've told her about him. Some were lies, most were the truth.

My father was a bit harder to convince. Especially after lying about being at Sage's, giving him a false address, and sending his goons on a wild goose chase. I told him that the building's landlord put us up in hotels for the time being, and he demanded I tell him where so he could send his cronies to come get me. New bodyguards because Bryan and Ryan were fired—or killed—after I ditched them.

I force myself out of bed and dress in a pair of sweats and a tank.

I lost everything I owned in that explosion. My photos—including ones of me with my mother—some of my favorite outfits, little things I've collected over the years while traveling. Del managed to salvage a few of my clothes but not many, so I ordered a whole new wardrobe express delivery.

I make a pit stop in the bathroom before heading out to the kitchen to find something to eat. The clank of a pan stops me in my tracks. I grab a vase from a table in the short hallway and lift it as I silently walk into the kitchen.

My heart beats faster and my vision blurs because all I see is a man with a weapon. I run towards him with the vase over my head. Seconds before I crash it down, he turns around and grabs me by the throat. His strong fingers squeeze the column.

"Del?" I wheeze out.

"Hello, Skittles," he muses, still not letting go.

I whimper because I'm a little bit turned on. Definitely not thinking about him slamming me down on the table and fucking me while choking me and calling me his dirty little slut.

The whimper surprises him and he lets me go, taking the vase out of my hand and setting it on the counter. He turns back to the stove and... he's holding a spatula, not a weapon.

He's making breakfast?

Not only that... he's making breakfast *shirtless* while wearing low-hanging gray sweatpants and an apron.

"What are you doing here?" I ask, surprised to see him.

"I live here?"

I scoff. "I mean, yeah, but you've barely been here since the explosion."

He shrugs. "I ran into dead ends. So, now I'm back."

He places two plates of food on the table.

I gasp. "You made waffles?"

"Sit," he says and points at a chair. It was bossy, and I want to defy the order, but my stomach growls.

He set out all my favorite toppings. How did he know? I ignore how suspicious that is and prepare my waffle: butter, drowned in maple syrup, and topped with strawberries.

I cut into the pillowy bread and savor the sweet tastes, moaning my appreciation.

"Holy fuck, Del. You're a fantastic cook."

"I know," he says, while pouring me a mug of coffee. He adds a shot of creamer and one packet of sugar since he apparently knows how I like it.

He really is a stalker.

He hangs up the apron, but declines to put on a shirt, and prepares his waffle—no butter, but he adds syrup and whipped cream.

The fun we could have with that whipped cream.

It's probably best he hasn't been around this past week. I needed to heal from my injuries, but that wouldn't have stopped me from jumping his bones. I constantly think about our kiss before he stabbed me, and I'm more than ready to continue what we started.

We eat in silence, and my thoughts turn to our conversation before the explosion. I've been wanting to ask him more about what happened the night he was forced to kill his mother, specifically the men who made him do it. Were they ever caught?

He said he was twelve when it happened.

So, how long has it been? Since I still don't know a lot about Del—including his last name, that fucker—I assume he's my age, give a year or two. So that means it's likely been twenty years for him as well.

Huh.

That's got to be a coincidence. I mean, murders happen every day. I'm sure our mothers were killed weeks or months apart.

"How old are you?" I ask, then take a bite of my waffle.

"Thirty-one."

Okay, so that would mean his mother died nineteen years ago, not twenty.

"Why?" He looks up at me, his brows pinched.

"I think we can help each other."

"Yeah? With what?"

"Find our mothers' killers. You tell me everything you have, and I'll share all the evidence I've compiled. It's helpful to have a second set of eyes on things like this."

He narrows his eyes at me. "Hmm. Maybe."

He returns his attention to the newspaper he's holding while eating and sipping his coffee. All he needs is a pair of glasses and he'd look so studious at this moment.

I scoff, and he looks back up at me.

"What?"

I cross my arms and lean back in the seat. "You don't trust me, do you?"

"I didn't say that."

"Then why?"

He sets the paper down and crosses his arms to match my stance.

"Fine. What do you want to know?"

Oh. Okay. I didn't think he'd give in that easily.

"You were twelve when it happened?"

He nods. "It was my twelfth birthday. Christmas Eve."

"What?"

"We celebrated my birthday that morning and then that night—"

"You were forced to kill your mother on your birthday?" My voice cracks as I ask the question, and my vision blurs with tears.

"Yes," he says and clears his throat.

"It snowed." Del continues, surprising me that he wants to talk about it. "I was excited that it was going to be a white Christmas..." His words trail off. "But after what happened... it's why I no longer celebrate my birthday. Why I hate Christmas."

My mind races with this information. My stomach souring as I make the connections.

Twenty years ago on Christmas Eve...

Is Del... a QBM or Lords heir? No. He can't be... I thought I knew all the heirs... Elias Carter and Cillian O'Connor. Did I miss one?

That's the only explanation. I'm scared to voice this suspicion because I could be wrong. But if I'm not...

We sit in silence for a few seconds before I speak. "My mother was killed the day before Christmas Eve. Twenty years ago."

Del sits up straight, finally understanding my words.

"Our mothers' murders are connected. They have to be," I whisper, barely able to process this revelation. "Del, if we compare notes—"

"I know who killed my mother." He stares down at his half-eaten plate of food as if that would have all the answers.

"Who?"

He grinds his teeth, his nostrils flaring.

"Who, Del? Tell me."

I watch him silently battle over whether he'll share this information with me. I need to know if my suspicions are correct. I almost grab him by the throat and yell in his face to tell me when he blurts out, "Gio Lenetti."

My entire body stills, only my heart beating wildly in my chest.

"What?"

"The leader of the Empire Mafia."

"No."

His head jerks back up at me.

"What do you mean, no?"

Within seconds, Del stands and grabs a knife from the bamboo block on the counter. I hop off my chair and get into a fighting stance.

"What the fuck do you know about Gio Lenetti? Who is he to you?"

This is it. This is when he finally kills me.

"He's my... my..."

"He's not..."

"He's my father."

"Of course." Del laughs like a maniac and rubs a hand down his face. "Barry McAllister. Your dull fake life. How could I be so fucking stupid?"

He did a background check on me? Of course, he did. He's the Marionette. That smart, cautious mother fucker.

Del rushes towards me, knife over his head. I block his arm coming down, but the blade slices my cheek.

Oh hell no.

I slam the heel of my hand into his Adam's apple, and he wheezes, grabbing his throat and stumbling back. While he's distracted, I swipe my leg out, taking him down to the ground. The moment I climb on top of him, he tries to grab me, but I take hold of his hand and twist. He cries out, letting me know I've done some damage.

"Stop. Fighting. Me."

"You killed her," he growls, attempting to hit me with his other hand. I scoop up the knife he dropped on the ground and stab the blade through his right palm. "God-damn it, Noah."

"Fuck you!"

I punch him and his head ricochets to the side.

His eyes flutter as if he's about to pass out, so I give him a titty twister, which makes him growl. "Stay awake so we can talk about this."

He tries to buck me off him, but he's still somewhat dazed by my sucker punch.

"I was eleven when your mom was killed. Obviously, it wasn't me."

"It was your father. He ordered her death."

I pause because this all but confirms my suspicions. Del is a mafia heir. And he believes my father is the one who targeted all the mob wives and their children? Gio would never risk starting a war... At least, I don't think he would.

My distracted thoughts allow Del to buck me off him. He flips me over onto my back, hard enough that the air leaves my lungs. Now he's straddling me. He slides the knife out of his palm and tries to stab me, but I swat it out of his grip, and it goes flying across the hardwood floor.

His hands latch around my neck, and he presses both thumbs against my trachea. The pain and lack of air excite me, and I can't help moaning.

The muscles in Del's clenched jaw ripple, and he glances down at my breasts, noticing my hard nipples through the thin fabric of my tank.

"You love when I'm rough with you, don't you?"

Okay. This is good. He's getting turned on. Maybe that means he won't kill me.

I nod at his question since I can't speak.

"Do you want me to fuck you while I choke you?"

I nod again.

He leans down, his mouth grazing against mine. "I should kill you right now."

I'm seconds from passing out before he lets go and stands.

I rub my neck, which is covered in blood from his stab wound, and savor the pain. It's going to be bruised tomorrow.

"I didn't do anything, Del. We can figure this out."

He looks at me with a mixture of disgust and lust. He wants to fuck me, but he also wants me dead.

"Your father is a monster. You're the heir to the Empire. You're just like him. Do you kill for them too, Colpa Sicario?"

"No! Never. I don't want anything to do with my father!" I cry out. "Del, you know me. Even though we've only been neighbors for a couple of months, and we hate each other, I never lied about who I am—"

"Except your real name is Noemi Lenetti!"

I'm taken aback as if he'd lashed out with a slap to the face.

"No," I begin, my voice shaking, and my heart thundering in my chest. "I'm not that person anymore. Noemi Lenetti died twenty years ago when my mother was murdered. I'm Noah McAllister now. I work at a bar. I'm horrible at cooking and singing, but I'm fantastic at sex and killing dirtbags. And I fucking *hate* the Empire. I don't want to take over, Delancy. I want to bring it fucking down."

"You need to go." Del's voice is low and dangerous. "Go, Noah, before I kill you."

"No."

He pulls a gun out of a hiding spot underneath the table next to where he stands, then storms me until the barrel digs into my forehead.

"Del, if he's responsible, I didn't know. Let me help you. Let me question him. I can find out for sure. I would never support him—"

He cocks the gun's hammer. "Did you move next door to spy on me? To kill me?"

I shake my head. "No. I swear on my mother's grave that I didn't know who you were when I moved in. This is just... an odd coincidence."

"I hate coincidences," Del says, his voice shaken. "You have ten seconds or I'm pulling the trigger."

"No. You won't kill me, Puppet." I'm not confident in that declaration, so I keep talking, distracting him. "My mother was murdered too. We can help each other."

He studies my face for a painful minute, at least, before lowering the gun and grabbing my arm to drag me to the door. I dig my feet into the ground to try and stop him, and he responds by throwing me up against the wall. He leans in, his mouth hovering over mine.

"I fucking hate you," he seethes.

"Yeah? Well, I don't hate you, Del. I never have."

We stare at each other, breathing hard and not saying a word for nearly a minute.

Then he kisses me.

It's rough and not at all romantic. He bites my lip, making it bleed before shoving his tongue in and caressing my own in desperate lashings. His hands cup my face, coating my cheek with blood from his stab wound.

I fish his cock out from his sweats and wrap my fingers around the thick shaft. He groans into my mouth as I fist him up and down. I use his precum to lubricate the length, squeezing just enough to hear him moan.

He moves his hand to my nape and fists my hair, tugging my head back so he can kiss and bite along my jaw and down my neck. The bites aren't gentle either. I'm positive bruises will be left behind and my pussy gets wetter thinking about seeing his marks every time I look in the mirror.

We enter a competition. Every rough bite is met with me squeezing his cock harder. I'm not even sure if it feels good for him, especially when he reacts by biting my shoulder and breaking the skin. I gasp at the sting, and he laughs proudly. The asshole.

He swings me around, so my back is flush with his front, then walks us to the chair in the living room. He folds me over the back, my ass in the air, and tugs down my leggings.

He takes handfuls of my ass cheeks and squeezes.

"Is this what you want? For me to fuck you?"

"Yes, Del, please. Call me your slut and ruin me."

"I don't have a condom."

"I don't care."

He runs the thick head of his dick up and down my wet pussy and nudges the tip in, holding it there.

"Beg for me, Vixen."

"Please, sir. Fuck me. Don't be gentle."

"Not good enough," he says and slaps my ass so hard, the sound ricochets around the room. I savor the ache.

"Fuck my pussy, Delancy. I need your cock. I need you to choke me until I can't breathe. Slap me, bruise me, use me."

"Poetic," he says and thrusts into me to the hilt.

"Oh, God."

"Not. God," he says and pistons into me at a damning pace. He wraps his hands around my neck for leverage, restricting my air and transforming it into pleasure.

"Play with your clit, slut," Del growls, viciously pumping into me.

He's hate fucking me, and I don't fault him for it. I *crave* it.

My fingertips press onto my clit, and I rub it in circles. Del groans as my walls suction around him.

"Yes, Noah, that feels good."

The sound of our bodies slapping together fills the quiet loft, our mingling moans adding to the chorus.

"Can I come, sir?" I beg, struggling to get the words out because he's still choking me.

"No, not until I say so."

"Please. Can't. Hold. Much. Longer."

He slips out of me, and I nearly gut punch him at the loss.

"Get on your knees and open your mouth. Play with yourself while I come down your throat."

I don't question him and drop down to the ground. I open my mouth and he grabs my hair at the nape to hold my head still. My fingers return to my clit and it's so swollen, so worked up, that I'm orgasming seconds later. Del follows, giving himself a few more strokes until jets of cum hit my tongue.

When he's finished, shaking out every single drop, he scoops up the cum that dribbled on my chin and shoves the finger in my mouth.

"Swallow, slut."

I shouldn't like him calling me slut, but I really am a slut for degradation. I swallow all his cum, like a good girl.

"Fuck, Noah. I haven't come that hard in... well, ever."

A smile spreads across my face, ear to ear.

He rolls his eyes. "So proud of yourself. Fine, we can talk. But that doesn't mean I still won't kill you."

"You won't kill me, Del," I say, standing. "Because that was just a taste. A preview of how good sex with me can be."

I kiss him, letting my tongue slip between his lips so he can taste himself.

When we part, I look down at my frontside. "I'm covered in blood and cum. I could really use a shower."

I walk away, glancing over my shoulder to see if he's going to follow. He doesn't, but I didn't think he would.

He just fucked the daughter of the man responsible for ordering his mother's death. I really am lucky he didn't kill me.

Sex might have just saved my life.

Chapter 15

Delancy

I hate her.

I hate her father.

I hate that I wasn't strong enough to resist her.

I want to kill her, but she's right. She did nothing wrong. As far as I know.

So, we'll talk. I'll find out how deeply ingrained she is with the Empire Mafia. She says she doesn't kill for them like I do for the QBM. She said she wants nothing to do with her father after he wouldn't talk to her about her mother's death.

It's why I didn't fight harder to make her leave. I was relieved when she stayed.

Then I was furious.

She taunted me, and I took the bait.

And, God, did her pussy feel fucking fantastic. Perfectly made for me.

She let me rage fuck her, choke her, do things I've wanted to do during sex, but I was afraid I'd go too far.

I want to destroy her.

Fucking Noah didn't help my growing obsession for her.

"Stop gawking at me and start talking, Puppet."

I both love and hate the nickname. Anything but Laptop and Computer. Del is also growing on me. But when she calls me Delancy, I go feral, as if her velvety voice saying my name awakens my cock and begs to be hers.

"Why do you think my father ordered the kill on you and your mother?"

I sip on my coffee, still struggling to trust her with this information.

She doesn't know I'm QBM. At least, I don't think she's figured it out.

Who am I kidding? She's fucking smart as hell. What if she knows and is playing me?

"My father had files on the men who broke into our house that night. It had their photos, names, addresses. Over the years, I tracked them down, tortured, and killed them. The first two held out, never revealing any useful information. But the last man... he gave me your father's name."

"That's it? Just a name?"

"Which is why I kept digging. I realized I needed to get access to the Empire. I went to your father's gun range to find a way in. Instead, I found you."

I should have known she was connected to Lenetti that day. Instead, my lust for her overshadowed my critical thinking skills.

"Did you find what you were looking for at the gun range?"

I fist my hands on the countertop. The pain from the hole in my right palm sends a shot of lust throughout my body. Noah stabbing me shouldn't have been so sexy. My cock was hard the entire time I wrapped it with a bandage while she was in the shower.

"I was working on it. I needed to make friends with the employees, get behind closed doors. I couldn't just break in. Places like that are well protected."

"You're smart. You would have been killed."

"What's behind the locked doors at the gun range, Noah?"

She sighs and takes the towel off her head. Bending over, she shakes her dark red hair and combs her fingers through the wet locks.

She's wearing a teddy—hot pink with sheer lace and satin trim that does nothing to hide her dark nipples and the patch of hair on her cunt. I know she dressed like this on purpose to tempt me.

"Gun running, money washing, murders... the usual," she says the moment she's upright.

"Noah," I warn at her playful tone.

"I'm sorry, Delancy, but I have no idea. I told you; I'm not interested in my father's mob business. He wants me to take over someday, but I refuse. I don't want this life. I never wanted it."

I fucking hate the Empire. I don't want to take over, Delancy. I want to bring it fucking down.

The confession surprised me. I want to ask her about her plan to bring the empire down, but she continues speaking.

"My mother might still be alive if Gio Lenetti would have been satisfied running restaurants instead of ruling a crime organization. He was greedy. Plain and simple."

She props her hands on her hip, narrowing her eyes at me.

"Who was your father, Delancy?"

I stand and walk over to her, hoping to appear intimidating. Instead of fearing me, she holds her head up high and juts out her tits.

"I think you've already figured out who my father is."

"Maybe I have, but I need you to tell me."

"Percy Carter."

"I don't understand." Her words come out as a whisper, confusion taking over her face. "Percy had two sons?"

"Yeah, but he made sure to erase me from his life for what I did. Not many people know I exist, which works out great for my line of work."

She shakes her head as she processes this information.

"How did he die? Rumors were he got sick."

"He did. Lung cancer. He spent his last few months in hospice. I didn't even get to say goodbye, not that I cared to. He refused to let me or my brother in to see him. He didn't want us to remember him that way."

Her palms flatten on my chest, and she slides them up to my tension packed shoulders. The tightness slowly unravels the longer she touches me.

"You're the QBM's enforcer, aren't you?"

I nod.

She steps away from me to pace the living room while rattling off words. "This is insane. My father would never put out hits on all the mob wives and their kids. He'd never start a mafia war. He's always been at the top. Why would he target the other mobs when he's the most powerful?"

"Why do you think, Vixen? To have claim over all five boroughs."

She stops pacing and wraps her arms around her stomach.

"Then what about my mother?" she asks, her voice full of tears. "I know she died the day before, but it's too odd of a coincidence."

Fucking coincidences. In my experience, the majority of coincidences are suspicious or manufactured to appear coincidental.

"If my father was responsible, why kill her too?"

"I don't have an answer to that, Noe. The city was led to believe Gio Lenetti's wife and daughter were both killed, so to find out you're alive…"

"Tell me again about the men in the file."

I join her in the living room, arms crossed while watching her pace.

"I'll never forget their faces and names. Francesco Ricci, Dante Amato, Luka Candreva. Recognize them?"

She shakes her head, her brows pinch as she thinks. I know she doesn't want to believe her father could be responsible, but it's time she wakes up and realizes just how horrible that man is.

"It doesn't make sense. Unless…"

"What is it, Vixen?"

She tries to fight the smile at the nickname.

"What if my father reacted because he found out who killed my mother? What if he believed it was QBM?"

"That doesn't explain the Lords."

"What if it wasn't Gio at all? What if someone targeted all the mobs, someone who wanted to weaken them with the deaths of loved ones? What if my father was framed?"

This is something I've considered. Something I asked Elias about. All the mob bosses' wives and children were killed or attempted to be killed. I'd be interested to know who the Lords believe were responsible for that night.

"As if someone was trying to pit the city mobs against each other," I say.

Noah collapses on the couch, her tits jiggling in the teddy, which does nothing to support her melon-sized breasts. She sighs and covers her eyes with her forearm as if discussing this has exhausted her.

She's splayed out on that couch, legs spread, inviting me to bury my head between them.

She knows exactly what she's doing.

I kneel on the couch, the cushion dipping under my weight. Noah doesn't remove her arm to look at me or question what I'm doing. Instead, a wry smile spreads across her gorgeous face.

"An hour ago, you wanted to kill me. Now you're between my legs?"

"I still might kill you," I say.

My palm smooths over her legs, from her ankle up to her dimpled thigh. She holds her breath, waiting for my next move, yet she doesn't remove her arm.

Would she like to be blindfolded? I stand and nearly run to my bedroom, opening the drawer holding all my ties. I take out two and when I return to the living room, Noah is peeking beneath her arm.

"Sit up and put your arms behind your back."

"Ooo, kinky."

"No talking, slut."

She purrs at the derogatory endearment, but does as I say. I wrap my tie around her wrists a few times then thread it through, tightening it hard enough that she lets out a tiny gasp.

I pull the other tie from my pocket and her cheeks redden.

"What's that one for?"

"I said no talking."

She scrunches her nose at me, and I assume it's because no one's ever ordered her around. Not my vixen. She likes control and power. She wouldn't be a successful contract killer if she let people tell her what to do.

Yet, she's more than willing to hand over control to me.

She sucks in a sharp breath when I cover her eyes with the tie, securing a knot at the back of her head.

I lean in and brush my lips over hers.

"Good girl. You're mine now. You'll take the pleasure I give you and you're going to like it. Do you understand me, Colpa Sicario?"

She groans. "Yes, sir."

"Now, lie back down."

I tug the lace of her teddy away from her breast, exposing her nipple. Taking it between my fingers, I squeeze and twist. Her back arches, and a moan escapes those plump pink lips. I cover the hardened nub with my mouth and lap it with my tongue.

She pants and squeezes her legs around my body, squirming beneath me, and desperate to use her bound hands.

"I want to hear you, Noah. I want you to scream my name when I make you come with my mouth. Do you understand?"

"Yes, sir, please."

I peel off her sheer pink panties over her hips and pocket them, then run my palms back up her inner legs.

"Keep these apart," I demand.

The tip of my finger traces up and down her opening, enough to know she's soaked. I slowly insert a finger down to the last knuckle, garnering breathy pants from Noah.

I add a second finger and pump into her lazily, enjoying her writhing because it's not fast enough. When I add the third finger, I lean down and cover her clit with my mouth.

She bucks off the couch and moans.

My thrusts pick up, but barely, and I can tell she's getting frustrated. I suck her swollen clit into my mouth and tongue graciously.

"Delancy, please," she begs.

Only because I love the sound of my name coming out of her mouth do I give her what she demands.

My fingers piston into her as I suck her clit harder, my tongue lashing out more viciously. Her pussy walls clamp down, and I know she's close.

I reach up my hand to pinch one of her nipples. The combination of sensations sets her off. She arches, her orgasm rippling throughout her body. I wait until she comes down from climaxing before removing my fingers.

"Open your mouth," I say. When she does, I stick my fingers inside. "Suck. Tell me how good you taste."

She wraps her lips around the digits and licks them clean, making my already hard cock jump. I remove my fingers and kiss her, long and hard.

"Do you want more?"

She nods. "Yes. Fuck me, Delancy."

I pull my cock out of my sweats and rub the thick head up and down her slick opening. It's leaking precum, just as excited as I am to fuck her again.

I nudge the head in an inch. Noah fidgets, anticipating me being inside her.

"You're being so patient, Noah, and patient girls get rewarded."

I enter her in one solid thrust and stay seated to the hilt. She screams, letting me know how good it feels. Her pussy pulses around me, still sensitive from her first orgasm. I slide back out, then pound into her again, savoring the way her body bounces.

The small moans and whimpers that come out of her mouth as I fuck her nearly put me over the edge. I'm reaming into her, hard and fast.

"Slap me," she breathes. "Call me your slut."

I don't even think about it and smack her across the cheek, making her head whip to the side.

"You're my perfect slut, Vixen."

Her pussy responds wonderfully, squeezing my cock as I drive into her. I slap her tits next, leaving a red mark, and she arches off the couch again.

My orgasm builds as I watch her destruct beneath me; her cheeks, neck, and chest flush because she's on the cusp of another orgasm.

"I need you to come, Noah. Now," I growl, and when I rub her clit with my thumb, she shudders. Her release takes over, sending her body shaking. This orgasm wasn't a quiet one, either. She screamed loud enough that I'm sure the pizza patrons downstairs heard.

I thrust into her a few more times before my cum coats her pussy walls.

When I collapse on top of her, breathing hard, she wraps her arms around me. Of course, she was able to free herself from her binds.

"Fuck, that was good," she whispers.

Noah's right. Sex with her *is* good. As if my addiction to her wasn't bad enough.

But it's more than that.

Noah is forcing me to face parts of myself that I thought were long gone... like my humanity. Perhaps all I needed to send the violence craved monster retreating was my missing piece.

Chapter 16

Noah

My pussy is pleasantly sore.

Delancy fucked me on the couch. Then he dragged me to the bedroom and fucked me on his bed. Then we made our way to the shower where he ate me out *again* before fucking me against the tiled wall.

Maybe I *am* a fan of shower sex.

The way he dried me off after... It was gentle, caring. I never imagined him to be so loving.

Like right now. My period is about to start. I woke up with debilitating cramps. I'm spotting this morning, then it'll be a day or two of heavy bleeding and more cramps. The hormonal IUD I got barely helped with my PCOS symptoms. Some months are worse than others.

I just don't have time for this. I can't wait until menopause, and I'm done with periods. I've known since I was eleven years old that I didn't want kids and yet every month I'm reminded about my body's failure to get pregnant.

"I got the stuff you asked for," Del says entering the bedroom carrying a plastic bag and tray. He hands me the bag with my pads inside and sets the tray down on my blanket covered lap.

"Are these chicken wings?"

"You said pads with wings."

I cover my mouth, trying to hold back my laughter. This sweet, adorable, clueless man.

"I didn't mean chicken wings." I hold up the package of pads and point to the word. "The pads have wings."

"How the hell was I supposed to know?"

"What else do you have here?"

His face lights up with excitement.

"A heating pad, chamomile tea, berries, Midol, and..." He takes his phone out of his pocket and taps at the screen for a few seconds. Smooth instrumental music starts playing. "Soothing tunes to ease your stress."

I pop a blueberry in my mouth. "Did you Google things to help with period cramps?"

He frowns at me. "Yes, why?"

I shake my head but smile at this thoughtful man.

He leaves the room and returns with a bottle.

"Want a full body massage? What?" he asks at my confused face. "The Internets told me it would help. Don't look at me like that, woman."

"The Internets? With an 's'?"

"Shut up. You know what I mean. I fucking hate the *Internet*. I'm lucky I found this information. So, humor me."

I take a sip of the tea he brought and hum.

"You like it? I can bring you something else if you hate it."

"No, this is perfect." I twist off the cap to the Midol and pour out two pills. After popping them into my mouth, I chase them down with another long sip of tea.

I could get used to this pampering.

"So... massage?" Del wags his eyebrows at me and waves the bottle of massage oil.

"You just want to get me naked and put your hands all over my body."

"That's true, but I also want you to be comfortable. Tell me what you need from me."

My face drops because I've never had anyone offer to take care of me. My father doesn't count. He cares too much. My father cares when I don't want him to, when he doesn't give me the choice.

"Thank you, Puppet. I appreciate this. All of this. I'm just really tired, so... rain check on the massage?"

"Of course." He leans in and kisses the top of my head, then stands up straight with an awkward look on his face. "Um, sorry. I hope that wasn't weird. It just felt... like a natural thing to do."

I laugh. "You can kiss me on top of the head anytime."

Del leaves, taking the chicken wings after telling him my stomach will not be happy eating them. I finish the bowl of berries and drink all the tea. The Midol is already helping, so I lie back down and place the heating pad on my lower stomach.

I must have dozed off because now I'm on my side. The bed behind me dips, and a pair of strong arms wrap around my body. The heating pad fell during my tossing and turning, so Del picks it up and holds it in place over my cramping uterus.

"Goodnight, sweetheart," he whispers next to my ear before kissing my neck.

"Don't call me sweetheart, asshole," I mumble.

His soft laughter at my feigned anger is the last thing I remember before falling back asleep.

Five days pass and my period kept me and Delancy from fucking. Don't get me wrong, I have nothing against period sex, but this cycle was a rough one. I did *not* feel sexy. Which was good because keeping our hands off each other was productive for our plans to figure out our mothers' murders.

Well, sort of.

Del asked his brother to contact his law enforcement source to see if police reports were filed on the Christmas Eve murders and my mother's death the night before. Surprisingly, there were. Of course, most of it contained fabricated details. Same with the FDNY's report on the deadly fire at the Lords Mansion.

The police report on Sasha Lenetti's death is somewhat how I remember the night. After I was found hiding in my room, a detective brought me downstairs. My father was there, which as a kid I didn't find strange but now... He was supposed to be in the Bronx all night finishing up work before the holiday. How did he get to the Lower East Side so fast?

I remember seeing my mother's body covered in a white sheet with deep red blood soaked through at the head.

Nothing else was out of place. The men didn't go through our belongings or steal anything, yet the police report marked my mother's murder as a deadly home invasion and burglary.

It's bullshit.

The men spoke Italian and while I wasn't fluent in the language, I remember them saying Lenetti several times.

They also kept saying *figlia*—daughter—as if they'd seek me out next to kill.

Maybe this is why I feel so connected to Del. We both experienced something no child should ever have to go through. We both got a second chance at living.

And now we both *kill* for a living. We seek out revenge by ridding the world of the bad.

Fingerprints were taken from the scene of my mother's murder; DNA was collected but neither garnered a match in police databases.

Too many details were left out of these files because it's the mob. They only included what they wanted the government to know. Which made our investigation that much harder.

The file on Imogen Carter didn't have any information on Del. Nothing on a child being found in the snow, nearly dead.

His father really did erase him from existence.

The FDNY file on the fatal fire at the Lords Mansion was so fabricated, the information was useless. The cause was listed as a wire malfunction in the laundry room. The cause of death for Cillian's mother and sister was listed as smoke inhalation. Cillian made it clear over the years that an accelerant was found in the bedrooms. He also claimed an autopsy—that remained off record—revealed his mother was raped, stabbed, and strangled.

But can we really trust Cillian's words?

"That's the third time you've looked over those reports. Find anything new?" Del asks. He's sitting across the kitchen table from me, drinking a mug of coffee and eating a crème filled donut from a shop down the block.

"Nothing. We need to find the mob reports."

"You know we don't leave paper trails."

"Your father did."

"Yeah, well, that was a dumb thing to do. He knew better."

"But then you'd never been able to kill the men responsible—"

"I know," he says, his voice short and clipped.

I frown at him. "Was your mother... did they..."

"Yes," he answers the question I struggle to ask. "They raped her just like Cillian's mother."

"But my mother wasn't..."

I stand and pace, hoping the movement will trigger a memory or... something.

"This was a planned attack. Why hasn't anyone connected the murders until now? Why has everyone moved on as if it never happened?"

Stopping in the middle of the space between the living room and kitchen, I put my hands on my hips.

"Fight me."

"What?" Del pauses mid-bite and he stares at me as if I've gone mad.

"Fight me. I do my best thinking when I'm beating the shit out of someone."

He laughs. "And you think I'm going to let you kick my ass?"

I shake my head. "No, I think you're a competitive asshole like me and you're going to push me to my limit."

His humor drops from his face.

"Challenge accepted." He stands and walks into the living area. "Let's move all the furniture back to give us more space."

By the time we're done, a big empty circle remains.

"Should we do a countdown or—"

I don't let him finish and kick out my leg, aiming for his chest. He catches it by the ankle and twists, sending me to the ground. I ignore the shot of pain to my hip from the impact of the fall and swipe my foot, striking him in his Achilles tendon. He topples over, knees and palms hitting the hard floor right next to me.

"Goddamn it, Noah."

He's in the perfect position for me to implement a triangle choke hold. I wrap my legs around his head, squeezing tight until his face turns red.

He claws at my leggings, and I almost let go but seconds later he swings his legs around, twisting his body to turn me on my side. I lose my hold, my legs parting enough for him to free his head and the next thing I know, I'm on my stomach, and he's smashing my face down on the cement floor.

"Ready to tap out?" he whispers next to my ear.

"Fuck, no."

He slaps my ass hard before getting off me to stand. I scramble to get to my feet, huffing because it's pissing me off that he's winning. I adjust my tank top and swat a piece of hair out of my face.

"You look sexy all flushed and disheveled."

"Shut up, Puppet."

He slowly walks to his right, so I do the same and we move in a circle, sizing one another up. Looking for a tell or a weakness to implement our next attack.

"It's hot in here. Don't you think it's hot in here?" I stop to fan myself, then hook my fingertips behind the band of my leggings.

"Don't," Del warns.

"What are you talking about?" I peel them down over my ass and hips. "I'm just trying to cool off."

I step out of the pooled fabric, then shed the tank top, tossing it into a corner.

Del groans and adjusts his cock. "You're not playing fair," he says, his heated eyes scanning my body from head to toe.

I look down at the sheer black lace bra and matching thong I'm wearing. "Oh, this thing? Isn't it cute? I wore it just for you."

I turn around to shake my ass, fluttering my eyelashes at him over my shoulder. He runs at me, but I bend down just in time, grabbing his arm to catapult him over my back. He hits the ground with a heavy thud, knocking the air out of him.

I mount him and grind my pussy in circles over his groin. He closes his eyes and runs his hands up and down my thighs.

"Does that feel good, Marionette?"

He nods and swallows hard.

"I want to eat you out. Straddle my face, Vixen."

"We're supposed to be fighting," I say, but he tugs me down until his nose and mouth are buried in my pussy.

He moves the thin fabric of my thong out of the way and plunges his tongue inside me. I toss my head back and moan.

His nose rubs against my clit while he thrusts his tongue in and out at a damning pace.

He digs his nails into the meat of my thighs and scratches thin lines down to my knees, hard enough to break skin. The pain mixing with the pleasure has me quickly building up to an orgasm.

I speed up the grinding of my hips, and he spreads my legs further apart to give him more access to my cunt. He takes my clit into my mouth and sucks hard, then grazes his teeth over the sensitive bundle of nerves.

"Fuck," I yell out and bury my fingers into his hair, tugging at the strands as his magical mouth sucks and laps and bites.

His palms skim over my thighs, spreading the blood from the scratches. When his hands reach my ass, he smacks both cheeks hard. My pussy reacts with a spasm.

I'm close so I pinch both of my nipples and Del nips my clit with his teeth, taking me over the edge.

When I'm done shaking, I fall to the floor next to him, breathing hard.

Del turns to his side and rests his head on his palm.

"I almost lost consciousness from lack of oxygen there at the end," he says and a laugh bursts out of me. "What a way to go, though, right?"

He leans in for a kiss and despite his face being covered in my release, I part my lips for him. He doesn't hold back and plunges his tongue inside my mouth. I taste myself; salty and somewhat sweet. I groan, and Del reacts by getting on top of me.

He pulls his hard dick out of his sweats and without warning, thrusts into me in one slick move.

"Fuck, Delancy, don't stop," I say as he pounds into me.

He pushes my hair out of the way to gain access to my neck where he leaves rough kisses and love bites. He sucks one patch of skin hard enough to leave a hickey, and I don't even care at the moment. He's not being gentle, and I wouldn't want it any other way.

"Harder," I moan, and he abides. His balls slam into my ass with pleasant slaps.

"I'm close," he groans.

Two more thrusts later, he's fully seated, emptying his cum inside me.

Once he's done, he slides out and presses a thumb against my clit. I jolt at the pressure since it's still sensitive from him eating me out.

"I need you to come, too, Vixen."

"I already did," I say, my voice breathy.

"Come again for me, sweetheart."

"Don't call me—ah."

He presses harder, massaging in tight circles. He notices his cum starting to leak out of my pussy and pushes it back in. When he slaps my tits, hitting my aching nipples, my orgasm erupts throughout my body, and I scream.

"That's a good girl, showing me what my touch does to you."

My vision blurs with how hard I came. I'm breathing like I just ran up ten flights of stairs, my skin slick with sweat.

"So," Del begins, lying down on the floor next to me, "did the fighting or fucking help your thought process?"

I smile drunkenly because that's how I feel right now.

"Actually, yeah. It did help."

Chapter 17

Delancy

This is a bad idea.

This is a bad idea.

It's not going to work.

He's going to murder me.

"He's not going to murder you," Noah says, and I realize I'd been nervously muttering to myself.

"Have you ever brought someone to meet him?"

"Well, no."

"Exactly. He's going to kill me."

She's putting on gold hoop earrings and pauses.

"You're being dramatic."

"You're his only child, and he wants you to take over the Empire someday. That means he'll probably want you to marry someone of his choosing."

"Well, he should know by now that I do what I want."

"Right. Like gallivanting around the world, killing the corrupt and powerful?"

"Who even says gallivanting anymore?"

I ignore her sass. "Your father seems insanely protective. How did he allow that?"

"Oh, I noticed his protection detail no matter where I went. He always had eyes on me from the moment he sent me away. It made it harder for me to take on hit jobs, but I managed to ditch his goons."

She picks up a gold chain with a single diamond in the middle and puts it on.

"Why didn't your parents have kids after you? Wouldn't Gio want to make sure he had someone to take over the organization once he's gone?"

Noah stares into the mirror with a frown, her fingertips on the chain. It's clear she's thinking about her mother's necklace, which she lost in the explosion. I've yet to return it to her. I'm waiting for the perfect moment.

"My mother struggled getting pregnant with me. She had complications throughout. I was born, and the doctors basically said she could die if she got pregnant again."

She gives herself one final look in the mirror, smoothing her hands over her black dress. It's absolutely stunning on her. Form-fitting on top with a dipped neckline showcasing her cleavage. It has puffed sleeves that fall off her shoulders and a full skirt with pockets.

The pockets were important.

"I'm surprised my father didn't cheat so he could have more. I know he desperately wanted a son and got me instead."

She walks to where I stand and adjusts my tie. Her father is hosting a Christmas party—something he does every year. Despite being back for a few months, Noah is announcing her official return tonight.

And since most of the underworld believes she's dead, tonight's expected to get... interesting.

"You think bringing me tonight and introducing me as your fiancé is a good idea?"

She sighs and places her palm flat on my chest.

"I'm not going to lie; he's going to be pissed, but he'll get over it."

I'm fucking screwed. She came up with this fake engagement idea as a way to bring me into the Empire so we could dismantle it together. I know this is what I wanted. I needed to work my way in so I could get to Gio. But my plan was always to target his associates, not bypass them and go straight to the man in charge.

Did Noah consider that her father might not accept me into the family? We plan to use one of my aliases. I can't exactly go into an Empire party and introduce myself as Lance Carter. I may be an unknown QBM heir, but my last name could spill blood.

"It feels weird to be celebrating," Noah says, frowning. "I wanted to stop celebrating Christmas after my mother's death, but my father turned the holiday into a memorial for her. It's the only reason I returned every year to visit. I wanted to honor her."

Noah looks down, and I cup her chin, lifting her head.

"We're going to get our answers. What we find might hurt, but we'll get closure. We'll have each other to lean on. Okay?"

She nods, her eyes glazing over with tears. "Okay."

I place a soft kiss on her lips.

"Do you still want to kill me?" She pouts, fluttering her lashes.

"I'm not ruling it out just yet."

Her laughter makes my heart dance, and I smile at the fact that I turned her grief into a happy moment.

"You won't do it."

"Yeah? How do you know?"

"You'd miss this body if I were to die."

"That is true," I say, silently adding that I'd miss *her* more.

I smack her ass when she walks past me to open the door.

She holds out her hand. "Ready fiancé?"

I hire a car to take us into Manhattan. Her father's Christmas party is being held at the Wyndock Hotel in Midtown. It's a five-star luxury hotel with all the amenities you can think of and views of the Empire State Building. Rooms cost thousands of dollars, including the penthouse, which goes for about $50,000 per night.

The lobby is two stories high with sleek black and silver marble floors. I count four round columns, two crystal chandeliers, and an elaborate painting on the ceiling as if this place is the freaking Sistine Chapel.

On the left, a woman decked out in a fur coat, a pearl necklace, and white gloves leads a worker pushing a luggage cart full of bags to a row of elevators to head to her room.

How cliché.

We pass the bar area on the right where a man in a tux plays a Christmas song on a grand piano. Just past the bar is a hallway that leads to the grand ballroom.

We turn the corner and encounter a line of about six people waiting to be let in. Two women wearing earpieces hold clipboards checking names, two other workers check coats, and three Goliath security guards wave metal detectors over bodies.

"Daddy's not playing, huh?" I say out of the corner of my mouth.

I glance at Noah when she doesn't answer. She's wringing her hands and fidgeting on her feet while we wait.

I grab her shaking hand and squeeze.

"It'll be fine." She squeezes back and nods. I point my chin at the double doors that lead into the ballroom. "Can't we skip the queue?"

"I don't want to bring attention to us. Not yet. I want to get in, see who's all in there, then find my dad before we make our announcement."

I bring our embraced hands up to my lips and kiss her knuckles. "Have I told you how beautiful you look tonight?"

"Yes, about five times now." She smiles, some of her anxiety slipping away.

"Well, it's still true. Even though you wouldn't let me fuck you in the car ride over."

"I didn't want to wrinkle my dress."

"You could have at least let me fuck you with my fingers," I whisper, though not quiet enough because the elderly woman in front of us turns around and scowls. I wink at her, and she clutches her pearls. Literally.

"Don't worry, Puppet. I plan to reward you for your patience tonight. I'll let you put it any—"

Before she can finish, it's our turn. Noah is immediately let in without giving her name or going through any security checks.

She tries to pull me in after her, but one of the older guards, who I just know gets off on power trips, stops us. He scans me for weapons and goes the extra mile patting me down, swiping his hands up my legs too close to my crotch. I almost ask if I can buy him a drink with how frisky he's getting. Noah is about to step in when the man finally releases me.

"Sorry about him," she says, handing our coats to a worker. They give Noah a ticket, which she puts in her clutch. "That's Vershun, my father's head of security. I'm sure he's already called him to let him know I'm here... with a man."

Fuck.

I'm going to die tonight.

The ballroom is decked out in red, green, and gold. The Christmas tree that's nearly as tall as the room is packed full of decorations. Bows are wrapped around columns and gold streamers hang from the ceiling. A string quartet plays an instrumental version of a popular holiday song while a handful of people dance along to the music. Others stand around drinking, eating, and chatting.

"Is it always this..."

"Gaudy? Tacky? Extravagant? From what I can remember, yes." She grabs two champagne flutes from a server making rounds and hands one to me. "When I used to come to this thing, I'd never stay long. I'd have a few drinks, eat the hors d'oeuvres, and find someone to fuck."

I break the stem of the champagne glass.

"Aw, does that make my puppet jealous?"

"Yes."

The grin she gives me tells me she's up to no good.

"What? You don't want to share me? Come on, Deli Baby. Let's find someone to take home with us tonight."

She wags her eyebrows at me.

"Someone?" I ask, even though I know she's attracted to all genders. I want to hear her say it.

"Man. Woman. Nonbinary. I find beauty in everyone." She runs her lower lip between her teeth. "What about you?"

"I'm bi, and while I do enjoy a threesome... you're mine, and I'm greedy, and I don't want to share you with anyone."

Her cheeks warm to a beautiful red, and she swipes her tongue over her plump lips.

"Stop thinking about me fucking another man."

She snorts. "I was actually thinking about you fucking a woman while I ride her face. But now that you mention it..."

"Lance?"

My brother's rough voice startles me, and I whip around, snatching Noah by the wrist to pull her behind me.

"Del, why are you trying to hide me?" She peels out of my grip and steps to my side.

"Hi. I'm Noah."

Elias scans Noah's body and rubs his thumb over his bottom lip, letting me know he likes what he sees.

"Elias. This idiot's brother," he says, pointing his thumb at me. He takes her offered hand, but instead of shaking it, he lifts it to his mouth to kiss her knuckles.

"A gentleman," Noah purrs.

The fury that races through me is nearly debilitating.

"He's not a fucking gentleman!" I growl.

Elias laughs, the asshole. "I have to say... I've never seen my brother so... protective of another person before."

Noah takes my fisted hand and opens it to weave her fingers with mine. She squeezes my arm, then rubs her palm up and down.

She's trying to calm me.

"What are you doing here?" I ask, my voice low. "If anyone were to find out the leader of the QBM is at an Empire party..."

Everyone knows Elias Carter leads the QBM, but few people know what he looks like. He rarely shows face. Sometimes he'll send a body double with similar hair and build to business meetings while acting as a right-hand man. He's present but in the background.

I think it's clever. He's a mystery, and he has a reputation of no mercy for violent criminals who prey on the weak and poor.

Preying on the rich and powerful and corrupt is a different story.

"I was invited," he says with a shrug and takes a sip of his whiskey.

"By my father?" Noah asks, and Elias whips his head over to her. His eyes narrow.

"You're Gio Lenetti's daughter? I thought Noemi Lenetti—"

"Died? No. It was a lie." She snorts. "It's weird hearing my birth name again after all these years."

Elias turns back to me, questions filling his face, but he doesn't ask them. He wants to know how long I've known Noah is the enemy and why she's latching on to my arm. Yet, he's the one eating and drinking at the party hosted by the man who ordered our mother's death.

"We're working together," I say.

"And fucking," Noah adds, which makes Elias's face turn crimson.

As much as I enjoy Noah messing with my brother, his temper is unpredictable. I wrap my arm around her waist, bringing her flush with my side.

"I wanted to meet yesterday to tell you everything," I say. "But you never answer my text messages. I even called and left a voicemail. So, don't act surprised. I tried, like I always do. We'll meet tomorrow to talk."

"It better be a good fucking explanation, little brother," Elias seethes.

"It will be," Noah says, trying to ease the growing tension between us. "Oh!"

She squirms out of my hold and waves at a thick blonde woman walking through the crowd towards us. She's the same woman I saw at the restaurant and again at the club with Noah the night she killed Cillian.

"Sage," Noah says, hugging her bestie. "You look amazing."

Sage poses with one hand on her hip and the other in the air. She's wearing a red sparkling strapless dress and elbow-length white gloves. Her hair falls in curls over her shoulders and down her back.

"Thanks, Noey!" She blows a kiss at her best friend, and I'm tempted to grab it because only I should be blowing kisses to Noah.

A stupid thought, which is why I keep my hands in my pockets.

"Sage, you've met Del before."

Sage scans my body from head to toe. "Oh, I remember." She gives Noah a not-so-discreet wink of approval before turning her attention to my brother.

"And this is Elias—"

"Oh, fuck," Sage's cheeks pink with... embarrassment? I don't know this woman at all, but she doesn't seem to be the type to embarrass easily.

"You," Elias growls.

"I'm sorry," Noah begins. "Do you two know each other?"

"We fucked, and she disappeared," Elias bellows, garnering the attention of a few people nearby.

"Tell the whole room, why don't you!" Sage huffs. "And it's called a one-night stand for a reason."

"Do all your one-night stands give you multiple orgasms? Do they fuck you until your eyes cross and your brain stops working? Isn't that what you said to me after the fifth round?"

Sage opens her mouth, then immediately clamps it shut. She can't argue with that.

"Is this the unbelievably earth-shattering mindless sex guy you told me about that you met at a club in Brooklyn a few weeks ago?" Noah asks, attempting to ease this tension.

"You mean the club *I* own? Underground Park Slope?" Elias asks.

"Yes! That's the one!" Noah giggles. "Oh, Sage... after what you told me... why would you ever deny yourself another night with The Boss?"

"The Boss?" Now I'm intrigued.

"Yes, why, *Sage?*"

My brother's words are full of hate, but his eyes can't stop devouring the woman's body. Elias isn't like me. He needs companionship. He needs someone to love and take care of. His girlfriend of two years broke up with him last month. They always do when they find out who he is and what he does. Or he breaks it off with them to protect them from this life.

He desperately wants to marry and have children.

"Anyone going to address Sage calling Elias 'The Boss'?" I ask, desperate for an explanation.

"Because he owns the club, obviously," Sage says.

Elias smirks. "Or is it because I owned your pussy? Made that cunt sore and stretched to fit my cock that no other man will be able to live up to the job of pleasing you like I did."

Sage walks up to him, her nose high. The top of her head barely reaches his chin. Elias's large and wide form towers over her. She doesn't realize the dangerous and powerful man she's challenging.

Crossing her arms and with a sneer, she says, "I've had better."

"Okay, while what's happening between you two is... interesting," Noah says, grabbing Sage's arm to pull her back next to us, "the show's about to begin."

Noah nods to the stage where her father is off to the side talking to white-haired and wrinkled men who are probably important.

"What show?" Sage asks, her button nose scrunching.

"I'm sorry I didn't get to tell you before. Please don't be mad," Noah says to Sage, then turns to my brother. "Can you watch over her? She means the world to me."

She then treats Elias like a doll, moving him to stand next to Sage, and she lifts his arm to snake it around Sage's waist.

Sage wiggles to get out of his hold, but Elias clings to her tighter.

"Let's go," Noah says, taking my hand and walking us into the crowd toward the stage.

"Babbo." She greets her father with a kiss on each cheek. His eyes are filled with love when he looks at her.

"Mio angelo." He takes her small hand in between his large ones. "I wish you would have told me you were coming tonight."

His eyes move to me. I swear I see him snarl.

"And with a... friend."

Noah laughs. "He's far more than a friend, Babbo. In fact, we have some news."

She takes my hand and leads me onto the stage. She taps on the microphone to make sure it's on.

"Excuse me, everyone. Can I have your attention?" The conversations slowly die out and heads turn to the stage, some with confused faces, others lighting up at the prospect of a performance. There will definitely be drama. "My name is Noah McAllister. Well, I suppose you'd know me as Noemi Lenetti, Gio Lenetti's daughter. Surprise! Not dead."

Chatter fills the room. I glance at her father, and his face deepens red. His fists ball at his sides.

"Noah, what are you doing?"

Noah ignores her father and keeps talking.

She waves her hand at me. "This is Lance Carter. Son of Percy Carter, brother of Elias Carter."

My stomach sours as Noah goes off plan.

She didn't use my alias for the announcement.

What the hell is she doing?

The voices in the room grow louder. She has to yell her next words.

"And we're engaged to be married."

Chapter 18

Noah

The stare of murder I got from my father after that announcement almost made me drag Del out of the party and go into hiding.

"I hope you know what you're doing," Del says next to my ear while we slow dance to "I'll Be Home for Christmas."

I've had three chutes of champagne and a vodka soda cranberry, and I'm feeling pretty freaking good.

"It's going to work."

"Your father is going to kill me."

"Don't worry about him. I can handle my father. Once I tell him that I'm ready to learn the business, he'll be too excited to care about killing you." I think. "Besides, it's just temporary. No one will question the fiancé of "Noemi Lenetti" being in Empire territory. This makes it easier to snoop around for answers about our mothers' murders."

"But they will question Lance Carter, QBM heir. Your father's not going to trust you now that he knows you're engaged to the enemy. Honestly, I'm surprised I'm not already dead."

I'd considered this. I didn't mean to out Del too.

"Okay, now hear me out."

"This ought to be good."

Rude.

"I had this idea after seeing your brother here at the party that maybe we can bring the two families together and become one crime organization. We'd be powerful enough to take over the Lords' territory on Staten Island."

The Lords are such a waste of space, it's time for them to go.

They run illegal gambling rings and black-market trading schemes. They're also a hotbed for sex trafficking.

Not that the other two mafias are angels. The QBM controls all the drugs that come in and out of the city.

And the Empire has majority power over guns.

I know each organization deals in other illegal activities: extortion, fraud, loan sharking. Up until now, I haven't cared to learn all those details.

I *still* don't want to know all the details, but if it will lead us to answers, then I'll learn.

Speaking of answers... We've yet to figure out who's trying to kill me. Am I being targeted for being a mafia heir or contract killer?

"I don't know about this, Vixen."

"I'll talk to him. I'm surprised he hasn't come over here to steal me away."

He's been busy doing damage control over my little stunt.

"He won't touch you if he knows how important you are to me."

"Am I important to you?"

"Yes. I need you to help me snoop through my father's stuff."

"Is that all I'm good for?"

Del's hands smooth up and down my back, inching dangerously close to my ass. He leans in and sniffs my neck.

"Basically."

"I'm not good at eating you out and fucking you until you're sore?"

"You're definitely not good at that. You're fucking fantastic."

Del growls in my ear. "Fuck it. Talk to him another night. I want to take you home now so I can devour you."

"Home? And where might that be? Your safe house?"

"Yes, the safe house." His soft lips press against my neck. "Or wherever you want. I'll buy you a penthouse with the best views of New York City if that's what you'd prefer."

More kisses, this time along my jaw.

"Mhm. Moving in together so soon? We barely know each other."

Even though we've technically been living together since the explosion.

"Good thing we're engaged, *fiancée*. We have until our dying day to get to know each other."

"It's a fake engagement, and you know it," I say, breathless as his eager lips leave no part of my skin untouched.

"Nope. We're getting married."

"What if l want a divorce?"

"Not happening. You're mine forever."

"Should I be concerned about this obsessive behavior of yours? What's next? Are you going to tell me you love me?"

He answers by nipping at my jaw.

I need to stop Del's PDA, because he won't hesitate to fuck me in front of everyone in the middle of this dance floor.

I glance around the crowd. I was hoping to talk to Sage. I know she's probably pissed about me hiding this part of my life from her. When I invited her tonight, I didn't think she'd accept since she's not a fan of my father. But I think she misses me. Fuck, I miss her. Del has been taking up too much of my time. So, yeah, she was thrilled to attend. She told me she was going to find a rich sugar daddy to take her home.

She either found that person or a handsome mobster stole her away.

"Where's your brother? I don't see Sage, and I'm worried he kidnapped her."

"He might have. I saw the way he looked at her."

He twists me around, crushing his front to my back and crosses his arm over my stomach. His lips return to my neck, and I close my eyes at how wonderful they feel.

"You better behave," I whisper. "My father has not let us out of his sight."

"We want to be believable, yes?"

"I also want you alive."

At that, he stops and swings me back around.

"I spoke too soon. We're about to be summoned." I nod at Vershun approaching us.

"Miss Lenetti," he says coldly. I blanche at the use of my birth name. "Your father has requested an audience with you and your... friend."

"I think you mean fiancé," I hold up my ring finger, flashing the white gold, five-carat, pear-shaped diamond ring. I nearly passed out when Del gave it to me. He claims it's not real, and it cost next to nothing, but I know my diamonds. It's the real deal with a $100,000 price tag. "Lead the way, Vershy."

He snarls at the nickname, and Del snarls at Vershun's reaction. My puppet is so adorably protective, and I'm quite enjoying this possessive side of him.

But right now? He's raging.

"Are you trying to break my hand?" I ask as we walk through the crowd.

"Sorry," he says and loosens his hold.

He might be nervous too. I mean, I'm nervous, but at least I know my father won't hurt me.

Vershun leads us out of the ballroom to a conference room with a long table and twelve chairs around it. My father sits at the front, or I guess the back, smoking a cigar.

"Sit, daughter."

The moment my ass hits the seat, my dad has a gun in his hand, and he pulls the trigger.

Despite the silencer masking the noise of the shot, Del was prepared and dodges the bullet to hunch over me like a shield.

"Impressive. Your reflexes are fast, and your first instinct was to protect my daughter."

"Is this really necessary, Babbo?"

"No, but it's fun."

I grab Del's hand and sit him down next to me, weaving my fingers with his; a sign of solidarity for my father.

"What is this about?" I ask.

"What is this about?" My father laughs. Then he laughs a little more until his face is scarlet and tears are in his eyes. He might have gone insane.

In a flash, my father's gun is back in his hands.

"No!"

It's too late. The bullet pierces through Del's shoulder. It would have gone in his chest if I hadn't tugged on his arm, out of the line of fire.

I stand up and press my hands over the wound.

"What the fuck, Giovanni?!"

"Watch your mouth, little girl," he says, pounding a fist on the table. "You disappear for over a week after the apartment you rented in neutral territory blows up. And you return only to be engaged to the enemy? Then you tell everyone your *true* identity? After everything I've worked for to keep you alive and safe?!"

"You wanted me back and now I'm here. Everyone was going to find out who I am."

My father's face is as red as his tie, and I worry he's going to have an aneurysm.

"Tell me this engagement isn't real."

"It's real, Babbo. I love him."

"You love me?" Del wheezes through the pain.

"After, what? A week? Bullshit."

Del's face pales and sweat coats his forehead. He winces when I ease pressure off the wound to swipe a piece of stuck hair back. Maybe I do love him. At least, I can see myself loving him.

"We've known each other longer. Almost three months now."

"He's QBM," my father says and spits on the ground beside him.

"I think him being QBM can help us," I say, my voice shaking because my father's face reads pure murder. I might not be able to talk myself out of this one.

His eyes narrow before he stands and walks to where we sit. He raises his gun and presses the barrel to Del's head.

"Tell me why I shouldn't kill him right here in front of you."

My throat aches with the threat of tears. I rarely see this side of my father. Ever since my mother's murder, I knew there were two versions of him: the man who loved and cared for me and the murdering mobster. But part of me didn't want to believe he could be the latter. I never wanted to believe he could be capable of ordering the hit on the wives and children of rival mobs.

Now I can see it. I see the true Gio Lenetti.

"Because to the world you may be a dangerous criminal, but to me, you're Babbo. My father," I say through tears. "You love me and if you care about me, you won't kill Lance. Let me explain. You at least owe me that."

He presses the barrel harder, and I can hear Del grind his teeth in response. My father finally lowers the gun with a sneer, leaving an indentation of a ring on Del's forehead.

Before I can breathe a sigh of relief, Gio pistol whips Del and knocks him out cold.

"Seriously?"

My dad shrugs. "I don't like the way he looks at you."

I pinch the bridge of my nose.

"Can you please call someone to stitch him up so he doesn't die?"

Gio stares me down as if he's about to say 'maybe I want him to die.' He glares at me, well, more at Del, then flicks his wrist at Vershun and the other guard with blond hair whose name I can't remember right now.

No name guy gives my father a snarl—or maybe that was meant for me—and leaves.

"Okay," my father waves his hand over the table. "Talk."

My eyes move to Vershun. I'd rather not have him here either. My father must see my hesitation, and with a silent command, the big security guy exits the room.

"Why him?" my father asks the moment the door closes.

I grab a bottle of water on the table to try and rehydrate after all the booze I drank tonight. The champagne kicked my ass. I'm not used to the bubbly stuff, and it made me a little lightheaded. I need clear thoughts to have this conversation.

"He saved me from the apartment explosion. We were... out on a date and when we returned, the building blew up—like I said, an accident because Mrs. Crowley's gas oven broke and was leaking, and she lit a cigarette. May she rest in peace." I do the sign of the cross to drive my point. "Lance found me, treated my wounds. I was underneath debris. Who knows how long I would have been there before someone found me?"

Not entirely the truth but close enough.

"You told me you were fine," my father growls.

"I was! I am. I'm just saying he was there for me!" I'm digging myself into a deeper grave. I should stop talking about me being injured. "Anyway, yes, Lance is QBM but Babbo, think about it. If I marry into their organization, then we can work together. We can unite and have majority control over the city. Together we can take down the Lords."

He puffs on his cigar and rubs his chin as he considers my words.

"The Empire will never work with the enemy."

"What makes them the enemy?"

"When you're the most powerful mafia in the city, everyone else is insignificant. Uniting with QBM will show weakness."

"Or our combined forces will show even more power and the Lords will be no match to a united front." I sigh, knowing he will never agree to this. Still, I have to try. "Besides, didn't you invite Elias Carter tonight? What was your plan with that?"

His eyes jerk up to mine. "What? I didn't invite that lowlife asshole."

I open my mouth, then clamp it shut.

Okay, I suppose I didn't get an answer from Elias when I asked if my father invited him. He got distracted when I revealed I'm Gio Lenetti's daughter.

Then who invited him? How did he get in?

"I don't like this plan, mio angelo. This man could be playing you. How do you know he didn't seek you out to get close to me?"

"He lived in the building before I moved in. Babbo, look, this is real. Like it or not. Either you're on board or Lance and I will run off together and elope, and you'll never see me again."

"You think you can go anywhere without me having eyes on you?"

My stomach drops and my heart thumps rapidly against my chest. I've always known he's kept tabs on me. Still, hearing him *say* it infuriates me.

What did he see?

If he knows about me being a contract killer, why hasn't he said something about it? Or utilize my skills? Or stop me from killing because every hit I accept puts my life in danger? Maybe he knew that if he forced me to return home, dragged me back against my will, I'd hate him forever.

And I'm all he has left in this world, so he lets me think I have my independence.

"Babbo... I came back because I'm ready to start learning about the Empire so I can take over some day."

My father's face brightens with shock... and pride. It's the words he's been waiting to hear for years.

"Tell me you are not joking."

I ease my pressure on Del's wound—and hope he doesn't bleed out in the next five minutes—and stand to walk to where my father sits. I lean over and hug his head. "I'm not joking. These last few months with Lance have opened my eyes. I want a future and that includes leading the Empire."

My father grumbles at the mention of Del being the one to open my eyes, but his excitement over me learning the job is overshadowing his apprehension.

"At least agree to a meeting with Elias. Just you, me, him, and Lance. No guards, no guns–"

"There will always be guns."

"Fine, then no shooting those guns and no violence. A civil meeting. Elias is doing good things with the QBM. He runs that organization smoothly and effectively. He has connections, Babbo, maybe even more than you."

He scoffs and before he can respond, the door opens. A woman with a medical bag enters, and I point at Del. She rushes to him and gets right to work.

He looks so innocent right now while passed out. I love watching him sleep. It's not often I wake before Del, but when I do, I perch my head on my palm and watch his eyes flutter from whatever he's dreaming about. The first night we fell asleep together, a nightmare woke him up. I can't imagine what he went through being forced to kill his mother. The second night we fell asleep together, he slept through the morning.

Now that I think about it, my own nightmares are few and far between now that I have him by my side every night.

"You really do love him. I can see it. Your mother looked at me the same way," my father says, his voice soft and sincere.

I want to ask him about that night again. I want to tell him that we're investigating her death and the murders of the other mafia families on Christmas Eve. But what if he's responsible? I don't want to tip him off and have him come after us or try to destroy any remaining evidence.

So, until then, Del and I have our way in. We'll get access to the Empire and, hopefully, track down information that could lead us to answers.

"I do love him," I say and walk back to my seat next to my puppet. He's slowly coming out of it. I hold his hand while the woman takes the bullet out and stitches him up.

I want to say that my confession of love is a lie, but if I'm honest with myself... I think I'm falling hard for this man. I can see myself loving him, and it's a feeling I've never had with anyone.

Still, it seems too soon, and my gut is telling me not to trust him just yet.

What if my father is right and Del is playing an angle? Why was Elias here tonight if he wasn't invited? Something's not adding up, and I'm going to be a paranoid bitch until I find out the truth.

Chapter 19

Delancy

It's been a week since that asshole shot me. My shoulder is still sore as hell, and I haven't been able to properly fuck my vixen. She's been adamant about me resting and healing, and all I want to do is sink inside her wet pussy.

"Why are you pouting?" Noah asks, setting a tray of food on my lap.

"Thinking about how desperately I need to fuck you."

I inspect the plate of bacon, scrambled eggs, and toast. Either she's getting better at cooking, or she ordered this from the deli a few streets over.

After taking a bite of the eggs, I decide she definitely ordered this.

"Yeah? Tell me what you'd do to me? Would you fuck me hard enough to leave bruises and make my pussy ache?"

She snatches a piece of bacon and pops it into her mouth.

"Mmm. Salty." She licks her fingers, sucking them greedily before swiping her tongue over her lips.

She's teasing me.

I place the tray on the bed and stand directly in front of her. She sucks in a breath as I tower over her five-foot ten height.

My fingers wrap around her neck, and I squeeze.

"Stop being a brat," I growl and kiss her roughly.

She gasps against my lips, parting her mouth to let my tongue caress and explore her sweet taste. She had an iced coffee this morning, and it mixes with the smoky and salty flavors of the bacon she just ate.

"Careful," she says after I release her. "You're going to break open the stitches."

"It was five stitches and they're nearly dissolved." I toss her on the bed and the tray full of my breakfast rattles. I swipe it out of the way, and it clatters onto the floor below.

"What the fuck, Del? You just wasted a shit ton of food. You're cleaning that up."

"Flip over, slut."

She thinks about defying my order, pissed I made a mess of the lovely breakfast she brought me. I'll make it up to her later. She sighs heavily before flipping on her stomach. The minute she does, I pull down her sweats and panties. My hand comes down hard on her ass, causing her cheeks to ripple like waves.

She lets out a grunt and when I do it again and again, she buries her face into the bed to muffle her screams of pleasure.

I run the tip of my finger up and down her ass crack.

"I want to fuck this tight hole. Will you let me fuck you here?"

She pushes against my finger, and it sinks between her cheeks. When I reach her puckered ring, I press the tip in.

"Yes," she pants.

"Are you a good little slut who's had men here before?"

"Yes, Delancy. I'm a slut. I'm your slut. Fuck my ass. Make it hurt."

I spank her again and she moans.

"No longer concerned about my stitches?"

"Fuck your stitches. I need you, now, please." She gets on her hands and knees: an invitation.

I take a bottle of lube out of the bedside table drawer and squeeze the thick gel on two fingers.

"Let me see just how tight you are."

I push one finger in slowly and she arches her back.

"Oh, yes, you're tight. Are you sure you can take me?"

"Yes, sir. I'll take it all, please, give me your cock."

My hand crashes down on her left cheek. "Good girls get rewarded, and you're being a brat right now. Be. Patient."

She whimpers as I push my finger all the way in. I ease it out, then begin pumping. I'm slow at first, then speed up when I add a second finger.

"You're doing so well, Noah. Are you ready?" I ask after stretching her asshole enough it won't hurt.

"I'm ready, please," she rasps.

I remove my fingers, and she whines at the loss. After stripping my sweats, I grab my dick and soak it with lube. I line the thick head to her asshole and push in barely an inch.

She sucks in a sharp breath.

"Relax, sweetheart."

She groans, and I press in halfway.

"Yeah, yeah, don't call you sweetheart," I say at the same time she does and thrust in, to the hilt.

She screams at the sudden sensation of my size but, if it hurts, she shows no signs of pain.

I move in and out slowly.

"Delancy, go faster, please," she begs.

The hairs on the back of my neck rise, and I hear the soft shuffle of feet behind me.

"Well, isn't this a sight to see?" a familiar voice chuckles.

My gun is sitting within reach on the bedside table and it's in my hand before this asshole can finish speaking.

"What the fuck are you doing in my safe house, Elias?" I point the gun at him while my cock stays fully seated inside Noah's ass.

She looks over her shoulder at the intruder.

"Hey there, Elly," she says, and he narrows his eyes at her. I don't even remember telling her my brother's nickname but hearing her say it makes me proud.

"I could join," he offers. "See which brother fucks you better?"

"Mhm... tempting," Noah says and starts bouncing on my dick. I know she's not joking either.

"Get the fuck out, Elias," I growl and drop the gun so I can hold Noah down. I spread her cheeks and pound into her ass. She moans with every rough thrust.

"And miss the finish?"

He walks over to the wingback chair in the corner of the room and sits, propping his ankle on his knee. He has a glass of whiskey in his hand—my whiskey, the bastard—and takes a sip.

"Let him watch," Noah cries out, her voice a mix of pleasure and pain. "It's turning me on."

I don't mind a little voyeurism, but not when it's my asshole of a brother. But Noah's into it, and I'll do whatever she asks of me, *begs of me*.

I'm still pissed, though, and take it out on Noah's asshole.

I slap both of her cheeks hard enough to leave a red outline of my hand and she moans. She's being so vocal for our guest.

Which pisses me off even more.

I thrust into her at a damning pace until her tight hole clenches around my cock and an orgasm washes over her. I reach my climax soon after.

"I see you're recovering well from being shot," Elias says as I lean over Noah's body, huffing and sweating.

After removing my cock from her ass, I watch my cum leak out and push it back inside where it belongs.

Elias sighs, the impatient fucker.

I grab Noah by the neck to bring her in for a kiss.

"Go clean up," I whisper against her lips.

Noah nods and crawls off the bed, not an ounce concerned about being half naked in front of my brother. She gives him a little wave as she walks by, and he watches her every step of the way.

"What do you want?" I ask the moment Noah's in the bathroom.

"Gio Lenetti shot you."

"He did."

"And why did I hear about it from Sa—someone else?" He takes another sip of his whiskey. "Not to mention that stunt you two pulled at the party. Engaged to Lenetti's daughter? Seriously, Lance?"

He sets the glass down on the small round table next to the chair.

"What's the goal here? Are you making a play—"

"We have a plan," I say in a low, warning voice.

"*We?*" Elias shakes his head. "You're pussy whipped. What is this plan? Are you sure she's not using you? Leading you to a trap?"

"If she wanted me dead, I'd be dead. We know what we're doing. We don't need your help."

"Actually, we do need his help," Noah says, coming out of the bathroom. She's found a pair of underwear, but the sheer fabric does nothing to hide her trimmed bush peeking through. Elias is also staring, so I punch him in the jaw.

"What the fuck, Lance?"

"Stop looking at her like that."

"Boys, stop fighting," Noah stands between us as Elias puffs out his chest and raises his chin, ready to hit me back. She raises a brow at Elias. "And your brother's right. Stop looking at me or I'll tell Sage."

Elias narrows his eyes at Noah, calling her bluff. She picks up her phone off the bedside table and taps away until finding Sage's phone number.

"Okay, fuck."

Elias is trying to get a rise out of me. I have no doubt my brother finds Noah attractive, but he'd never act on his feelings. Especially with his sights set on Sage.

"Now, Elias, we need you to join us for dinner tomorrow night at my father's townhouse on the Lower East Side."

"Absolutely fucking not."

Noah holds up a finger to stop him from further protest. "I promise it will be worth your time."

N oah has no idea what she's doing. Inviting the leader of a rival mob into the home of New York City's most notorious mobster is begging for someone to be shot and killed.

And I doubt we'll be planning Gio Lenetti's funeral.

Noah says her plan is to convince these two powerful men into working together and forming one mighty mafia—her words, which I pointed out that mighty mafia sounds like a cartoon that airs on Saturday mornings. I don't see how this will work. It would still mean putting one of them in charge of the combined organizations while the other plays right-hand man.

Gio Lenetti will kill Elias before letting him rule. My brother is also a stubborn asshole and won't give up control. He only agreed to dinner because Noah explained that combining the mafias is temporary until we can uncover the truth about our mothers' murders.

"If it's my father, he will pay for what he did, and Elias can take over sole control of the combined organizations."

Noah says to me in the car, heading to Gio's townhouse on the Lower East Side.

She's too scared to say that her father must die. She knows that's the only answer. But who kills him? Me or her?

I don't think I could let her live with that. I know what it's like to kill a parent and the trauma that never goes away. Even if she finds out he betrayed her, she still loved him. He still cared for her for the past thirty-one years.

"We're already planning to dismantle the Lords, so if it was Finn O'Connor who put out the hits twenty years ago, then he dies. Either way, we offer his soldiers and associates immunity for providing us insider information that will help us absorb their organization or threaten death if they refuse."

"You're too trusting, Noe. We shouldn't let any of the Lords live."

"They're just following orders. We can vet them. Or torture them. I'm sure you'd love doing that."

I would love that. Still, we'll have to discuss this further. I've yet to meet a Lords soldier who isn't as corrupt as their leader.

"What if it was my father?"

"If it was Percy, then there's nothing else to do since he's dead."

"I'm not convinced your father will agree to merge with the QBM. It's unprecedented."

"I know it's a long shot, but I have to at least try. That being said, I came back with a promise to destroy the Empire. That hasn't changed. My anger has always been with my father for letting the underworld kill my mother."

"Instead of bringing the Empire down, why don't you steal it from him?" I offer. "Take over and lead it your way."

"I don't think I'm strong enough to lead. Not yet. I'm more than happy to let Elias have it. Do you think he'll help me?"

I take her hand and kiss her knuckles. "I have no doubt."

Elias has slowly been gaining more control over city officials and law enforcement. The QBM is aiming for the top spot, so if Elias has a chance to take it from Gio, he will.

"And if none of the three mafias were responsible for the murders?"

She meets my eyes. The thought has crossed her mind, and she's scared that will be the outcome.

"I don't know," Noah answers.

Is it possible that whoever tried to kill Noah with the explosion is the one who put out the hit all those years? Are they trying to tie up loose ends? If that's the case, why didn't they douse my apartment with gasoline too?

It doesn't make sense.

We sit in silence for a few minutes, Noah's head rests against my shoulder. It's such a normal thing for someone to do. A gesture of love and trust. It makes me feel human—which is still a strange sensation for me.

"Can I ask you what happened after the gun range? You disappeared for a week. Where did you go?"

She looks up at me, fluttering her mesmerizing brown eyes. I tuck a piece of her hair behind her ear, and she closes her eyes at the move.

"I didn't lie," I say. "I really did have a job."

"Oh, right, your private investigator job." She giggles.

"Technically, I do investigate and research each kill. Don't you?"

She shrugs. "Not really. I mean, I'll do a bit of recon to track behavior and lock down their schedule, but I don't need that much from my targets. I'm also not as concerned with setting the murder scene like the Marionette."

"I really hate that name."

She laughs and wraps her arm around my stomach.

Her jasmine and citrus scent envelops me, and my hand falls to her thigh. I rub my palm up and down, desperately wanting to go between her legs to sink my fingers inside her cunt. She already teased me by not wearing underwear with her dress.

"You're nervous about telling me?" she asks.

I am. Can she hear my heart thundering in my chest? Or maybe it's because I can't keep my hands still when I'm anxious. Can she see me sweating?

I'm nervous because I'm still not used to sharing my life, or my feelings, with another person. I remember after her father shot me. I was delirious with pain, yet I swear I heard Noah tell her father she loved me. I haven't asked her about it. I'm scared she might think I'm crazy because we haven't known each other long. Or what if she says she never uttered those words?

And if she did say it, was it only to convince her father that the fake engagement is real?

"When you hugged me, I don't know, it surprised me. I hadn't hugged anyone like that since my mother died. So, I needed to get away from you, clear my head. I took a job. A sexual predator who was released from prison on some dumb technicality. The mother of the teenage girl he raped didn't have a lot of money to pay me, so I took the job pro bono."

"You're a good man, did you know that?"

I laugh. "I kill people for a living."

"We're good people who do bad things. But we're also killing the monsters who are pretending to be humans."

"And what does that make us?"

"We're angels disguised as monsters."

She looks up at me with a smile. I press a finger underneath her chin and tip her head up allowing me to press a kiss to her plump, dark red lips.

I want to ravish her in the back of this car. Kiss her until her lipstick is smeared and lips swollen. But she's pulling away before I can follow through with my plans.

"We're here," she whispers against my mouth.

The car slows to a stop and my door opens. A blond man in a suit and earpiece stands back, waiting for us to get out. He flashes his gun at me, a warning not to try anything.

"Fuck. I told Gio no soldiers," Noah murmurs to me.

"Like I said, too trusting, Vixen. That's a bad quality to have for a contract killer," I tease.

She punches me in the side, a little too hard, making me oomph as we approach the building where another huge man in a suit stands at the entrance. Noah takes my hand, interlocking our fingers as she stares him down.

"Let us by, Vershy," Noah commands.

"I have to pat him down."

"This is a peaceful dinner. Del's not going to be a problem. Trust me."

"I wouldn't trust you as far as I can throw you, and, well..."

He waves his hand up and down the length of Noah's body and it takes everything in me not to snatch it and twist his wrist until it breaks.

"All that tells me," Noah begins, "is that you're weak. I bet you've got a small cock too. You wouldn't be able to get it past my cheeks, huh, Vershy?"

A blond guard, who I think is Vershun's second in command and looks more like he should model for men's fitness magazines, barks a laugh at Noah's insult.

Vershun doesn't find it amusing and takes a step forward. I pull my gun and point the barrel at his forehead.

"Del, don't—"

Too late. I pulled the trigger. Vershun falls to the ground, blood pouring out of the bullet hole in the middle of his forehead. The rest of the security team surrounds us, guns drawn. If Noah hadn't been here, and moved in front of me as a shield, I'd be dead, lying next to Vershy.

Or maybe it's because GQ has his hand up, a silent command not to shoot.

That's... *interesting*.

"Dumbass," Noah mutters out of the corner of her mouth. She has her hands raised so I follow suit.

"He insulted you," I say. "And he lunged at you."

"I'm pretty sure I insulted him worse, and he didn't lunge. He took a step. One step, Laptop."

Oh, she's angry. She pulled out the old nickname.

"Let them in," a booming voice behind us says.

Noah lowers her hands and turns, grabbing my arm to twist me with her until we're facing her father.

"Babbo."

He doesn't look at his daughter. His eyes are on me. I expect anger to greet me. I expect him to raise his gun and fire, launching a bullet between my eyes or through my heart.

Instead, Gio Lenetti stares back at me with respect.

"I heard what Vershun said about my daughter. I commend you for defending her."

He waves his hand at the men surrounding us. They've lowered their guns but are still on edge. They just witnessed their colleague get shot point blank.

"Take the body down to the basement then call the cleaner," Gio says to his soldiers. He points at the blondie. "Matthew, you're now head of security. You come with me."

He doesn't wait for an answer before turning and walking off down the hallway, Matthew following with a scowl on his face.

Handsome and grumpy. Noah is going to love him.

I already hate him.

I check my pants to make sure I didn't piss myself.

"You lucky mother fucker," Noah says, amusement filling her voice.

Yeah. Maybe I do have a guardian angel.

Maybe it really was luck, and I should go buy a lottery ticket. Either way... dinner is going to be interesting.

Chapter 20

Noah

My father disappeared to his study, leaving me shocked that he let Del live. Vershun had been his head of security for the past thirty years.

I remember being a kid and Vershun would make snide remarks about my weight or snarl at me because I was too loud, too hyper, too much.

Did my father know the man was a fucking tool and had always been an asshole to me?

Still, I'm not going to ask him why he let Del live and give him any ideas.

I give Del a tour of the townhouse while we wait for the rest of our dinner guests. Sage texted me five minutes ago saying she's ten minutes away and the butterflies in my stomach start stirring.

She showed up at Del's apartment the day after the Christmas party and demanded an explanation. I'm guessing Elias gave her the address since he showed up uninvited a few days after her. Sage and I talked for hours. I told her everything about my mother's murder. About my father protecting me by changing my name and letting the world believe I was dead.

She said she understood. She wasn't mad that I kept it all a secret to protect her, only that I kept this badass part about myself from her.

And now, Elias, with his heart eyes for Sage, has dragged her deeper into our world.

It's not her fault she became best friends with the daughter of one of New York City's most notorious mob bosses. I should have pushed her away like I do everyone else. But the moment we met, we clicked. She matched my energy. When I was sad? She'd buy Ben & Jerry's and join me on the couch to watch movies that made us cry. When I was mad? She was furious, and she'd take me to one of those rage rooms where we paid money to break stuff.

Nothing seemed to shock her about my chaotic and unhinged personality... like when I go from laughing at the smallest thing to ready to murder someone. She was there for it... well, not the murder part. Though, now I wonder if she would have held down my marks while I stabbed them through the heart.

Sage makes me feel... accepted for who I am no matter what. There was no way I was letting her go.

But will she accept me after I tell her I'm a contract killer?

Will she hate me for being a monster?

Will she fear who I truly am?

"You're fidgeting."

Del's voice pulls me out of my thoughts.

"I want to tell Sage about Colpa Sicario."

"Are you worried how she'll react?"

"Yes. She's going to hate me or never want to see me again because I'm a killer."

I shift on my feet and twist my hair and nibble on my fingernail. Del tugs my hand away from my mouth and sticks my index finger in *his* mouth, down to the knuckle. He sucks and flicks his tongue over the pad. My breathing falters, and I squeeze my legs together.

He's distracting me from my thoughts with his talented tongue.

"She won't," he says after releasing my finger. "Sage is a smart girl. She'll understand."

His words ease my nerves. Not entirely, but at least I'm thinking about sneaking off to fuck Del instead of confessing my darkest secret to my best friend.

We continue walking through my father's brownstone, holding hands. I'm taking Del from room to room, telling him stories from my childhood or showing him photos hung up on the walls and the story behind each one.

We stop at my mother's small office—a room I haven't stepped foot in since her death.

"You don't want to go inside?" he asks.

I shake my head, tears burning the back of my throat.

"This room holds too many memories."

"Tell me a happy one."

Del smooths his palms over my shoulders, letting me know he's listening. He's shared so much about his life with me, and I've yet to open up to him.

"She'd sit in here for hours journaling or reading or creating new fun recipes. She'd let me help her in the kitchen, teaching me how to cook and bake. I even wanted to be a chef at one time. Of course, that was twenty years ago, and I forgot everything. Maybe that's why I'm so horrible at cooking and baking now."

I point to the oversized white cotton chair in the corner.

"I'd sit there and just watch her. She was so beautiful. She modeled in Italy before moving to the U.S."

The cushion of the chair sinks slightly from how much my mother and I used to sit in it. The fabric on the arms is worn down and stained, mostly from Mom spilling her wine or me dropping random foods on it: ice cream, candy, Cheetos powder.

"She'd read to me in that chair. Everything from fantasies about dragons and damsels in distress to travel books where we'd pick out our next adventure. Gio stayed busy, so we didn't see him a lot. That didn't matter. My mother and I had fun without him. We traveled a lot. With a security team, of course. My favorite trip was to Egypt, where we went inside the pyramids and rode a camel through the desert.

"This office was our little space. We felt powerful in this room. She'd tell me affirmations to live by, and I'd repeat them every day until I memorized them."

"Tell me one," Del says, placing a soft kiss on my shoulder.

"Everything I need is within me," I say, tears claiming my voice and streaming down my face. "I am beautiful, inside and out. I am radiant and bright."

"Yes, you are, my beautiful, radiant, *Rainbow* Bright."

I let out a combination laugh and sob at Del's favorite name for me. My mother always called me her brilliant star. A bright light in a sea of darkness. I never knew what she meant until now.

Was she miserable in this world? Where my father was dangerous and cruel? She married him in Italy, and they moved here together. They were young when Gio opened Lenetti's. He struggled for months until deciding to get into illegal business dealings to make ends meet. That's how it all got started. Maybe my mother never wanted to fall in love with a mobster.

I turn around to face Del, and he swipes a tear off my cheek.

"That was a great memory. She sounded like a wonderful mother."

"She was."

I don't share my memories of her often, keeping them locked deep down. I'd always been afraid to access my trauma.

But with Del... he makes me want to remember.

We move on, down the hallway and enter a music room where I begged my parents to buy me all kinds of instruments to learn how to play: piano, violin, and cello.

Instruments I lost interest in after my mother was killed.

It didn't matter what dream I had; she'd always encourage me to follow it. Even when I wanted to learn archery and accidentally shot the instructor in the ass cheek the first day. When I wanted to ride horses, but the teacher turned their nose down at me because of my weight. And when I wanted to become a pop star despite my horrible singing voice.

Del sits on the bench in front of the baby grand. He skims his fingers over the top of keys as if he's refamiliarizing himself with them.

When I sit next to him, he starts playing.

The song has a classical vibe with a fast and whimsical melody. It reminds me of books I've read that send me to forests full of fae kings and magical creatures. Del's fingers dance across the keys, his eyes closing as he becomes one with the music. He doesn't miss a beat, and I don't think another human has amazed me more than this mystery of a man.

The song doesn't last long and Del finishes with a dramatic slowdown as he gently presses the final two notes.

"Holy shit," I whisper. "What song was that? It was beautiful."

He smiles and looks down at his hands in his lap.

"'Great Fairy Fountain' from *The Legend of Zelda*. Elias and I used to play the game every day before he decided he was too cool to hang out with his annoying younger brother. Then when my mother died, I didn't have the heart to play it anymore. It reminded me of when she was alive, and she'd yell at us to come downstairs for dinner, but we were in the middle of a big battle, so we'd argue with her until she'd come in and turn off the game. We'd get so mad at her." His smile drops and his Adam's apple bobs as a painful memory resurfaces. "She's no longer here, and I wasted time being mad at her over a fucking video game."

I push the hair falling on his forehead back and run my fingers through the locks. He closes his eyes at my touch and clears his throat.

"She loved the piano. She taught lessons—taught me and Elias how to play too. Elias wasn't interested. I don't think he remembers how to play, but I do. Even after she died, I kept playing. That's when I learned the Zelda song.

I couldn't bear to play the game, but the song was like an ode to her."

He shrugs and looks away to wipe a tear off his cheek.

When he turns back to me, he's smiling.

"I want to eat you out on this piano."

I frown, and his smile drops. I palm his cheek.

"You know you can talk to me about anything, right? You can be vulnerable with me. This was a beautiful moment, a wonderful memory you shared with me. That's all it needed to be."

"So you're saying I ruined it?"

I laugh this time and bring him in for a hug.

"You didn't ruin anything."

He melts against my body, squeezing his strong arms around me. I inhale his citrus and woodsy scent.

"I'm never letting you go," he whispers against my neck.

"I'm not going anywhere."

Two voices arguing downstairs break up the moment we're having.

"Sage," I say at the same time Del says, "Elias."

When we get to the sitting room, Elias has Sage pinned to the wall and... they're making out?

What the hell?

Del clears his throat.

Sage tears herself from the kiss and slaps Elias, the sound ricocheting throughout the small room. She wipes her mouth and walks over to where I stand to hide behind me.

Elias has his back to us, his hand on his face where Sage hit him.

"Are you okay?" I ask.

"I'm fine," Elias answers.

"I was asking Sage."

His frustrated and somewhat embarrassed expression from Sage's slap turns murderous. He balls up his fists at his side.

"She's the one who slapped me," he growls.

"He kissed me without my permission," Sage counters.

"I haven't seen you in a week, and you didn't seem to mind when you moaned the moment I slipped my tongue inside your mouth."

"Okay," I say, breaking up whatever this is between my best friend and Del's brother. She told me they slept together again the night of the Christmas party but didn't go into details, despite how much I begged. She claims it was just a one-time thing.

Which is the same thing she said the first time they fucked.

I think she likes him but is terrified that he's the Don of the QBM.

"Excuse me," a woman says, appearing at the opened door to the sitting room. "Dinner is ready to be served."

"I thought you said there'd be no soldiers here," Elias says as we filter out of the room.

"There wasn't supposed to be, but did you really believe my father would agree to that?"

Never mind that I trusted his word. Though, now that I think about it, he never actually said there wouldn't be guards.

"No, which is why I brought three of my own men."

"Were they allowed in?"

"Nope, but they're on standby."

"Good. Just... behave yourself. My best friend is here, and I can't have you or Del pissing off my father, and a gunfight breaks out."

"I'll keep her safe."

"I'm sure you will."

Elias smiles, and it might be the first time I've seen something other than anger on his face.

The dining room is large and dark, the lights dim except for a bright crystal chandelier above the long table where my father hosts casual dinner parties.

We sit at one end. Me and Del on one side, Sage and Elias on the other with my father at the head. A server comes around to get our drink order then disappears.

"Who is this?" Babbo asks, pointing his chin at Sage.

"My best friend. I told you she was coming, remember?"

He's not a fan of bringing 'civilians' into our world. Which is why I made sure he knew Sage was cool. I basically named her my associate so Gio wouldn't see her as a threat.

He looks at her again and gives an approving nod. His brown eyes slide to Elias, and they narrow.

"Elias Carter. Never in my life did I think I'd be serving QBM swine in my own home."

Sage's hand disappears underneath the table and the fury that was building within Elias settles.

"You can thank your daughter for that, Lenetti."

My father takes a sip of his whiskey and turns his head to me. "Yes, what is my daughter up to?"

"Well," I begin, swallowing to wet my suddenly dry throat. "As you know, Lance and I are getting married."

Elias and Gio scoff at the same time.

"Oh, fuck off, the both of you," I say. "It's happening and when we're married, our organizations will be connected. We should take advantage of that. We need to work together."

"You betray the Empire to sleep with the enemy. Now you want me to do business with QBM rats?"

Elias tries to stand but Sage stops him. She saved his life without even knowing it.

The server returns with our drink orders and places them on the table in front of us before disappearing in an instant, likely sensing the tension in the air.

"Look, the Lords need to go. They're beginning to gain the attention of the FBI. It's a matter of time before Finn O'Connor is arrested on RICO charges. You know he'll sing once he's in custody to get a plea deal. Then the government will target us. Your FBI sources can't protect you forever. So, let's unite and take control now before that happens."

My father shakes his head but doesn't say anything.

Elias stares at the utensils on the table as if they're the most interesting thing in this room.

No one speaks, so I continue. "The Empire runs guns. QBM handles drugs. QBM also takes down sex trafficking rings. The Lords are the biggest offenders when it comes to exploiting sex workers. Lance has recently come into information that they're recruiting teenagers. Babbo, we could help the QBM shut it down. We merge our organizations and become powerful enough to dismantle the Lords."

"And who will be in charge?" Elias asks, now focused on a fork he's twirling in his hand.

"You still control Queens and Brooklyn. My father will cover Manhattan and the Bronx. And..." I take a deep breath. "Del and I will control Staten Island."

"Oh, we will?" Del whispers next to my ear.

Yeah, I didn't really run that by him. It just popped into my head. But it doesn't matter. This is a temporary plan until we can figure out who is responsible for the deaths of our mothers.

That revelation could change everything.

"Big decisions will be made by the four of us. Like a counsel," I add.

Del has been holding my hand through my entire speech. He squeezes it and smiles when I glance at him. He approves of this plan.

"You don't know anything about running a mafia," my father says after a few moments of silence.

"You're right," I say. "But you want me to learn the business. Here's my chance. Let me shadow you over the next few weeks or months. Show me what I need to know."

My father takes another sip of his whisky, then pets his clean-shaven face.

"We need a plan." I pause when three servers enter, carrying large bowls of salad and baskets of bread. They set them down on the table in front of us.

A woman dishes out my father's salad. No one else moves a muscle until I start scooping the leafy greens and veggies onto my plate.

"We work together—all of us—to form this plan to take down the Lords. *You,* me, and Elias. You know, teamwork? One big merged mafia? A mighty mafia?"

Elias sighs at the name.

Rude.

Sage tries getting a helping of salad for herself, but Elias insists on doing it for her. She wants to fight him so badly, but glances at my father and changes her mind. I didn't want to invite her into the Lion's den tonight but having her here means my father is less likely to murder Del or Elias.

I think.

Gio takes a bite of his salad and chews. And chews and chews and he's driving me insane with the silence.

"Fine."

"Really?"

"I agree to work together to destroy the Lords. We will *not* combine our organizations. That will never happen, mio angelo."

Well, that's a start. I never expected him to agree to combine the Empire with QBM. Still, I clap and bounce in my seat, celebrating my victory.

But my excitement dies the moment my father leans over and stabs his fork through Del's left hand, nailing it to the table.

"What the fuck, Giovanni?" I scream, standing up in shock. My chair topples to the floor.

Sage also stands and backs away from the table. Elias moves in front of her.

Del grunts and rips the fork out of his hand. Blood pours out of the top and bottom, soaking the white table-cloth red. I grab my napkin and start wrapping the wound.

"That's for killing my head of security," my father says. He sits back down, picks up a clean fork, and resumes eating his salad.

Chapter 21

Delancy

Like father, like daughter.

It's been a week since Gio Lenetti stabbed me with a fork, giving me a scar in the middle of my left palm to match the one Noah gave me on my right.

Jesus fucking Christ.

Literally.

I haven't seen much of Noah. She's been staying at her father's townhouse and riding with him to his office at the gun range in the Bronx. He also has an office in Harlem, yet he takes her to the one furthest away from me.

We haven't been able to lock down a day to discuss our plan to take control of the Lords because Gio is an asshole and won't commit, and Elias is in the middle of an operation to take down a sex trafficking ring on Long Island.

I've been accepting easy hit jobs to kill time and feed the monster that craves violence.

He hasn't been as hungry since meeting Noah, but with her being away, I want to kill every person who irritates me.

Not to mention that tomorrow is Christmas, and my trauma from twenty years ago is trying to consume me.

I pull up to the Brooklyn apartment that's now more a home instead of a safe house and park my motorcycle at the side of the building. After locking it up, I take the stairs to the second floor.

My body aches from the work I did tonight to clean up my kill. But the exhaustion biting at my heels fades the moment I hear soft music playing through the door.

Noah is home.

The scent of home-baked cookies hits my nose, "Santa Baby" plays over the radio, and Noah is dressed up in a vintage dress—red and green with a built-in corset. The colors match her newly dyed hair, styled in curls like a pinup girl from the 1940s.

My rainbow bright.

She looks fucking fantastic.

"Welcome home, fiancé," she says, flashing me her sexy smile.

Fiancé.

The word coming out of her mouth makes me groan. It would only sound better if she had said *husband*.

The moment we agreed to the fake engagement, I knew it would be anything but fake. Does she feel the same?

"You cooked?" I asked, impressed.

She removes a tray of cookies from the oven and sets it on top of the burners. She takes off the oven mitt and waves her finger to correct me.

"I baked. Well, not *really* baked. I just had to break off the pieces and put them on a tray. Easy, right?"

She picks one up and takes a bite. She immediately spits it out and frowns.

"I burned the bottom."

I laugh and hang up my jacket. When I walk into the kitchen, the burned cookies are in the trash, and Noah is plating Chinese food take out. She pours two glasses of wine.

"And what are we celebrating?"

I lean in and claim her lips. It's a soft kiss that she doesn't allow to go further.

"It's your birthday."

"You want to celebrate my birthday?" The voice that comes out of my mouth doesn't sound like mine. It was at least an octave higher.

Because this woman has left me speechless. She surprises me every day with her humanity. She's slowly dragging *my* humanity out of me.

"Of course, silly."

Noah turns me towards the bathroom and pushes my back.

"Go clean up and then we'll eat dinner. After, we'll have cake—"

"Did you bake the cake too?"

"God no."

"Oh, good."

"Don't make me take your birthday gift back!"

She got me a gift too?

I stumble away in pure shock. I haven't celebrated my birthday in twenty years. I haven't *wanted* to celebrate my birthday. But Noah has me excited.

I'm turning thirty-two and for the first time in twenty years, I'm going to be happy on the anniversary of the worst night of my life.

Noah ordered my favorite, Kung Pao chicken with a side of crab Rangoon. She got sesame chicken with rice for herself. We eat in silence, enjoying the meal while sipping on Pinot Blanc.

Once we're stuffed, she takes a single slice of chocolate cake out of the fridge, still in the plastic container from wherever she bought it from and sticks a lonely candle in it.

"I'm not going to sing to you because I'm a horrible singer—"

"Oh, I know. I've heard you through the walls at the old apartment."

She flips me off.

"Anyway, I know this day holds a lot of pain for you, but we're getting so close to finding closure. I can feel it. So, I thought this year could be different and we celebrate both your birthday and Christmas."

Last night, on the anniversary of *her* mother's murder, we honored Sasha Lenetti by visiting her grave at Bronx Cemetery. We brought books and sat at her headstone, reading for hours.

Noah confessed that she's only visited her mother's final resting place a handful of times. She said it was too difficult seeing her name etched into the headstone. It was too final. A reminder that she was never coming back.

Talk to her, I said.

She'd never done that. She never sat and talked to her mother like I do when I visit Imogen.

She said she felt silly but after a few sentences, I could see the weight of her grief lift off her shoulders. Noah told her mother everything. About me, about us investigating her death, about her plans for the Empire.

Before we left—Noah heading back to her father's townhouse and me to plan a kill—she thanked me and said she now plans to visit her mother's gravesite more often.

But tonight, apparently, is my turn to face my past.

She lights the cake's solo candle.

"Make a wish, Puppet."

I close my eyes and wish for a normal life with Noah—no QBM, no Empire, no goddamn mobs.

I want a two-story home, white picket fence and all. A corgi running around the front yard—I've always wanted a dog and corgis are so damn cute. Maybe we could get a black cat too because they're considered bad luck and evil, like me, but they're not and maybe in the future, I don't have to be evil either.

Kids? I don't need them unless Noah wants some, then I'd love to make a baby with her. Though I doubt she does. She has an IUD and has said several times how she's glad it's there since we never use protection.

I open my eyes and blow out the candle. Noah's dark red lips spread into that contagious smile of hers again.

She stabs the fork into the cake, breaking off a bite and holding it up to my mouth.

"Open wide for mommy," she says with a wink.

"Never say that again." I laugh and take the offered bite. Sweetness bursts in my mouth, and I groan. I'm not a cake fan—ice cream is my go-to dessert—but this is good chocolate cake.

"You should try this."

I use my fingers to grab a good chunk and smash it into Noah's mouth.

Barely any gets inside so I smear the rest down her chin and neck, stopping before it gets on her pretty dress.

Maybe she'll remove that dress for me.

"You did *not* just do that!" she giggles and licks around her mouth.

She takes a handful of the cake to do the same to me, but I stand out of her reach. That just eggs her on and she starts chasing me. *I'm* laughing as I dodge her grabby, cake-filled hand. I jump onto the couch, then the ottoman, the chair, and the coffee table before running into the bedroom and climbing onto the bed.

"Are you going to come up here and get me?" I taunt.

Noah hunts me, walking slowly around the edge of the bed.

"What do I get if I catch you?" she asks.

"My cock."

"Hmm. I don't know. I can have that at any time."

"True. Then why don't you tell me what you want, sweetheart."

She lunges for me, and I jump off the bed.

"Don't fucking call me sweetheart, asshole!"

She lands on top of the bed on her stomach, so I take advantage and crawl up there with her. I flip her onto her back and straddle her.

She smears the cake all down the front side of my shirt. I remove the soiled piece of clothing and toss it to the floor.

She still has leftover cake and frosting on her palms and rubs it over my abs.

I inhale sharply at how strange yet fantastic the food feels on my skin.

"Tell me what you want, *Vixen*. Skittles. Crayon. Rainbow Bright." I lean in and place a soft kiss on her lips. "Kevin."

She tries to buck me off, so I pin her arms to the mattress.

She's huffing and puffing at her attempt to break free, but I'm stronger than her. She eventually gives up.

"Tell me."

She bites her lower lip and smiles.

"I want to peg you."

"Oh yeah?"

She nods.

"You don't think I've had a cock up my ass before?"

"I know you have."

"You don't think I've let women peg me before?"

She moans.

"Does that turn you on, Vixen?"

"Yes."

"Here's the problem." She holds her breath, anticipating my next words. "I'm the one who caught you."

I release one of her pinned arms so I can slide my hand underneath her dress. She's wearing tights so I rip them to shreds. Her panties go next, allowing me to sink my fingers inside her wet pussy.

"Always so ready for me, Noah."

I pump in and out and flick her clit with my thumb. She arches off the bed and groans.

I remove my fingers and stick them in her mouth.

"Suck."

She greedily laps up her pleasure, then I kiss her, getting a mix of sweet cake and her cunt.

I grab her hair at the nape and bring her mouth to my torso. "Clean me off."

Her tongue swipes through the mess she made, licking up the frosting. My cock grows harder with every greedy stroke across my abs.

I release the tight hold on her hair, and she falls back onto the bed, allowing me to finish removing her underwear and tights. I use the now-torn material to tie her hands to the bed frame and place her panties over her eyes.

"I want to hear you, Noah. Tell me how much you love my cock."

I strip out of my sweats and take hold of my dick, then slide into her in one brutal thrust. She rewards me with a scream of pleasure piercing through the silence of the bedroom.

"That's right, Noah. This pussy is mine, and you will only come when I tell you. Do you understand?"

I pound into her, using the fabric of her dress as leverage. I want to tear it off her so I can see her tits bounce, but the outfit is too beautiful to destroy.

I'll just have to patiently peel her out of it. I pause inside her, to the hilt, to unbutton the front of the corset.

She gasps and squirms because she can't see what I'm doing.

She can only *feel* it.

Once the fifth button is undone, her breasts pop out and jiggle. I lean over and take one of her nipples in my mouth.

She bucks at the sensation and moans her sweet song as I flick my tongue and suck as hard as I can. I scrape my teeth over the hardened bud.

"Delancy," she pants. "Please."

I continue moving inside her, slow at first before picking up speed.

"You feel so good," I say, driving into her.

When I slap her breast, her cunt constricts around my cock.

"Can I come? Please, sir."

God, I love when Noah begs.

"Yes," I answer, slapping her other tit this time.

She explodes with an orgasm. I pause to let her come down from the high, then resume my thrusts.

"Give me another one, Noah."

I adorn her throat with the finest hand necklace and squeeze, confining her breaths as I piston into her tight pussy.

She tugs at the tights I've used to bind her hands and the material digs into her wrists. She winces at the pain, which only adds to her pleasure.

I can already feel her next release building.

Her face darkens red from the lack of air, and I let go when she snaps her fingers—since she can't tap on my arm to let me know she needs to breathe. The rush of air mixed with pleasure sends her over the edge again, and this time, I go with her.

In one final thrust, I douse her pussy walls.

I've never come so much and so hard in my life.

I lie on top of her, panting and sweaty.

She's freed her hands from the binds and runs her fingers through my hair.

"Time for your present." Noah says and pushes me away so she can sit up. "Let me clean up first."

She gives me one final kiss, then smacks my ass as she walks by me to the restroom.

While she's in there, I change into clean clothes, remove the cake-smeared sheets, and wipe down the kitchen. I manage to salvage a few more bites of cake for myself.

I'm pouring two glasses of wine when Noah emerges. She's dressed in a mouth-watering red and green silk pajama set. The shorts ride up her ass and show off her dimpled thighs.

"Don't look at me like that. We can't get distracted again!"

She reaches for the cabinet above the fridge and pulls out a wrapped box, not too large but big enough to make me raise an eyebrow. She holds it out to me.

"Don't tell me I shouldn't have because I wanted to, and I'll fight you if you argue with me."

I open my mouth to argue because I love fighting with her, but I can see how much this means to her. I take the box and we sit on the couch in the living room.

"Hurry up," she says with a smile. She's excited. Maybe more than me.

I tear into the rainbow and unicorn wrapping paper to reveal a brown box. It's taped all to hell, so I grab my pocketknife to cut through the packaging. Noah eagerly bounces on the cushion beside me. When I open the flaps to the box, I find two Nintendo Switches inside and two copies of the latest *Legends of Zelda* game.

Tears build behind my eyes, my throat aching as I hold in my elation.

"Noah," I whisper.

"We can play together. Will you teach me?" She places her palm on my arm, glancing up at me with a look that says I'm here for you and your past doesn't scare me. The trauma you experienced won't push me away.

At least, that's what I hope that look tells me. Tears blur my vision so I can't really see her face clearly anymore.

"I'd love to," I say, swallowing hard.

She kisses my cheek and stands.

"Teach me tomorrow, because now that we fucked, I want you to make love to me. Then we'll cuddle and fall asleep. And tomorrow we'll wake up and you'll make waffles—"

"I will, huh?"

"Yes, I'm a horrible cook. And we'll open presents—"

"You have more?"

"Then we'll go to my father's for dinner."

I groan.

"Elias will be there, and we can finally come up with a plan to take down the Lords."

And just like that, my happy birthday turns sour.

I really don't want to get shot or stabbed again, and every time Noah's father sees me, he puts a new hole in my body.

Chapter 22

Noah

The sweet smell of waffles wakes me up, and I follow my growling stomach into the kitchen where Del is making breakfast.

I come up behind him, wrap my arms around his waist, and kiss between his shoulder blades. He stiffens for a second, his killer instincts kicking in until he realizes it's just me.

My stomach twists in the best way at how domesticated this feels right now.

I'd never imagined myself wanting this type of life. A normal one where I wake up happy and in love with a man who spoils me with waffles and fantastic sex.

Love?

It's a strange word. One I've never experienced with someone. It's the only word that makes sense to describe the way I feel when I'm around Del.

He makes me feel safe. He makes me feel wanted. He makes me feel whole. I've spent my entire life wondering if I'd find someone who could handle my trauma. Who isn't scared away by my violent side. Who doesn't mind that I'm a kaleidoscope on the inside and out.

My rainbow bright.

Pet names used to piss me off. They always seemed so impersonal. Never clever or unique. Del managed to put meaning behind each one.

Except maybe sweetheart. I don't know why he likes calling me that one.

"Merry Christmas, Puppet," I say and release him. I ignore how rough my voice sounds. My throat is sore from how roughly Del fucked it last night.

My pussy also aches.

I'll gladly suffer these pleasurable pains night after night.

"Merry Christmas, sweetheart," Del says with a grin the moment he spots me. "Don't you look... well fucked."

I didn't care to fix my red and green hair standing up all over my head. I'm also covered in bite marks and hickeys, which I'll have to cover with makeup when we go to my father's.

I flip off Del for both pointing that out *and* for calling me sweetheart and take a seat at the table. He brings over a plate with my waffle and a mug of coffee—made with a shot of creamer and a packet of sugar, just how I like it.

We enjoy breakfast in silence because neither of us are fans of small talk in the morning. Not until we're both full of caffeine.

Once our food is gone and coffee drank, we grab each other's gifts from their hiding spots and head to the living room. I sit on the couch, tucking my leg underneath me.

"Mine first." I hand him a large manilla envelope.

He opens it and peeks inside.

"Noah," he whispers, taking out a stack of papers. He swallows, his Adam's apple bobbing.

"It's for your new piano," I say as he shuffles through the sheet music. He pauses and glances up at me, his eyes glazed with unshed tears.

"You got me a piano?"

"Not just any piano," I begin and open my phone to show him the pictures. "Your mother's."

He takes my phone and swipes through the photos.

"You told me your father sold it after your mother passed."

He nods. "Elias said Percy hated seeing it because it reminded him of her."

"I asked your brother if he knew who bought it and he didn't, but his underboss did. He was the one who took care of the sale for your father. So, I called the piano store it was sold to, and they got rid of it years ago, but the piano store owner is a hoarder and kept a record of every purchase made, including contact info. I called the number on the receipt and a woman answered. She said she'd bought the piano for her daughter who grew up and no longer plays it."

Del barely lets me finish before I'm in his arms and he's hugging me. We've come such a long way since the gun range. I think this is the first hug he's initiated.

"We pick it up tomorrow."

When he releases me, he picks up the wrapped box he set on the floor and hands it to me. There's a card on the top. When I open it, Christmas music starts playing. I giggle at the thought of Del perusing the card aisle for this.

Inside are two pieces of folded up paper. I close the card and set it aside... but the music doesn't stop playing.

"What the hell?"

Del covers his mouth with his palm, hiding his amusement.

"How do I get it to stop?"

Now Del is giggling like a child up to no good.

"Delancy William Carter! Did you buy me a prank card?"

That did it. He loses control and falls back onto the couch with laughter.

I stand up and stomp to the window, opening it to toss the card outside.

"Hey!" Del protests. "Rude!"

I ignore him—even though my face hurts from smiling at his stupid prank—and pick up the first folded paper.

"What is this?" I ask, confused because all it has is a poorly drawn plane, two stick figures, that I believe are me and Del, holding suitcases. "Did you draw this?"

He nods and smiles ear to ear.

"What does it mean, though?"

"A vacation. You and me. Whenever and wherever you want to go."

"Really?"

"You travel a lot, right?"

"Yeah, how did you know?"

"The photos inside your apartment. You had a lot in front of international landmarks. Were you traveling for pleasure or Colpa Sicario business?"

"Both. Some hit jobs needed me to travel. My favorite one was in a small town just outside of Florence, Italy. My target was a woman who was stealing money from organizations that help people in need. She had a laundry list of shitty things she'd done. After killing her, I had time before my flight back to the states to play tourist. I took so many photos. I'm sad I don't have them anymore. They were all in the apartment that blew up."

I never got a chance to go back and try to salvage my belongings following the explosion. Del got some of my things, but me going myself was too risky. We worried about the person who was trying to kill me scoping out the place to see if I'd return so they could finish the job.

We still haven't figured out who wants me dead. But whoever it is hasn't tried again. I don't know if that's good or bad.

"Now this one," Del says and hands me the other folded up paper.

This one is also hand drawn by Del. It's him and me in the kitchen, wearing chef's hats and aprons.

"Is this you making me a meal?"

He shakes his head. "This is you and me cooking together."

Then it sinks in. He wants to teach me how to cook like my mother once did. He remembered I'd told him that.

"You said how much you love baking and cooking. I'm decent at it. I thought I could show you a few things."

I place my palm on his cheek, and he turns his head to kiss it.

"I love it."

"Good, no refunds allowed."

I pick up the box next, shaking it. The heavy contents inside rattle against the sides.

"So what's in this?"

"Open it and find out."

I tear into the paper and rip off the tape. Inside is a single photo placed on top of red and green tissue paper.

"Puppet," I whisper. It's a picture of me at the leaning tower of Pisa doing the iconic pose trying to hold it up. "Where did you get this?"

"I stole it from your apartment."

I slap him playfully. "I knew something was off with my bookcase!"

He laughs, and I cherish the sound. He's laughed more today than any of our previous times together.

"Keep going. There's more."

I remove the tissue paper and find one of my romance books and my bullet vibrator.

"Seriously?"

He shrugs. "I thought about taking all your toys. I know how reliant on them you were after bringing home your one-night stands."

Yeah, because of you, I add silently. He was the reason I couldn't get off because all I wanted to do was fuck him.

"Keep going."

"There's more?"

He nods, and I remove the last piece of tissue paper. Underneath are more photos.

My photos.

The rest from my bookcase and the small photo albums I kept in a laundry basket.

I'm crying as I pick up a framed photo of me and my mother on my eleventh birthday. The last birthday I spent with her.

"How?" I ask, my voice full of tears.

"I salvaged whatever I could. The photos were likely saved because they were on the ground underneath a metal door or other debris. Some of the edges might be burnt though."

He pushes aside some of the photos and reveals a black box.

I gasp. "My mom's necklace?"

It's a simple gold cross. I'm not religious, but I kept the necklace after she died. I wanted to have something she always wore close to her heart. I thought I'd never see this again.

"Oh, Delancy," I sob and now it's my turn to hug him.

But this time, the hug turns into kisses, which turns into both of us naked and we're making love—and using my bullet vibrator—on the living room floor.

There's no way I wasn't going to thoroughly thank him for the best gift I've ever received.

D el is nervous, and it's adorable. A little sexy too.

He's also sweating, and he keeps rubbing his palms on his jeans.

"He's not going to hurt you this time," I say and place my hand over his knuckles.

"Two times, Vixen."

"It's Christmas. My father won't be violent on a holy day."

At least, I hope not.

My father is extremely religious. I believe he still goes to church every Sunday. Sometimes he'll attend mass other days of the week.

I just find it strange to be a criminal who murders one day, then asks for penance the next. I don't think it works like that, Babbo. At least not with serious crimes like murder.

We pull up to the Lower East Side townhouse, and I get out first. My father's new head of security nods as Del and I walk up the steps. He's the guard whose name I couldn't remember the night of the Christmas party.

Matthew Dalton is younger than Vershy. Probably thirty-five or forty. He's one of my father's top soldiers and he was Vershun's right-hand man, so it makes sense that he'd get the role.

"Miss Lenetti," he says, and I cringe.

"Please, call me Noah."

I suppose I'm going to have to get used to that name now that I outed myself at my father's Christmas party.

Matthew smiles and looks me up and down with his dark blue eyes. He seems to like what he sees even though I'm wearing a Santa hat, leggings, and an ugly sweater that says 'Jingle My Bells' with Santa bent over showing off his 'balls.'

Del tightens his hold on my hand and makes a noise that might have been a growl. Awe... my jealous puppet. Matthew's eyes move to him and scan over his body the same way he did mine.

Matthew just let me know he's into both of us, which gives me an idea.

Instead of me pegging Del, would he let me watch while Matt topped him?

Nah. I still want to peg Del.

"What," Del begins, "no pat down?"

Matthew quirks a perfect brow. "If that's what you're into, I'll pat down whatever you'd like."

Del chokes on his words, and I tug on his arm to walk us inside.

"Rain check, Matty."

"What the fuck was that about?" Del asks as we head down the hallway.

"I think he likes you."

"No, he was checking *you* out."

"Maybe he's into both of us?"

Before Del can respond to that, we've arrived in the sitting room. Elias is already here, sipping on a glass of whiskey.

"Finally," he sighs and peers around us. "Where's Sage?"

I walk straight to the booze cart and make myself a vodka soda because I'm already stressed about dinner.

"It's Christmas, Elly," I say. "She's with her family."

"She's not coming?" His blue eyes widen as big as a puppy dog's. The poor lovesick man.

"She told *us* she wasn't coming. She didn't tell you?" Del asks, preparing to taunt his brother. "Wait, are you not in the group chat? Weird."

Elias tosses his empty glass at Del's head and hits him just underneath his eye. I can't help the laugh that bubbles out of me.

"You fucking dick!" Del grabs a metal fire poker next to the fireplace and juts it at his brother like he's a sword fighter.

The tip nicks Elias in the arm and he stands, managing to pry the poker out of Del's grip. Then hits him over the head with it.

Great, now Del's bleeding, and he's going to have a nasty bruise under his eye from the whiskey glass.

I sit my ass on a chair out of the way, sipping on my booze while watching the immature children fight.

Elias is twice Del's size, so I'd put my money on him. He currently has his little brother in a headlock while Del punches his jiggly gut. Elias is unfazed and tightens his arm around Del's neck. My puppet's face turns deep red and just before I think he's going to pass out, he claws at Elias's arms, drawing blood.

Elias lets go and Del bends over, hands on his knees to catch his breath. Elias takes advantage and kicks him, sending Del to the floor.

I clap at the move, and Del gives me a scowl for cheering on his brother.

"You're not going to win, Lance. It's like when we were kids. I'm bigger and stronger than you. And I don't lose."

Del charges at his brother like a bull seeing red and bends over just before crashing into Elias's midsection. The two go flying into a table with a stack of books and magazines on top. The wood crumbles underneath their combined weight.

Elias quickly jumps on top of Del and starts punching, but Del isn't giving up. He grabs a splintered piece of wood and smacks Elias over the side of his head. The big man falls to the ground onto his back and the two lie there, huffing and puffing, out of breath.

Del manages to punch his brother one more time before one of my father's staff appears at the entrance to the room.

"Um..." she begins, her eyes wide. "Dinner is served."

"Thank you, Natalia. Can you have someone..." I wave my finger at the mess.

"Of course," she says and turns on her heel.

I walk over to the two men lying on top of all the debris caused by their fight and cross my arms.

"Dumbasses."

"He started it," Del says.

"And I ended it," Elias adds.

"You both lost," I say and hold out my hand to Del. "Dinner's ready. Help your brother, then you two go clean up."

"You could have stopped us, you know," Del growls.

I shrug. "True. But watching you two fight was fun... and sexy."

I turn and walk away, hearing a grunt behind me. I don't know which one it was from, but someone sure got in the last punch.

Chapter 23

Delancy

Fucking Elias.

I won that fight, and he knows it.

Tussling with my older brother was oddly nostalgic. When we were kids, we'd have wrestling matches like the WWE wrestlers on TV. Elias would also teach me karate or other martial arts moves that he learned by watching movies.

He had no clue what he was talking about, but it was the most fun I'd ever had as a kid.

He used to be the best big brother.

Until my father demanded he grow up when he turned thirteen, and Elias no longer wanted to hang out with me.

I can't imagine how beat up we both look. Noah's father narrows his eyes at us when we walk into the dining room, one after the other, tails between our legs.

He immediately sees our disheveled appearances, cuts, and bruises and shakes his head like a disappointed father.

"Where is the other one?" he asks, returning his attention to the paperwork set out before him.

"At her family's place in…" Noah begins but pauses and looks over at Elias. "She's at her parents' house."

Gio nods and signs one of the white sheets, then hands it to a man standing off to the side.

"Are you seriously working on Christmas?" Noah frowns.

"I am always working. I get no vacations. No sick days. Have you learned nothing, little girl? You've been shadowing me all week. You need to know this when you take over for the Lords."

"Speaking of," Noah says, ignoring his scolding, "we need to talk about a plan."

"We will do nothing until after the new year," Lenetti immediately interjects.

"Fine, but we can still talk about it," Noah counters.

He grunts but doesn't respond and before Noah can continue, the food starts rolling out.

Baked salmon and Italian dishes like tacchino ripieno, antipasta, salad, charcuterie, and traditional American foods like ham, green bean casserole, mashed potatoes and gravy, macaroni and cheese, and deviled eggs.

Once everything is on the table, Noah says, "So, I was thinking–"

"No." Gio's booming voice scares Noah enough that she jumps in her seat. My hand falls to her thigh, and I squeeze. My touch barely soothes her. "We eat, then we talk."

Noah shrinks into herself, and I want to murder him right now for making her feel this way. He's lived his life getting his way, but he agreed to work together to bring down the Lords. He needs to learn to listen to others.

Noah must sense my anger and shakes her head subtly. She doesn't want me to argue with him. Not today.

We eat in peace; only me, Noah, and Elias making conversation. Once dessert is served and Gio finishes eating two pieces of pie—pumpkin and pecan—Noah opens her mouth to speak.

"I was thinking I could lead a meeting with Finn—"

"Absolutely not," Gio growls and slams his fists on the table, causing dishes and silverware to clatter. "You will not be going anywhere near the Lords. Do you understand me? You let these two men handle taking them down. After every one of those assholes is dead and there is no more danger, then you can claim leadership over Staten Island."

"I'm an adult, Giovanni. I can protect myself. I know how to shoot a gun."

Barely, I silently add. Which reminds me, she needs to do more sessions at the gun range.

"If I'm going to lead, I need to show my face. Let people know who they're dealing with. And we're not going in there with guns blazing. We don't want a bloodbath because that will only gain the FBI's attention. Which is why we need a plan. We should set up a meeting. If I can't lead it, then *you* should, Babbo. Finn might not even agree to meet with me or Lance. Maybe Elias, since he's the QBM boss, but it should be you."

A man who I believe is Gio's consigliere enters the room. He walks to Gio's side and leans down to whisper something in his ear. Lenetti glances at Noah, then me and Elias.

"I'll take care of it," Gio responds then stands. "I'm sorry mio angelo. I have to go."

"Dad," Noah sighs, and he scowls at her. It's the first time I've heard her call him dad instead of Babbo. He must hate it.

"Is this Empire business?" I ask as Gio turns to leave. "If so, shouldn't Noah be shadowing you?"

"Careful, young man," he warns.

"Careful?" Elias scoffs. "She's going to take over for you someday. She should know what's taking you away right now."

"Someday. But not today."

I stand, refusing to back down and walk around Noah's chair. She tries to grab my arm to stop me, but I yank it out of her reach.

"Let her join you," I say, chin raised.

Matthew, who'd been standing against a wall with his arms crossed over his chest on guard, steps closer. Gio lifts a hand to stop him.

The blond man clamps his jaw shut, the muscles rippling.

So much for that rain check. We just became his enemy.

"Where I'm going now doesn't concern you or her or your lowlife brother."

Before I can take a swing at him for calling my brother a lowlife—I mean, he is, but only I get to call him that—Noah steps in front of me. Elias stands, but he at least has enough sense to stay back, unlike me.

Gio points at me over Noah's shoulder. "You're lucky my little girl loves you, because you would be dead right now for speaking to me like that."

When he reaches the dining room door, he pauses and focuses on Noah.

"You want to learn this business?"

She nods.

"Stay. Alive. Never take meetings unless they're on your territory, and you're surrounded by guards. Finn O'Connor does not deserve the courtesy of a meeting."

"Then tell us what to do, Babbo."

"You will do nothing. You send others to die because the only way to successfully bring down a crime syndicate is to go in with 'guns blazing.'"

And with that, he leaves.

I'm breathing hard, adrenaline rushing through my body. It's making me lightheaded, and I might just pass out from hyperventilating. Noah takes my hand and leads me out of the room, beckoning Elias to join. We return to a freshly cleaned sitting room and Noah sits me down on the couch. Elias sits on the love seat across from me.

"He's hiding something," I seethe.

"Probably," Noah sighs. "But attacking him and getting yourself killed won't help us figure it out."

"He told you to send us in guns blazing. Sounds like a setup to me," Elias says.

"I agree, but I refuse to do a hostile takeover. We'll come up with a plan ourselves. Then I can present it to my father and let him know we're doing it with or without him."

"We shouldn't tell him anything," I nearly bark.

Noah scowls at my tone, and I immediately offer her an apologetic look.

"Or we tell him a fake plan and see if he turns on us," Noah concludes.

"You have an idea?" Elias asks, sipping on a glass of whiskey that he brought from dinner.

"Maybe."

"Is it a good one?" I ask.

"I guess we'll find out."

It's been two weeks since the Christmas day dinner.

Noah and I rang in the new year on the couch, cuddled up with champagne, chocolate-covered strawberries, weed, and the ball drop on television.

We kissed at midnight, got high, made love, then fell asleep shortly after.

The best new year's celebration of my life.

Elias disappeared after we formed our plan and said he'd be back in time to implement it. I have a feeling he left to go find Sage, the poor girl. When my brother has his mind set on something... or someone... he won't back down until he gets what he wants.

Noah told me a little bit about Sage's past and her ex-husband and how he damaged her. It's all she said since it's not her story to tell, but I made sure Elias knew. He's coming on too strong and if he scares her, or worse, hurts her, Noah will not hesitate to kill him.

And I won't stop her.

I asked Noah what she plans to tell her father, and she said she'd figure it out. I've learned over the past few months with Noah that she's not a big planner. She's spontaneous and loves surprises while at the same time hates surprises. She craves adventure and adrenaline and the idea of meeting with the Lords' Don has her squirming with excitement. I took advantage of that excitement a few times, fucking her until that adrenaline melted into lust.

Word spread fast about mine and Noah's engagement. Speculation that it was a move to gain power blossomed to do exactly what we had intended: put the Lords on edge.

"I was thinking about the trip you got me for Christmas. We'll be pretty busy this first half of the year, so why don't we plan something for the weekend of my birthday? Make it a celebration," Noah says as we sort through paperwork in her father's office at the Bronx gun range.

"And where do you want to go?"

"Scotland. I've never been. I want to find the Loch Ness monster... and chase waterfalls." She starts singing the TLC song, off key, but it still makes me smile.

Because Noah is perfect in every way... except when it comes to singing. And cooking.

"When is your birthday, anyway?"

"Puppet!" Noah gasps. "You don't know? I thought you did a background check on me."

She smiles despite her offended tone.

"Well, that fake ass file said September 29th, so I'm not sure if I believe it."

She laughs and places the stack of papers she's holding inside a folder and files it in a drawer.

"September 29th is my real birthday."

"What else in your background check is real?" I ask, walking to where she's still shuffling through all the files in her father's cabinet. Since we're at the gun range, I made Noah practice her aim for an hour before coming into his office to snoop around.

Noah's back is to me. I wrap my arms around her, bringing her flush with my front and grind my cock into her ass. It awakens, growing harder as her jasmine and citrus scent overtakes me.

"Most of it... especially the places I worked, which were all fronts for Colpa Sicario. My education, my finances—well, the legal transactions," Noah says, her voice breathy. "All real."

I kiss along her neck, and she hums at the feeling of my lips on her skin. She shuts the drawer and turns around in my arms.

"You really want to do this here?"

I take her plentiful ass in my hands and squeeze. "Yes," I say and crush my mouth against hers.

I swing her around and sit her on the desk.

"Even when my father could walk in at any moment?" she asks as I slowly unbutton her jeans.

"You said he's at the Harlem office tonight."

"Yes, but—oh."

Her words are cut off the moment I slide my fingers behind her panties and inside her wet cunt.

"What was that, Vixen?"

"Nothing, keep going."

"You're such a little slut, aren't you? Begging for me to fuck you when anyone could walk in and catch us."

"Yes, Delancy. I'm your slut. Fuck me on this desk."

I pump my fingers in and out of her pussy, and she bites her lips to suppress a moan.

"Oh, no you don't," I say, tugging her lip from her teeth. "You want to put on a show? Do it. Don't hold back. Your pleasure is *mine*. I want to hear all your noises. Let everyone hear how good my fingers feel inside you. Scream for me."

My thumb brushes against her clit and she bucks, almost falling off the edge of the desk.

There's my moan.

I adorn her neck with a hand collar and tighten my hold, making her whimper at the pressure.

My fingers thrust into her faster.

I bring her to the brink of orgasm, then stop, removing my fingers and releasing my grip on her neck. She whines at the loss.

"I'm going to eat you out now," I say and lay her back on the desk. Papers fall to the floor and her head hangs over the edge.

"Play with your nipples while I taste the rainbow."

"Ew. Don't ever say that again."

I snicker as I peel her jeans the rest of the way down her thick hips and thighs.

I'm impatient, so I rip her panties off, shredding the fabric. She finds a stapler to throw at my head, which I dodge.

"Unnecessary!"

I chuckle again and sit down in her father's oversized chair, then roll close enough to the desk so I can bury my face in Noah's pussy. Wrapping my arms around her thighs, I spread them apart so I can flatten my tongue and drag it over her opening.

"Yes, Del," she groans.

I take her clit into my mouth and suck, then thrust my tongue inside her. Noah's hands find my hair, and she tugs on the strands to bring my face closer.

My tongue pumps in and out of her until she's panting and squeezing my head between her legs. I'm about to add my fingers when the door bursts open. For a second, I fear it's her father, and I'm about to die. Instead, it's his head of security.

"Oh," Matthew says and turns to walk out. He pauses, glancing over his shoulder at us.

"Hey Matty," Noah says with a sweet smile.

He grinds his teeth, breathing heavily. I'm not sure if he's pissed, embarrassed, or turned on. Yet, he doesn't leave. He stands there, the door still open, and his hand on the knob as he watches me finger Noah. He sees how I make her squirm on top of the desk.

"Are you going to watch or join?" Noah asks, and I gently bite down on her clit, making her scream.

"So jealous, Puppet," she purrs. "Let him join us. I want him to fuck my mouth."

My possessiveness over Noah rears its ugly head but the moment Noah's cunt constricts around my fingers, I know how much she's turned on by this idea.

"Are you going to run off and rat us out, Matthew?"

Matt scowls at me, his face transforming from indecision to frustration. Or maybe it's anger. I don't care.

"He wouldn't do that, now would he?" Noah says, her voice straining from the pleasure I'm giving her. "Besides, we're engaged. We can fuck all we want."

But maybe not on her father's desk, I silently add.

Matt runs his hands through his dirty blond hair. His cheeks flare red, but I notice his cock pressing against his jeans.

He's enjoying this.

"Join," he finally says and shuts the door. He leans against the wood, hands in front of his groin. Is he hiding how turned on he is? I should punish him for that.

"Are you waiting for orders?" I tease. "I know you're Lenetti's little bitch, but you can be mine too."

I love the way my words make Matt's nostrils flare. He hates me, that much I can tell.

He walks to the desk where Noah's head hangs off the edge and reaches out a hand, ready to grab her by the hair.

"No touching her unless I say so," I growl. He jerks his hand back and nods. So obedient. "That's a good little bitch. Now, take off Noah's shirt."

She groans at my commands, and Matt eagerly strips off her top. His eyes widen as her large tits fall out. Of course, she's not wearing a bra.

"Play with her nipples," I demand, and he covers her breasts with his large hands.

He kneads them before taking her nipples between his fingers, pinching them hard enough that Noah arches her back off the desk.

She reaches for Matt's belt buckle, and I slap her pussy, making her yelp. "I didn't say you could suck his dick yet."

"Please, Del, I need him in my mouth," she whines. Matt sucks in a sharp breath and stiffens.

It's clear he's never been in a threesome. Or maybe he has but not with another man, or at least one who's dominant like me.

"Take your cock out, blondie, and rub the tip over Noah's lips."

While he gets to work unzipping his jeans, I pull down my sweatpants and run the tip of *my* cock up and down Noah's pussy. I glance up at Matt and see him following my order, spreading his pre-cum over my girl's swollen lips.

"Open up for him, sweetheart." She does, likely about to bitch me out for calling her sweetheart. The moment her lips part, Matt pushes his cock inside.

"Take him as deep as you can," I say and smirk. I want him to fuck her throat hard enough to make her gag and cry.

I thrust into Noah's wet pussy at the same time Matt slides his length all the way in. He's gentle at first, then Noah clutches his hips, digging her nails into his skin. That urges him to fuck her mouth harder. She gags around him, spit starting to drip around his length and onto the floor.

Okay, that's fucking hot. I set my jealousy aside and ream into my rainbow bright's tight pussy, massaging her clit with my thumb. Her walls clamp around me, and I moan at how amazing this feels.

"Fuck," Matt grounds out. "I'm not going to last long."

Noah hollows her cheeks as she sucks Matt's cock like the pretty little slut she is. The way her head is angled allows him to go deep and his balls slap violently against her nose.

"Smack her tits and pinch her nipples. She loves that," I say, and Matt abides as he pounds into her face.

I match his movements, not holding back, and between the both of us, Noah's orgasm breaks through. Her body tenses as pleasure washes over her. Matt groans and stills as he pours his cum down her throat.

Watching her swallow it down like the good girl she is has me coming too. I grunt as I splatter her walls until there's nothing left.

Matt removes his cock from Noah's mouth and sits down in a chair behind him, melting in satisfaction.

I pull out of Noah and walk around to the front of the desk where her head still hangs over the edge.

"Open. Lick it clean. I never want you to forget how fucking amazing you taste."

Noah greedily laps up her release coating my cock, sucking hard enough to make it twitch, ready for round two. Before that can happen, I tuck myself back into my sweats. Then I grab my knife from the desk.

I stab Matt in the thigh.

He screams bloody murder and clamps his hands around his leg. "What the fuck, you asshole?"

Noah shoves me from behind and I stumble, catching myself before my head rams into the door.

"What the hell is wrong with you?"

I stand up straight and shrug. "I told you, you're mine. I don't like people touching what's mine."

The next thing I remember is Noah's fist coming towards my nose and the room fading into darkness.

Yep. She punched me.

Chapter 24

Noah

"Dumbass," I mumble when Del falls to the ground, unconscious.

I turn back to Matt and squat to get a better look at the damage from Del's idiocy.

"Well, the good news is he missed your femoral artery." Barely, I add silently. "Let me call someone to stitch you up."

Matt nods, his tan face pale because he's losing a good amount of blood. He's also sweating, either left over from the threesome or from the shock of being stabbed.

I collect my clothes thrown everywhere—a chair, the ground, on my father's desk—and get dressed.

"I'm really sorry about Del," I say slipping on my jeans sans panties because that asshole tore them. "He has issues."

Matt waves a hand, looking away to give me privacy—despite having his cock in my mouth minutes ago.

"It's fine. It was kind of hot."

Okay, Matt's a psychopath like us.

Because it *was* super-hot.

I'm still mad he did it, though.

"I can tie him to this other chair and let you stab his thigh if you want?"

Matt laughs. "No... well... maybe. Rain check?"

He winks at me, and I grab my phone to call the doctor on my father's payroll.

"He said he'll be here within five minutes," I tell Matt.

"Thanks for punching him. That was also sexy as fuck."

I shake my head. "You're our level of crazy."

"Yeah, I guess." He laughs. "Um, but no offense... I don't think I want to do this again."

He runs his right hand over his face, and I notice he's missing a pinky.

"What happened?" I point at the missing appendage.

His face immediately falls into cold, hard nothingness and he looks away.

"I was punished."

"What? By whom?"

He laughs, bitter and unamused.

"Who do you think?" I open my mouth, at a loss for words at his sudden change of attitude.

"You really know nothing about how your father runs things, do you?"

"I don't. I'm sorry." There's an uncomfortable silence between us. "So my father did this."

He clenches his teeth, causing the muscles in his sharp jaw to ripple.

"It could have been worse. I could be dead."

"Matthew—"

Before I can offer him any assurance that things are about to change, the doctor arrives. Dr. Hager, an older German man with stark white hair, stitches up Matt, then he takes a look at the dumbass still passed out on the floor. The doc waves smelling salts in front of his nose to wake him up and checks for signs of a concussion. He gives Del the all clear before leaving.

"Oh," I begin and help Del stand. "I forgot to ask what you needed."

Matt tilts his head.

"You barged in here and caught us fooling around. Did you have a reason? Did you need something?"

"Right," he stands and hobbles to the door to make his exit. "Your father wanted me to assist you with your plan to take down the Lords."

Of course, he does. My father refuses to help, so I'm not even surprised he sent Matthew in his place. He wants to make sure I won't be putting myself in danger.

I'm not about to trust my father's new head of security. He's too... friendly. Too eager to help us out—and fuck us, apparently. Anyone who's loyal to my father sees everyone else as the enemy. But Matt might be different. What he just told me about being punished, the hatred in his voice and disgust on his face... he might truly be on our side.

I want to ask Matt what he did to garner such a harsh punishment, but my attention turns to Del when he grunts. He wipes his nose, which is still bleeding, and dark circles are starting to form underneath his eyes. I grin at the aftermath of my right hook.

"Proud of yourself?" he asks.

"You deserved it." I turn back to Matt. "We're meeting Friday morning, nine a.m. Whitehall Terminal. We'll take the ferry to Staten Island and have a driver meet us to take us to the Lords Mansion. Don't be late."

"You got it, boss."

I raise a brow at Matt, and he blushes. I really like the sound of a man calling me boss. I wonder if I can convince Del for another threesome with Matt if he promises not to hurt him again.

I turn to my puppet who glares at Matt's back as he leaves the room.

Okay, maybe not.

"Let's go, Stabby."

Del follows behind, head down, tail between his legs.

"Where the fuck have you been?" Del asks when his brother finds us at Whitehall Terminal.

"None of your fucking business, Lance-a-lot."

"I will fucking kill you," he warns.

I know Del despises the nickname. Well, he'd told me how Elias used to call him that all the time when they were kids and how he loved it, making him feel like a knight in shining armor. Then, after Del was forced to kill his mother, Elias refused to use the nickname again. As if he was punishing Del.

"Boys, let's behave. We can't walk into this meeting with tempers flaring, okay?"

I punch Elias in the arm. "Ow! What the hell was that for?"

"You went to Sage's parents' house uninvited."

"*That's* where you've been?" Del asks.

"What the fuck is this asshole doing here?" Elias avoids his brother's question and stares Matthew down, as if that will scare my father's head of security away.

"Gio sent him to help."

"More like sent him to spy," Elias scoffs. "And what's wrong with him?"

He points at Matthew's leg, noticing him limping slightly as we walk with the crowd to board the ferry.

"I stabbed him," Del answers.

"It was a threesome, Puppet. We invited him to join. You're just a jealous asshole," I sigh and turn to Matt. "I'm still so sorry."

He smiles at me but narrows his eyes at Del.

Matt is definitely not as harsh as Vershun was. Vershy wouldn't have hesitated to kill Del for what he did. Of course, we never would have invited Vershun to join us for a threesome. Vershun was closer to my father's age while Matthew is a few years older than us and looks like he could be a Hemsworth brother.

We find our seats outside along the side of the ferry away from other passengers. Thankfully, it's not too crowded, and we can have some privacy.

"Okay," I begin, "let's go over the game plan."

"We've been over it a million times," Elias whines.

"Boo hoo you big baby. We're going over it again," Del says, picking a fight with his brother. I give his leg a squeeze in warning.

These men, I swear.

"I reached out to Finn O'Connor for a meeting, telling him I have information on who may have killed Cillian. He's still under the impression that it was a home invasion gone wrong. At least, we think that's what he believes. We have connections across the four other boroughs that he doesn't, so he was quick to accept this meeting."

After Cillian's body was found, Finn went on the news vowing to find his killer. He put on a show, the grieving

Staten Island business owner who has already lost too many of his loved ones. We expected him to blame the other mobs but surprisingly, Finn went along with the cops' motive.

We know better though. He's up to something.

"Then, once inside, we threaten to turn him over to the FBI on racketeering charges. He has the choice to either hand over control of the Lords and work with us as a united crime syndicate or get locked up for the rest of his life."

"This is not going to end well," Del says. "He'll never believe Gio agreed to become one merged mafia."

"A mighty mafia," I add.

"He's going to fight back," Elias adds, ignoring my mighty mafia comment. It's a fun name and they know it.

"Look..." I sigh and rub my temples. I can feel a headache coming on. "It's time for this rivalry between the three organizations to end. We already have an advantage over the Lords. The underworld believes The Empire and the QBM will unite once Del and I are married, which has the Lords on edge. So, we go in and offer him a deal or threaten to turn him in to the FBI. He knows we have connections there. He knows Gio is desperate enough for power to do something this unprecedented. And if he refuses and opens fire, then we fight back and kill him."

I shrug as if we're not about to walk into the viper's nest. If I'm honest, I'm terrified.

"Your father was under the impression you were going to stay out in the car with me," Matt says, frowning.

"Yeah, about that. Change of plans. I'm not staying in the car."

Matt takes out his phone—certainly about to call my father—and Del snatches it from his hands and tosses it overboard into the New York Harbor. Matt takes a second phone out of his other pocket, holding it away from Del this time, only for it to be seized by Elias.

Matt stands, ready to throw punches.

"Sit down and shut the fuck up," Del orders, and I squeeze my legs together at the demanding tone. "Unless you want to be tossed over the side next?"

Matt clenches his jaw, and he scans the area, seeing passengers about thirty feet away. A few eyes turned our way at Del's outburst. Matt shakes his head and slowly sinks back down to the metal bench seat, deciding not to make a scene.

The plan I told my father involved me staying in the car with Matt while Del and Elias barged in with a team of Empire and QBM cronies to shoot up the mansion and kill Finn. Instead, we're doing it my way by blackmailing him into turning over control.

I'm also hoping we can ask Finn about the Christmas Eve murders during this meeting. He might have evidence to help us with our investigation.

After a thirty-minute ride, the ferry docks at St. George Terminal on Staten Island.

I lead the men out of the station and find our driver. He's one of a few dozen QBM and Empire soldiers who have already arrived on the island to prepare for this meeting. They'll be hidden on nearby properties, waiting for our call if things go south.

The SUV takes us to the hilltop community of Emerson Hill and turns into the driveway of a massive estate.

The Lords Mansion.

It's a Mediterranean Tuscan style villa painted pale orange with cherry wood trim. I count six balconies and terraces throughout the four floors. Sculpted bushes fill the front yard and about half a dozen luxury cars that I couldn't even begin to name are parked around the circular end of the driveway.

Elias exits the SUV first, followed by Del, me, and Matt.

A short set of stairs lead us from the driveway to the front door where Finn and his security team wait. Finn is in his seventies with dark gray hair and a leathery, tanned face. He's wearing a bowling shirt and slacks and shiny black dress shoes. He's a small guy, short and thin and frail. I wonder if the old man is sick as he coughs into a handkerchief. He also leans over slightly, relying on a cane to keep him standing.

Unless the cane is a weapon, and the sickly demeanor is all an act.

"What a pleasure to meet with not only the long-lost daughter of Gio Lenetti, but the Carter brothers," Finn says, his arms opening wide in a theatrical greeting. "We always wondered what happened to little Lance after that tragic night. Percy made sure to wipe you from existence, didn't he?"

I hold my arm in front of Del when he tries to take a step forward. Finn pays him no attention, focusing on me, and giving my body a once over before snarling.

"However did you convince these two QBM men to work with the Empire? And your father agreed to it? Call me perplexed."

He smiles, but it's all fake. Underneath, I know he's pissed... but maybe a little intimidated too.

We don't respond to his goading.

"If you don't mind, my team will need to check your weapons at the door," Finn says, raising an eyebrow at me.

Does he think I'm in charge? I'm not. Maybe he thinks being the daughter of Gio Lenetti puts me at a higher rank over Elias.

"We won't be doing that, O'Connor," Elias says, his hand near his belt where I know he's storing at least one of his guns.

"This is a peaceful meeting," I add. "We're not here to fight. Like I said on the phone, we have information about Cillian's death."

"And why should I believe you?"

"Because we know who's responsible."

"You could have told me who over the phone," Finn counters.

"Maybe we also have an offer for you," Del adds. "But in order for us to discuss that offer, we enter with our weapons."

Finn's eyes dart from me to Del, then to Elias. He could easily turn us away or start firing at this moment. But he must be curious enough to hear what we have to say because, after a few minutes, he nods at his security team and they back away.

"Only you, princess. The rest stay out here."

"Absolutely fucking not," Del says.

"We'll leave the blond one, but Lance and Elias are coming with me."

"Your father will kill me if I let you go—" Matthew begins, but Finn cuts him off.

"Fine." Finn waves his hand at us. "You three. Follow me."

I turn to Matt before leaving. "We'll be okay. Stay out here in case we need cover and a fast getaway. Take my phone since Del and Elias tossed both of yours." He clenches his jaw and hastily grabs the phone out of my hand.

He's definitely going to call my dad while we're inside.

Finn takes us through a wrought iron door and into a hallway, passing the living and dining rooms that are adorned with crisp white furniture, cherry wood floors, large windows, and French doors. We walk by the kitchen—which I hear is one of two—and I peek inside to see quartz countertops, a large island, sleek metal appliances, and another pair of French doors leading out to a backyard area.

Finn stops at the end of the hallway in front of opened double doors. One of his cronies gestures for us to enter. It's a cigar room with five large leather armchairs organized in a circle and a small table in the middle. Two walls are filled with floor to ceiling bookcases, another wall is full of windows, and in the middle of the fourth wall is a lit fireplace. The flames offer a cozy vibe during this intense meeting that's about to happen.

Someone comes around and offers us drinks, but we all decline, except for Finn who takes a glass of whiskey. The server also offers us cigars. Del and Elias take one and the woman lights it for them.

"I hear congratulations are in order," Finn says, holding up his drink. "Engaged. Is it true love or merely a ploy? What's next? Merging the QBM with the Empire? No, Gio wouldn't allow that. Does he know you three are here now?"

He's clearly not intimidated by our united front. He should be. We have triple the number of soldiers to his measly dozens of members.

"So, tell me... what is this information you have about my son's killer?"

"We know it wasn't a deadly home invasion," Del says.

"Of course, it wasn't," Finn scoffs.

"We believe it was one of the families Cillian had screwed over."

"Oh yeah?" Finn asks and takes a puff of his cigar, chasing it down with a sip of his booze.

I scrunch my nose at the smell of smoke filling the air and raise a brow at Del letting him know I won't be kissing him until he brushes his teeth. He looks back at me confused, so I guess my judgment wasn't all too clear.

"You don't sound surprised," Elias says, taking a drag and puffing out smoke rings. He appears relaxed with his leg propped on his knee as if we're not in the middle of a tense meeting with the leader of a rival mob.

"I know who killed my son," Finn says, his smile making my insides turn sour.

Something isn't right.

"Who?" Del asks, taking the bait.

"A contract killer," Finn answers, looking at me then Del. "Two, actually. The Marionette and Colpa Sicario."

This is bad. This is really bad. We need to leave.

"Don't know them," Del says.

"You don't, huh?" Finn laughs, and it's one of those villain laughs that sends a chill down my spine. "Imagine my surprise when I discover the two people I hired to get rid of my useless son are my two biggest rivals."

Finn pulls a gun from his holster and fires it at Del and Elias, who duck just in time, clamoring to the floor. I was sitting closest to Finn and before I'm able to take cover, the old man grabs me by the arm.

The cold metal of a gun's barrel digs into my temple.

"Let her go, O'Connor." Del says, scrambling to his feet and aiming a gun at the mob boss. Elias points his weapon at Finn's soldiers, who wait for his orders to open fire on us. "If you hurt her, I will make sure you die a slow and painful death."

The fear in Del's eyes ignites a fire in my stomach. I will not let this mother fucker kill me and leave my puppet alone again.

I ram my elbow into Finn's stomach, and he releases me. I turn around, slamming the heel of my hand into his nose, and he topples over onto his knees, clutching it as blood pours out.

"How did you figure out who we are?"

I kick him, and he falls to the ground.

Behind me, I hear Del and Elias firing their guns as they fight off Lords members.

Finn groans and I kick him in the stomach. "Tell me!"

"We need to get out of here, Vixen," Del yells as he stabs a man in the neck and lets him fall to the ground with a thud.

"Tell me, Finn!"

"Fuck you!"

"Did you blow up my apartment building?"

He starts laughing again, like a madman, and it's clear he's not going to talk. I pull my gun from my holster and fire, hitting Finn in the middle of his forehead.

I stifle the urge to celebrate the perfect shot. Those extra sessions at the gun range have really improved my aim.

"I'm so proud of you, sweetheart," Del says, appearing by my side and staring down at Finn's lifeless body. I relish his praise, not even caring that he called me sweetheart.

"Time to go, now," Elias says, shooting out of the door into the hallway.

The moment we step out, bullets fly by our heads.

"Fuck!" Del yells, pushing me behind him.

He shoots his gun down the long hall, and it's followed with a thud, letting me know he hit his target. We inch forward cautiously, dodging bullets and blasting our weapons in return.

Del won't let me on the front lines, so I stay behind, covering for them anytime they need to refill their ammo.

"Where's Matt? He should be in here covering us," Elias yells.

Minutes of constant gunfire go by before my cartridge empties. I step back out of the way and that's when two large arms grab me from behind. I scream as a hot, searing ache blooms throughout my stomach.

"Del," I wheeze.

He whips around at the sound of my voice and runs to where I've been left on the ground to die. I've never felt pain like this. Hot, sharp, throbbing.

"No, no, no, no," Del says over and over again.

"It's fine, it barely hurts," I lie, my vision starting to blur. The room is spinning, and I'm burning up. No, I'm freezing. I'm both.

"It's too much blood," I hear Del say. My eyes flutter as I weave in and out of consciousness.

"Don't fall asleep," Del says. It feels like I'm floating.

"I'm really tired, Puppet," I whisper.

"Please, Rainbow Bright, stay with me. Please."

And right before I pass out, I swear I hear Del say he loves me.

Chapter 25

Delancy

It's been four days and Noah is still in a coma. I tried to take her to a hospital, but Gio didn't want to deal with paperwork and police. He already had to send a clean-up crew to the Lords Mansion.

Finn is dead and most of his soldiers were killed in the shootout as well. Thankfully, fellow QBM and Empire members were on standby outside. We anticipated this would turn into a bloodbath. We just didn't realize it would happen so fast. It's almost as if someone tipped Finn off.

I suspect Matthew. He disappeared during the shootout, nowhere to be found when we emerged from the mansion.

Or maybe it was Gio. He refused to be a part of this plan. Did he have an ulterior motive? Is that why he told Noah to send me and Elias in? So we could be killed, and he could claim control of the QBM? Noah had mentioned she was suspicious of how quickly her father agreed to this plan.

After Elias and I carried Noah out to an SUV in the parking lot and told one of our guys to call her father, we went back inside, and I let my rage fuel the rest of the massacre.

Elias walked away with two bullet holes: one in his thigh and the other in his shoulder.

I got shot in the arm and one of the Lords soldiers managed to slice me on my neck, thankfully not too deep.

I was so proud of my lovely rainbow bright for killing Finn, shooting him in the head when he refused to answer her questions. Though, we probably should have kept him alive to torture him.

How did he know Noah and I were contract killers? He hired us to kill his son, but why did he want his son dead? And does this mean he's also the one responsible for blowing up Noah's apartment?

Maybe we were wrong about the Christmas Eve murders. What if it wasn't Gio but Finn instead?

I wouldn't think he'd set his own home on fire with his wife and children inside, but after finding out Finn ordered his own son's death, nothing's off the table.

Gio set up a room inside his Lower East Side townhouse for Noah's recovery with all the medical equipment needed to keep her alive. He has a doctor on staff who put her in a medically induced coma to help her injuries heal faster, especially since she was minutes from death by the time she arrived here from Staten Island.

Since last night, the doctor has been reducing the medication that's keeping her under and said she should wake today. They also removed the tube down her throat. Now, I sit next to her bed, holding her hand, waiting.

I've been a wreck without her. I haven't slept more than a few hours a night. What if she doesn't wake up? What if I lose her? I panicked and told her I loved her, but I wasn't sure if she heard me before she passed out from blood loss.

I meant every one of those three little words.

The doctor enters, and I stand to get out of his way. Gio lingers at the door and gives me a nod. He's furious that I let her get hurt, but at least he didn't kill me for it. One thing's for sure, Gio has a hit out on Matthew. He failed to follow orders by letting Noah go inside the Lords Mansion and she nearly died because of it. Gio wants his head.

I'd be more than happy to help find him. I still don't trust that fucker.

There's something about him rubbing me the wrong way. I swear I've seen him glaring at me... and even Gio when he doesn't think I'm looking.

"Her vitals are good," the doc says, adjusting his wire glasses on his nose. "If she doesn't wake up by the morning, call me."

He leaves and a nurse comes in to change her dressings. She marks things down on a chart and hangs it on the end of the bed before quietly slipping out.

Gio returns to Noah's side and pets her hair, then kisses her on the forehead.

"I know she'll want your face to be the first she sees when she wakes. Please call me when you two have had your time together so I can see her, okay?"

And with that, Gio leaves.

That man shocks me every day. Has he finally accepted that this thing between me and Noah is real? It may have started out as a fake engagement, but I have no intention of letting Noah go. If she'll have me, I'd love to make her my wife.

I doze off in the oversized armchair next to Noah's bed. I'm not sure how long I've been asleep before fingers combing through my hair startle me awake.

"You were having a nightmare," she says, her voice rough and raw from not speaking these last few days.

"Vixen," I whisper and stand to scoop her up in my arms. She hisses, and I immediately release her. "Fuck, sorry."

Her cold palm finds my cheek, and she smiles. "The pain was worth it. You never initiate hugs."

I try to kiss her, but she slaps her palm over my mouth.

"My breath tastes like death. I need to use the restroom and brush my teeth."

She moves to get out of bed, but a gazillion medical wires are still attached to her.

My heart races with panic. "You shouldn't be moving around like this. Let me call the doctor—"

"I'm fine, I promise," she says.

I purse my lips. "Please, just stay put while we wait for the doctor to check you out."

She searches my eyes and nods at whatever she sees in them.

"Lie down with me," she pats the side of the bed. I fire off a text to the doctor, then get in, tucking her to my side.

"I realize I wouldn't have gotten far because there are catheters in my ass and up my coochie," Noah murmurs.

A laugh bursts from my throat and it's a strange sound after not finding humor in things since she nearly died. Of course, Noah is the one to bring the light back to my darkness.

"That's why I wanted to call the doctor, Vixen."

She hums. "Call me that again."

"Vixen," I say and kiss the top of her head. Her arms are wrapped around me, and she nuzzles her nose into my armpit.

"You stink."

I laugh again. My cheeks already hurt from smiling, and she's only been awake for a few minutes.

"I haven't been concerned about hygiene."

"That's gross."

"Yeah? Well, you pooped and peed in bags for the past four days."

She tilts her head back to look at me. "It was that bad?"

"Yes, sweetheart. You were stabbed, and the knife nicked your liver. You had to get emergency surgery—did you know your father has an operating room in the basement—anyway, they put you in a medically induced coma to help you heal faster."

"Wow," she whispers.

Should I point out that I called her sweetheart, and she didn't yell at me?

No, I think I'll take that as a win. She's warming up to the nickname. I can't decide which one I like best, because Noah is, and has never been, simple. She's my beautiful rainbow bright, a colorful crayon, my sweet Skittles, a vivacious Vixen, my *sweetheart*.

I've never had a sweetheart.

She's Kevin, too, but I only pull that one out when I want to rile her up.

"Were you hurt too?"

Her hand roams over my stomach and up my chest to my neck where she finds the stitched knife wound. She skims her fingertips down my arm, causing goosebumps to rise, before she traces them over the sewed-up bullet hole.

"I've had worse."

She lifts my shirt, and her fingertips find my oldest scar. The one that nearly claimed my life. She likes tracing it anytime we cuddle after sex. It's along the side of my stomach. My father's doctor was surprised that all my vital organs were missed. It's why I didn't die sooner. Instead, I was left to bleed out. A painful, suffocating way to go.

Noah moves her freezing hands over more scars along my stomach and chest. My abs constrict trying to escape the icy touch.

"I killed Finn."

I smile and lift her chin with my thumb and forefinger. "Hell yeah you did."

The doctor walks in at that moment, followed by the nurse, and I hop out of the bed.

"I'm going to clean up while he's taking the poop chute out of you," I say, and Noah giggles.

"Good, your stinky ass was making me gag."

I almost make a joke about giving her something to gag about but hold back since there are other people present.

The shower was quick, and I feel one hundred percent better when I return to Noah's room. She's sitting up in bed, eating soup and drinking ginger ale. Her father sits in the armchair where I've been camped out for the past four days.

Shit, I forgot to text him.

Gio stands when he sees me. "I'll leave you two alone. I have a meeting at the gun range."

Once he's gone, Noah smiles mischievously at me. "The doctor said I can take a shower."

"Did he? I was kind of hoping I could give you a sponge bath."

SETTLE MYER

"Tempting, but a shower sounds heavenly. Will you help me?"

"Are you done eating?"

"For now."

"Okay, I'll help you. But it's only going to be a shower. No messing around."

Noah frowns. "Aww, you're no fun."

"I'm serious, Vixen. You're injured. No sex until you're healed."

She holds up her hands. "Fine. I'll keep it in my pants."

Noah hisses in pain with every step she takes, and I smirk.

"Oh, shut up."

"Recovery from surgery is no joke."

"Am I laughing?"

"You really thought we were going to fuck in the shower, didn't you?"

"Didn't I tell you to shut up?"

By the time we make it to the bathroom, Noah is sweating and panting. I help her shed the medical gown and turn on the water to the perfect warm temperature.

I carefully guide her under the stream, making sure her dressing doesn't get too wet. The nurse said it's waterproof but to avoid getting it soaked.

"Aren't you going to take your clothes off?" she asks and sighs as she lets the water cascade over her body. "I'll behave, I promise."

Despite showering just minutes ago, I strip my shirt and pants. I leave my boxers on, so Noah doesn't get grabby. She scowls, but I ignore her tantrum and pour shampoo into my palm to wash her hair.

It takes longer than normal to get Noah clean since I'm being careful of her injuries. After turning the shower off, I lead her out of the stall and dry her with a towel.

When I crouch down to get her legs, I look up at her. She smiles and runs her fingers through my hair. "Thank you for taking care of me," she says.

I give her a wink and kiss her thighs, just above the knees, then grab a robe hanging on the back of the bathroom door and help her put it on.

"Teeth next?"

She nods and watches me put the toothpaste on the brush. She tries to grab it, but I pull back.

"Open," I command, and she pouts, preparing to disobey.

I clutch her jaw and squeeze her cheeks.

"Open, Vixen."

She rolls her eyes, and I make a note to punish her for that later.

After her teeth and breath are minty fresh, I claim my kiss and lead Noah back to the room.

"Tell me what you need," I say, my arm wrapped around Noah's waist while she uses me as a crutch to get back into bed.

"You."

"Seriously, Noah."

She rolls her eyes. "More food? That soup did nothing for me."

I make a call to Gio's kitchen staff and ask them to whip up scrambled eggs, toast, and a bowl of fruit for Noah. She wanted waffles and bacon, but the doctor has a list of foods she can't have while recovering.

"And coffee," she adds before I hang up.

I order her apple juice. Coffee is on the list.

"Anything else while we wait?"

She pats the bed beside her. "More cuddling?"

I'm suspicious of her intentions, but crawl into bed anyway because I desperately need to be touching her right now. Noah curls up against my side and rests her head on my chest.

I've never been one to cuddle, but having Noah's body against mine is a luxury I never knew I needed. She's warm and soft, and I relish how the calm of contentment rushes through my veins. If we could only lay here forever and not worry about killing to survive and surviving to kill.

"Why were you such an asshole neighbor?" Noah mumbles. The exhaustion in her voice makes me want to go back to the Lords Mansion and kill every last fucker for a second time.

"Me? An asshole?" I laugh. "You must be confusing me with someone else."

"Um... waking me up at seven or eight in the morning blasting your music? That's an asshole thing to do, Puppet."

I smile at the memories that were only a few months ago.

"I can explain. You see, I'm quite shy," I begin, and Noah scoffs. "I am. So, I saw you moving in, and I thought you were gorgeous, but I don't like to initiate conversations. Never have. Then I thought, what if I annoy her enough that *she's* the one to come knock on my door? And that's exactly what happened."

She lifts her head to look up at me. "That was the dumbest plan in the world."

"Maybe, but here we are now. Besides, I liked that you got angry. You are undeniably unapologetic and when you started fighting back, it became a game."

"A game I always won."

"Wrong."

"What else do you like about me?" Noah rests her head back down, sighing. Her palm mindlessly rubs my stomach, and I'm doing everything I can not to grab it and move down to my hardening cock.

"I like that you look at me with no fear. You never saw the evil inside me like other people do. You didn't run away."

"That's the thing. I think I not only saw the evil, but I saw the pain in your eyes. I felt connected to you, and I couldn't understand why."

I kiss the top of her head and rub her back.

"Is that what you like about me? That I'm evil? Damaged?" I ask.

"You make me feel alive," she whispers, and before I'm able to do something dumb like flip her onto her back so I can fuck her properly for that response, there's a knock on the door.

Noah groans at the interruption. "Come in."

A woman carrying a tray enters with Noah's food. That was fast. I guess when the boss's daughter is injured and healing, she gets anything and everything she wants in record time.

I hop out of bed to take the tray from the worker. Noah sits upright, and I place her breakfast—even though it's almost seven at night—on her lap.

I squeeze some ketchup on her eggs, swatting at her hands when she tries to do it herself.

"You spoil me," she says with a grin.

"I do because..."

"Because?"

My heart pounds inside my chest at the near admission.

"Because you love me?"

I'm feeling dizzy. Lightheaded. I'm panicking. What if she doesn't say it back? I mean, we've only known each other for a few months. Is it too soon?

I can face down the barrel of a gun or sink a knife into a man's chest and not care about all the blood that follows, yet I've never been more scared in my life than at this moment.

"Tell me you love me, Delancy," Noah's voice is low, barely a whisper.

My phone rings, and I curse as I pull it out of my pocket.

"What?" I yell upon answering my brother's call.

"What the fuck is up your ass?"

"I'm in the middle of—"

"It doesn't matter. I need you to meet me at the Lords Mansion. I found something."

"I'm not leaving Noah here alone."

"Tell the guy you stabbed to stay with her," Elias chuckles, and I want to crush my phone in my hands.

I'm ready to argue and tell him that even if Matthew hadn't disappeared, I wouldn't want him anywhere near Noah without me here. Before I can say that, Noah stands and places her palm in the middle of my chest.

"Go. If he's calling you and asking you for help, it must be important."

I cup her cheek and run my thumb over her bottom lip. I've missed these lips. I've missed her. She's alive, but Finn is the reason she nearly died. Noah is right. If my brother has information about him, anything that could explain how he figured out we're contract killers, then I need to go.

"Fine," I sigh into the phone. "On my way."

I disconnect the call and angrily stuff my phone back in my pants.

"I'll be okay. Don't worry about me," Noah says. She takes one of my hands and peels my balled fist open so she can weave her fingers with mine.

I clutch the back of her neck and bring her mouth to mine, kissing her hard and deep.

She gasps for air when we part.

"Yes. I do love you, Rainbow Bright," I begin. "I love you so much it scares me."

And I walk away before she can react.

Chapter 26

Noah

Del leaves me in shock, my heart racing.

He loves me?

I knew he was obsessed with me, but I never thought a man like Del could fall in love. He's like me. He pushes people away because of trauma. The crushing pain of losing a loved one never seems to go away. It's why I've never been in a relationship. It's why I tend not to have friends.

Sage was an exception that I still regret now that she's part of this world.

Plus, Del and I are both killers. We crave violence. How can love play into the world we've created for ourselves?

The world that we fell into after a tragic night twenty years ago.

I text Del to send me updates, adding a heart emoji, then cringe because he deserves more than a heart emoji. Should I have texted him that I love him too? What if something goes wrong at the Lords Mansion? What if Lords soldiers—the ones who got away—show up for revenge? What if Del is hurt, or killed, and I never get to tell him I love him back?

No... I can't text him. No one wants to be told they're loved for the first time through a text message.

I barely eat my eggs, toast, and fruit before my stomach turns upside down with nerves. There are too many unanswered questions still.

Is Finn responsible for our mothers' murders? He's the one who put a hit on his own son, but I don't blame him. Cillian grew up to be a liability for his father. I doubt Finn wanted his wife and children to die all those years ago.

I am, however, convinced he's the one who ordered my apartment to be blown up.

My mind won't shut off and I refuse to lie here in bed letting my thoughts drive me crazy. The doctor told me I need to walk around so I ease myself out of bed and shove my feet into slippers. My injuries ache as I inch my way down the hallway, but the pain medication I'm on numbs it enough to be bearable.

By the time I reach the door to my mother's office, I'm sweating and fatigued.

For twenty years I avoided this room, which remained exactly how she left it.

The space is small, only big enough to hold the oversized chair in the corner, a desk, a bookcase full of books, framed photos, and other knickknacks.

Her desk is dust free and there's a closed journal directly in the middle with a pen beside it. I open the pink cover and flip through the pages. Most of them are full of recipes, random thoughts, or ideas for charities she loved to volunteer for.

Only a few pages remain blank at the back, and before I close it, I notice a page is missing. There's a sliver of paper at the bottom that lets me know it was ripped out in haste.

That's strange.

My mother would never be so careless when it came to her journal. Unlike me, she was always organized. She loved cleaning and decorating.

I leave the desk and walk over to the bookcase. The spines are color coordinated and resemble a rainbow. My mother was a fan of the old romance books that had bare-chested, long-haired men on the covers. She had three rows full of them, leaving the two bottom rows of the bookcase for my children's books.

I remember one day, not long after turning ten, she'd been in her office working on a letter to the city about a fundraising opportunity. Aside from volunteering, she'd donate tens of thousands of dollars each year to charities, especially ones involving children and animals. I ran in and begged her to let me read one of her adult romance books. She told me I was still too young, and I could read them once I turned eighteen.

Then I forgot all about these books after she died. At least, I didn't care to read them anymore.

A blue spined book has been mixed in with a red one, so I pull it out to put it back where it belongs.

Deadly Deceit.

The cover is gorgeous. It has a curvy blonde woman in a red dress, her leg poking out of a slit and a man with dark black hair beside her, wearing a suit and holding a gun.

I flip it around to read the back.

A woman discovers her husband has been lying. She stumbles upon his secret life as a mobster, walking in on him the moment he murders a man in cold blood. When she tries to run, he imprisons her in a cage. She's not alone. In the cell next to her is her husband's rival, who's been missing for the past five years. Together they form a plan of deadly deceit: escape and kill the most powerful and dangerous man in the city.

Damn. This sounds good. Maybe a little too close to comfort. I'm going to read it. I tuck it under my arm and head back to my room. After setting the book on my bedside table, I walk into my closet to change out of the robe.

I pick out an oversized green sweater and leggings then comb my red and green hair into a bun at the top of my head, making a mental note to text my hair stylist Jenny for a dye job since it's no longer Christmas. Maybe I'll go all green this time. Or blue.

Though, blue would open the door for Del to call me a Smurf.

I walk out of my room to wait downstairs for Del to return and run into Matthew in the hallway. Relief sweeps through me, and he smiles at my reaction.

"So my father kept his promise?"

An emotion flickers over his face, too fast for me to process what it was. He looks over my shoulder. "What are you up to? Are you okay? I heard you almost—"

"I'm okay. Hurting like a motherfucker, but alive."

He holds one hand behind his back and suspicion washes over me. My heart kicks into action, fueled by adrenaline.

I point my chin at him. "What are you hiding?"

"Nothing."

He takes a step back, and I match the move, hovering my hand over the knife I tucked into the band of my leggings—just in case.

Though, if he has a gun, my knife won't be much help.

"Stop," he says, his voice raised.

"I swear to God, Matt, if you're here to kill me, you better kill yourself too because Del will find you and make you wish you were dead."

"I'm not going to kill—"

He huffs and walks closer to me, into the dull light of the hallway.

"Oh, Matt," I whisper.

His left eye is bruised, and his lip busted. He's got tape over the bridge of his nose leading me to believe it's broken.

"I just wanted to thank you for talking to your father," he says.

After I woke up and Gio came to see me, I'd asked if anyone died in the Lords Mansion battle. He'd said five of his soldiers and when I specifically asked about Matt, his face turned deep red with fury. I found out about the hit he'd put on Matt, and I demanded he rescind it immediately. Matt was following *my* orders. I was the one who changed the plan. I explained to my father that if I'm going to lead someday, I can't have my soldiers defying me.

It took me about ten minutes, but I'd finally convinced him not to kill his new head of security. I may have threatened to leave and cut ties with Gio unless he promised to allow Matt to live.

It's clear my father still made sure to punish him.

"It's fine, Noah. At least I'm not dead."

I must wear a mask of guilt on my face. I sigh and nod. What more can I say? No words can undo what happened to him.

"Will you keep me company downstairs?"

Matt hesitates before answering, his face conveying an array of emotions. Is he hesitating because of my father?

"Del..."

Ah, the other protective man in my life.

"Don't worry about Delancy. I won't let him touch you again. Please, keep me company?"

Matthew relents, and we head into the living room. I hit a button, and a television emerges from behind the wall. I pull up a streaming app and select a comfort show.

"*Buffy the Vampire Slayer*?" Matt asks, amused.

"Don't hate. Buffy is a badass!"

Matt laughs and shakes his head.

We watch the first five minutes of the show in silence before I can't take it anymore. I have to know more about this man and his history with the Empire. I shut off the TV and turn in my seat to face Matt—who sits far away on the other side of the couch.

"Can I ask you a question?" His eyes widen, but he nods. "How long have you been a part of the Empire?"

"Since I was eighteen."

His face drops into a scowl.

"Did you want to join that young?"

He shakes his head as a darkness washes over him. "My father was a soldier."

"Was?"

"He got sick, and I replaced him."

"Wait, were you forced to join?"

He sighs. "It doesn't matter. I had to do it for my family."

He looks away, letting me know he doesn't want to talk about this anymore.

"Matt," I whisper, moving to sit next to him. He looks away, hiding the black eye. "I'm sorry these injuries happened because of me. I asked him not to kill you. I should have promised him not to harm you either."

"Did you really think there wouldn't be consequences for letting you go inside the Lords Mansion?"

"Show me what he did."

He holds up his left arm revealing his hand wrapped in bandages.

"All of it."

He stares into my infuriated eyes for the longest time before slowly raising his shirt.

I curse. His entire torso is covered in bruises.

"This is not how I will run things once my father is gone," I say quietly. "I won't do this. I wouldn't—"

"It's necessary. It's how mafias work. You'll see."

"No, Matthew. Fear is a tool, but so is unity... respect. I'll give you an out once I'm in charge. I promise."

He clamps his mouth shut and looks away again.

He doesn't believe me.

"How long have you hated him?"

"Del or your father?"

That makes me laugh and the tension running through Matthew's body eases.

"I was talking about my father but now that you mention it, what is it about Del that scares you? You've been an Empire soldier for twenty years. You've worked your way up the ranks, right? Killing an endless number of men? Probably dudes twice as big as you?"

"Yeah, I guess."

"So what is it about my fiancé?"

Matt's face turns crimson, and I wonder if he's about to pass out with all the blood rushing to his head.

"Um, well, he stabbed me."

"You've been stabbed before, Matthew."

He smiles at me saying his full name again. He must not hear it a lot. He's got a great smile. It lights up his tanned face. He's not as built as Del, or as tall, but he's definitely packed with muscle. Now, if only I could convince Del to have fun with Matt again.

"Yeah, but I've never been stabbed over a blow job." He sighs and rubs his palm over his face. "I'm not scared of Del. I mean, he's intimidating as fuck, but I mostly worry about your father finding out, and I really don't want to die anytime soon."

He laughs nervously.

"Don't get me wrong, Noah, you're beautiful, and your mouth is fucking talented, but now every time I see you or Del, I think about our threesome. As much as I would love to get involved with you two, I'd be the first one to end up dead if something went wrong."

By either my dad or Del killing him, I add silently.

"Well, that's a shame. I was desperately wanting to peg Del while he fucked your ass. Or maybe you fuck him while he fucks me."

Matt groans. "You're killing me, Noah."

I giggle and ignore the heat spreading across my skin as I imagine reaming into Del, him shuddering with an orgasm and pouring his cum into Matthew's tight hole.

It's going to happen. I just have to find someone who Del won't want to maim afterward.

The sound of car doors closing jolts us out of our conversation.

Matt stands. "That's my cue to leave." He doesn't let me protest and nearly runs out of the room.

It takes me a while to reach the hallway, and by the time I round the corner, Del and Elias are walking inside.

"What are you doing down here?" Del asks the moment he spots me. He rushes to my side. "You should be in bed resting."

He takes my arm and wraps it around his waist to act as my crutch. It's sweet but a tad bit overbearing. "I'm rested.

I was tired of being cooped up in that room and needed to walk around. The doctor encouraged it."

"Where's Gio?" Elias asks, glancing around.

"He had a meeting at the gun range. When he says meeting, he usually means a game of poker with his cronies. He'll probably be there all night."

At least, that's how it was when I was a kid.

"Good. We need to talk." Elias walks past us into the sitting room and goes directly to the booze cart. He pours himself a glass of whiskey and takes it to the couch.

"What did you two find?" I ask after Del helps me sit on the loveseat across from Elias.

"Security video of the two men dousing your apartment with gasoline and setting it on fire," Elias says.

"The video from my feed," Del adds. "Someone must have hacked it."

He curses, mumbling something about firing his hacker friend. Or maybe he said 'killing' his hacker friend.

"So he *was* responsible for blowing up our apartment," I conclude.

"I'm not so sure," Del says. "How the hell did he get that footage? Why would he want evidence to tie himself to the crime?"

"There's no way for us to know that those men in that video are Lords," Elias adds.

"Okay... but he said he hired us to kill Cillian. Why? He had no other heir."

"That we know of," Elias says.

"He could have left the Lords to any blood relative, not just his children. We all knew Cillian would have gone power hungry in the role. Maybe that's why he had him killed," Del explains.

"And as for hiring you both," Elias begins. "Double assurance? In case one of you failed?"

"But he figured out who we are. How?"

"We found pictures in a manilla folder addressed to Finn," Elias continues. "You and Cillian entering his apartment the night he was killed. Del showing up minutes later. Then pictures of you and Del leaving. Whoever was taking photos of you followed you all the way to Del's safe house. They staked out his place, then followed you the next day when you returned to Astoria and got shots of you both walking up to your apartment building. They must have been in communication with someone the whole time, making sure you two walked inside the moment it blew up."

"We think whoever took these photos didn't know our true identities until the night of the Christmas party. Then they saw an opportunity and sent them to Finn," Del says.

"Someone wanted him to retaliate," I murmur. "Our engagement connected our organizations, and they didn't like it."

Del and Elias nod simultaneously.

"But who? That's what I can't understand."

"Whenever we figure that out, we'll have the answers to who was behind the explosion... and possibly who was responsible for the murders of our mothers."

Chapter 27

Delancy

This has Gio written all over it. We just can't figure out why he would do any of this, especially blowing up the building where his daughter lives when he's so protective of her.

It's been nearly three weeks of snooping around his offices at the gun range. We've yet to go through paperwork at his other office in Harlem because he's there most of the time and we have no good reason to be there without him. At least at the gun range, we can cover ourselves with target practice.

Noah's injuries are all but healed, so we left Gio's townhouse and returned to the Brooklyn loft.

For the past few weeks at the end of the day, we'd both crawl into bed, make out or fool around a little or cuddle until falling asleep.

It's been nice having her next to me; in my arms, her soft body against mine, my face snuggled into her neck as I inhale her sweet smell.

"I got something for you," Noah says, walking into the living room after her shower. She's wearing a robe and has a towel on her head. In her hands is a box wrapped in black. "Go shower and I'll give it to you after."

Oh. This must be something sexual then. She wants me clean so she can get me sweaty and filthy again.

I don't think twice and jump off the couch.

It takes me five minutes to scrub my skin with the body wash Noah loves so much, the one with woodsy and citrus undertones. I don't wash my hair—no patience to do so—or shave because I know how much she loves the scratchy feel of my stubble along her thighs and cunt.

When I return to the living room, the lights are low, and she's lit a dozen or so candles around the room. She stands in the middle wearing a hot pink lingerie set to match her hot pink hair.

Pink like the first time we met.

My cock jumps as I take in her body. Her large breasts are barely held in by the fabric of the corset. Her dark nipples poke out because she's turned on and excited about the gift she's about to give me. A row of her skin peeks above the band of her panties, showcasing the beautiful pattern of the stretch marks along her round stomach.

Her thick thighs are adorned by garter belts that hold up knee-high stockings.

The thong she's wearing is sheer like the corset bra, doing nothing to hide her dark pussy hair. I want to bury my nose in the trimmed bush.

"I take it you like what you see," Noah hums, her eyes dropping to my fully erect cock pushing against the loose fabric of my gray sweats.

I stalk toward her, and she raises a brow, not even intimidated.

"Noah, I don't just like what I see... but I *love* everything about that body of yours. If it were up to me, I'd be fucking you in the morning, again after lunch and dinner, then once more before we go to sleep. If it were up to me, I'd fuck you hard enough that your pussy ached anytime you moved."

"Jesus, Puppet," Noah says, breathless.

Once I'm in front of her, I palm her neck and trace my thumb over her jaw.

"You are so beautiful," I say and lean in to place a kiss on her plush pink lips.

She parts her mouth, and I slip my tongue inside and lap up her minty taste. My hands bury in her long, dyed hair, the strands soft as I fist them to tug her head back. I trail my kisses down her throat, making sure to nip and suck her skin and leave my marks.

Wrapping an arm around her waist, I pull her body against mine and lower my greedy hands down to her plentiful ass, squeezing hard enough to make her cry out.

My hard cock grinds into her soft stomach.

"Can you feel what you do to me? How desperately I need you right now?"

She groans when I grab her breast and tweak her nipple.

"My rainbow bright."

She pushes at my chest, and I step back.

"You can't just come in here and take charge when I have plans for you!"

"I can't huh?"

"Yeah. I have a gift, remember?" She walks over to the side table where she set the box down and picks it up to hand to me.

She claps her hands and bounces on her feet with excitement.

I rip the wrapping paper to shreds, then tear the tape. Inside the box is another wrapped box.

"Really?"

"Gotta make you work for it," she says with a wink.

I get through this second box to find a third.

"Noah," I scold, and she giggles, her cheeks turning red.

The final box has cock-adorned wrapping paper, and I think I know what's inside.

Sure enough, I find a strap-on staring back at me.

"Is this my gift or yours?" I muse.

"Yours, I promise." She points at the image on the back. "Look, it has a clit massager for me!"

I sigh and shake my head but can't help smiling.

This is definitely for her.

"Okay, go grab my lube."

She squeals, claps her hands again, and skips down the hallway to the bedroom. She returns seconds later with my bottle of lube in her hands.

My cock is already leaking with how turned on I am thinking about Noah fucking my ass.

I've already taken the strap-on out of the box and set pillows down on the floor. Noah walks over to where I stand in the middle of the pile.

"Will you put it on me?"

I lean in and place a gentle kiss on her lips. "I'd be honored."

I inspect the strap-on. It's purple with buckles that click into place and the part that presses against Noah's pussy is flat except for an extended piece that will vibrate and massage her clit.

Once it's on her, she strokes her hand over the shaft. I hook my fingers behind the band of my sweats, too eager to have it inside me.

"Wait," Noah says, stopping me. "I want to undress you. Can I?"

I love that she's asking my permission. She never needs it, but I'll take it anytime she offers.

"Of course."

Her hands shake as she slides my shirt over my head.

Is she nervous?

"Have you pegged someone before?"

She bites her lip. "Yes, a few times, but pegging them was never important."

"Pegging *me* is important?" I laugh as she peels off my gray sweatpants.

"You're important. I want to explore the things that give you pleasure. I want our sex life to be fun and adventurous because that's who we both are, right?"

I nod. Can't argue with that.

She stares down at my chest and traces her fingers along the scars I've racked up over the years. Then her nails drag down to my abs where she places her palms flat. She leans in and kisses the same scars she just touched. All of them. Then her kisses reach the two on my face left by my father's abuse.

When she's done worshiping the evidence of my physical trauma, she smiles at me. "Get on your knees."

"Yes, ma'am."

A hand crashes down on my ass and I groan. In my twenties, I tried being submissive, but it wasn't my thing. I needed to be in control. Yet Noah being in control of me, spanking me just now, was intoxicating. I need more.

"Don't call me ma'am. Call me…" I glance over my shoulder and see her tapping her lip while she thinks. "Call me Madam Rainbow."

"Yes, Madam Rainbow."

"Much better."

I hear her pop the cap to the lube and seconds later, her slick fingertip teases the tight outer ring of my asshole. She presses the tip in, just an inch, and I inhale a sharp breath.

"Mhm… so tight for Madam Rainbow," Noah purrs, and my cock leaks at the sound of her sultry voice.

She adds another finger and slides both in slowly, letting me stretch around them until she's all the way down to the last knuckle.

I nearly come when she starts pumping.

Her other hand smooths up my spine and I moan, my balls tightening from overstimulation.

"Are you ready to take my cock, Puppet?"

"Yes, Madam Rainbow," I groan.

"I'll be easy on you since we didn't do much prep. I need a word for when it's too much."

"I don't need a word."

She spanks me, hard enough that I'm sure it'll leave a bruise tomorrow.

"A word, you brat."

Oh, she's going to pay for that. She's the one who's a brat.

"Kevin," I say, hoping to piss her off. Instead, she giggles.

The lube top opens again, and she slicks the gel up and down the dildo.

"I want you to touch yourself when I enter you, do you understand?"

"Yes, Madam Rainbow," I say.

The head of the silicone dick presses against my hole, and I fist my cock, like the good boy I am.

Noah enters me slowly. She slicks more lube on the shaft to help glide it in until it's to the hilt.

I clench around the sizable toy and moan.

"You like feeling this full, Puppet?"

"Fuck yes," I grunt.

She strikes my ass cheek again, and I buck away from the unexpected pain.

"Sorry, Madam Rainbow," I say, and she rubs the burning spot, pleased with my correction.

"Are you ready, sweetheart?"

I smile at the nickname she hates but has turned on me.

"I'm ready, Madam Rainbow. Do your worst."

I hear the soft buzz of the clit massager turn on and Noah gasps at the sensation. Then she pulls out of me and slams back in.

My hand squeezes my cock, and I fist myself to the rhythm of Noah pegging me. Her thighs slap against the back of mine as she picks up her pace. More cum leaks onto the blanket I spread out on the floor.

"I'm not going to last long, Noah," I groan.

I get a lashing for calling her Noah, and my asshole clenches around the dildo as the pain mixes with pleasure.

"You don't get to come unless I allow it," she says, breathless.

She pistons into me, harder, and I fist my dick vigorously.

"Please, Madam Rainbow," I beg.

She latches onto my hair, tugging my head back.

Oh, fuck, that feels good.

Her thighs slap against the back of mine, her cock grinding through my clinched asshole.

"Okay, Puppet, you can come. Can you do that for Madam Rainbow?"

When I don't answer, I get another smack on the ass and that's what breaks me. I scream out my orgasm and shoot jets of cum onto the pile of pillows below.

Noah stays seated inside me until I finish coming.

When she slides out, I flip her onto her back and frantically work to unbuckle and remove the strap on. Once that's gone, I rip her pretty lingerie, and she tries to slap me for it. I pin her arms to the floor.

"I think my forearm landed in your cum," she says, breathless.

I lift it up and sure enough, there's a patch there. I move it to her mouth. "Lick it up, slut."

She groans but does as I say, then I descend on her pussy, lapping my tongue up her slit to cover her clit. She arches her back when I suck and lash against the sensitive bundle of nerves. I slide two fingers into her soaked heat.

"You're dripping, sweetheart," I growl. "But here's the problem. That strap-on couldn't get you off, even with the clit massager."

I thrust my fingers into her at the same rough pace she just fucked my ass.

"My tongue, my fingers, my cock will always be better than your toys, do you understand?"

"Mhm."

I continue pumping my fingers in and out and suck her clit into my mouth again. It doesn't take long for her to reach her release, and she's shaking beneath me.

I crawl up her body, leaving kisses along the way; her stomach, her breasts, and take a nipple between my teeth. She gasps and my cock jolts at the sound.

It's already ready for more.

When I start kissing along her neck and jaw, I line up my cock to her still wet pussy. I don't give her any warning when I thrust in.

"Fuck, Del!" she screams.

I lift her leg and rest it on my shoulder, allowing me to fuck her deeper.

I watch her tits bounce as I drive into her. It's brutal, and I'm not holding back. She can handle it.

Reaching down, I massage her sensitive clit with my thumb.

"Ahh," she pants, and her walls choke my cock in response.

"Give me another, Noah."

She squeezes her breasts and pinches both her nipples while I continue to massage her clit. Her cheeks burn red with lust, and I drop her leg so I can wrap my hands around her throat while reaming into her pussy.

I'm choking her hard enough that she loses air quickly and just before she's about to tap me to let go, her orgasm washes over her.

I release my grip on her neck, admiring the redness that will surely turn into bruises tomorrow, and pump into her gripping pussy a few more times before I'm coming again, splashing my remaining cum against her walls.

"Such a good girl," I say and collapse beside her.

We lie there panting for a few minutes, then Noah turns on her side and traces her finger up and down my bare chest.

"You liked me pegging you?"

I nod.

"Would you let another woman peg you while you fucked me? Maybe that curvy redhead you had a date with that one day?"

"You're insatiable, Vixen," I laugh.

"What if Matthew fucked your ass while you fucked me?"

I jump up and start tickling her. She screams and giggles and curls her legs to try and kick me.

"I'm starting to think you like Matthew more than me," I say, continuing my torture.

"Never!" She laughs and manages to slip away from me. I chase her around the apartment and when I catch her, I fuck her again.

And again and again.

Chapter 28

Noah

Del is a man true to his word. He fucked me until my pussy ached and every time I moved, I thought about how he filled me, bruised me, claimed me. We spent two days together, forgetting about the world, the mafia, and the fact that someone wants me dead.

Now it's time to get back to work trying to figure out if Finn blew up my apartment, or if he was set up, and if he's the person responsible for our mothers' murders.

"I'm going to the Harlem office today," I say, walking out of the closet dressed in a crop top sweater and high-waisted jeans.

Del takes in my body, his eyes lighting up with lust like they always do when he sees me.

"He's going to let you inside his most protected space?" Del asks.

I shrug. "He doesn't know I'm coming. He can't cover anything up if I arrive unexpectedly. Besides, he's at the gun range today. Do you want to come with me?"

"Oh, I'm not missing this. Let me get dressed."

After about fifteen minutes, Del and I are on his motorcycle, weaving through lunchtime traffic.

We enter Manhattan, heading up FDR Drive toward Harlem when Del makes a sudden exit.

"Where are you going?" I yell, but he can't hear me through my helmet and over the motor.

Then a bullet flies by my head and lodges in the rear frame of the car in front of us.

What the fuck?

I glance over my shoulder and see a black SUV with tinted windows speeding up to us. We merge onto First Avenue, only to be met with heavy traffic.

I reach into Del's jacket for his gun and start shooting behind me. All three bullets hit the SUV, causing it to swerve. It veers off the road, jumps the curb, and crashes into an outdoor dining shed.

Those extra sessions at the gun range with Del really paid off.

Del parks his motorcycle nearby as people approach the driver and passenger sides of the SUV, trying to help the people inside. From what I can tell, no innocent bystanders were injured by the crash. Hopefully, it stays that way.

"Get the fuck out of here," Del growls at them and waves his gun around.

A woman and man take off immediately. A few other people linger either in shock or because they're not seeing a big gun in Del's hand.

But the moment someone inside the SUV fires a shot at us, the area clears.

Police sirens wail in the distance.

"We need to get out of here," I say, ducking behind a parked car on the street.

"Cover me," Del says and runs toward the SUV.

"Dammit, Puppet!"

I take a stance, ready to shoot, but whoever's inside the SUV must be injured, or they didn't see Del approach the passenger side. I assume the driver is dead, because Del returns with only one man, dragging him by his shirt.

"We can't take him on my bike. Do you know how to hotwire a car?"

"No. Do you?"

"Yeah, here, hold him."

Right before Del hands off his hostage, tires squeal behind us. I twist around and point my gun, ready for another attack.

An SUV comes to a stop and Matthew jumps out of the passenger side. He opens the backseat door.

"Get in!" he yells.

I don't hesitate and run to the vehicle, crawling in and sitting on the far side of the backseat. Del follows, but I can see uncertainty cross his face.

"Either get in or get arrested," Matt says, clamping his hand down on Del's shoulder.

I spot police cars a few blocks away, thankfully slowed down by the congested streets of Manhattan.

Del shakes off Matt's hand and curses before shoving his hostage inside.

Once Matt and Del are in the SUV, we take off.

"I need rope," Del says and within seconds, Matthew is handing him some.

Del cuts off a long strand with the knife he keeps hidden somewhere on his body and aggressively ties the man's hands together.

"We need to go back to my father's townhouse," I say, and the driver nods. He takes the first side street off First Avenue and away from heavy traffic.

Del gives me a questioning look.

"Gio has torture rooms in the basement."

The man between us squirms and squeals. Del punches him in the temple, causing him to pass out.

"Is this him?" I ask.

Del doesn't need me to clarify.

"It's hard to tell if it's the same guy from the explosion video since they were wearing masks, but he has the same build as one of them.

"This was messy. Whoever they are, they aren't professionals," I say.

Del grunts in agreement.

I glance at Matt in the front seat. "Were you following us?"

Matt doesn't even turn around to answer.

"Lenetti's orders."

Del doesn't like that answer and punches the seat in front of him. Matt launches forward, only for his seatbelt to stop him from smashing his head into the windshield. My father's head of security reacts by pulling his gun and pointing it at Del's head. Del's just as quick, his own gun in his hand and aimed at Matt's chest.

"Do it, blondie!" Del seethes.

"Can we not with the foreplay?" I sigh and pinch the bridge of my nose. "Both of you, lower your guns. Matt, you know Del is an asshole."

Matt keeps his eyes on Del, the two playing a game of chicken. But I know Del won't back down, so Matt takes the high road and lowers his gun first.

Del tucks his gun away in a holster and leans his head back on the headrest. He closes his eyes, finally relaxing.

My nerves are on edge, and I try to calm down by focusing on the landscape out the window.

I suck in a sharp breath. "Where the fuck are we going?"

"We're going to your father's," Matt says.

"This is not the way to the townhouse."

Matt turns his head, a vindictive smile spreading across his face causing my stomach to dip and my heart to drum in my chest.

"I wasn't talking about *your* father, princess." His eyes trail to Del, whose head is still leaned back, eyes closed, and mouth hanging open.

He's asleep?

No... he's been drugged.

By Matt?

Betrayal slams into me headfirst.

"Who the hell are you? What did you do to Del?" I try the handle of the door, but of course it's locked. Not that I would have jumped out. The driver is speeding, and I would never leave Del.

Matt laughs and pulls his gun on me.

"Just sit back there and look pretty. This will all be over soon."

It takes us about thirty minutes driving through traffic to Queens... QBM territory... before coming to a stop in front of a large three-story home painted an ugly shade of yellow green with dark forest green sidings.

"I'll bring *Rainbow Bright* inside," Matt says to the driver. "Untie Baron, and tell Percy his son is here."

Percy?

Del's father? He's alive?

My door opens and the muscular driver grabs my upper arm, his fingers digging into my fat. Great. He's going to leave a bruise.

He hands me off to Matt, who grinds a gun into my side, making sure I don't fight back.

I wouldn't even try, and it has nothing to do with Matt being taller, and probably stronger, than me. I'll play along so I can figure out how the hell Percy Carter is still alive.

Was Del playing me this whole time?

Fury ignites in the pit of my stomach.

"Why, Matt? You've been a part of the Empire for twenty years. Why are you betraying my father now?"

Why are you betraying *me*? I silently ask. I slap on a strong face because my heart is hurting.

We walk down a long sidewalk covered with snow on either side. The home next door has a snowman in the front yard, and I can only hope there are no kids nearby because this place is minutes away from turning into a bloodbath.

"Betraying *your* father? Seriously? After everything I told you?" Matt scoffs and shakes his head. "Princess, I've been wanting to do this from the moment he imprisoned me in this godforsaken mafia."

Fuck! I'm going to die today.

Matt shoves me inside the front door and the place reeks of piss and mildew. There's no furniture inside, clearly an abandoned home.

"Look, I know he did unspeakable things to you—"

"Not just me. He killed my mother and sister."

"Oh, Matt—"

"Don't. You're not allowed to feel sorry for me. You're just like him, *Colpa Sicario*."

What the fuck? How did he...? My chest aches with how fast my heart is beating. Am I having a heart attack? Panic attack?

"No. I'm not like him. I'm on your side. Let me go, and we can help you get vengeance."

He doesn't believe me. After everything we've shared, me telling him I would give him an out. A new life. Does he need money? I'll give it to him. But I say nothing because the Matt I've come to know is no longer here. Here is a man full of rage and retribution.

"Not going to happen, princess."

I really wish he'd stop calling me that.

We descend creaky and unsteady stairs into a creepy basement that's probably full of spiders and ghosts. A single light bulb hangs from the ceiling, and there's a solo chair in the middle of the room.

How cliché.

Matt sits me in the chair and pulls zip ties out of this pocket. He secures my hands behind my back, then binds my ankles to the chair.

When he stands, he cups my jaw and skims his thumb over my bottom lip. He grabs his cock with his other hand.

"You look devastating tied up like this. Can you see how turned on I am?"

I snap my teeth, attempting to take a chunk out of his thumb, but he jerks his hand back just in time.

The move pisses him off, and he slaps the shit out of me, which causes me to bite down on my tongue instead. I spit blood on his shoes.

I can't believe I let him put his cock in my mouth.

"No playing with my toy, Matthew," a deep voice says.

I turn my head toward the stairs and see a large man with silver and gray hair—who looks eerily like Elias—standing on the bottom step.

Percy Carter.

Two men, holding up a still passed out Del, emerge right behind him.

"Del!" I squirm in the chair, but all it does is tighten the zip ties around my wrists and ankles.

"Aww, how precious." Percy says, walking toward me. "You really do love him, don't you?"

He pulls a gun from his jacket and points it at my head.

I try to hold in the tears, but they're falling now.

"Good, because I plan to kill him first. Let you witness and *feel* the pain of losing a loved one."

"He's your son," I sob.

"He killed my wife... his mother."

"It wasn't his fault!"

"You're right," Percy says. "It was your father's fault."

He fires the gun, and it pierces my shoulder, sending a stinging, burning pain throughout that part of my body.

"Bring him over here," Percy says, and the two men drop Del at his feet.

He bends down and waves smelling salts underneath his nose and Del starts coughing. It takes him a few seconds to reorient himself. When he spots me, his eyes widen, then his vision focuses, and he finally sees his father.

He reacts by throwing up.

"Seeing ghosts, son?"

He wipes his mouth before standing, wavering slightly. "How?"

"Simple. I lied. I was never sick."

Del's confusion lingers so Percy sighs.

"I received a folder a few months after you killed your mother. It provided me with everything I needed to know, including photos, names, and addresses of the men who forced you to murder Imogen. There was a note with the name of the man who hired them. Gio Lenetti."

"We never saw a note with Lenetti's name. It took me years to figure that out," Del says and locks eyes with me. He mouths 'are you okay?' and I nod, despite the blood pouring out of my shoulder.

"Right. Well, I couldn't have you killing Lenetti. That was my job. I left the folder for you and Elias to find and seek out your vengeance while I planned mine. I had all the evidence I needed to prove Gio ordered Imogen's death, thanks to those files Matthew delivered to me. Lenetti needed to pay for what he did. But in order for Gio to grieve as I did, I had to aim for someone he truly loved, now that his wife was dead."

"Me," I whisper.

"You, princess. The heir to the Empire. I kill you and Lenetti has no blood relative to leave his organization to."

Both of my parents were only children. I never had aunts, uncles, or cousins.

"The Lenetti line dies out and the QBM can finally take claim as New York City's most powerful mafia."

"Elias would never allow this," Del growls.

"Perhaps not, but now that I'm back, he will have no choice but to hand over the QBM." He chuckles. "So, what happened to the little girl who saw her mother killed all those years ago? Lenetti let everyone believe she died, but I knew better. I had spies embedded in the Empire that told me you lived. I spent years trying to find you with no luck."

He turns to Del.

"Until my son, who led me right to you."

My heart stops working. I can no longer breathe.

"What?" I ask, my tears returning.

Del shakes his head. "I didn't. I would never. You have to believe me, Noe."

"Lance was stalking you. And I was stalking my son. Now, what was it about this woman that had him so fascinated?"

I'm shivering, and I'm not sure if it's the shock, the blood loss, or because it's cold as fuck down here.

"Lance couldn't watch over you all the time, but I did. Imagine my surprise when you led me right to Lenetti's restaurant. My spies were right. His daughter was alive and well and back in New York City. A miracle."

I'm going to die here.

"Then I was furious. My *son* was infatuated with the enemy's daughter. After killing my wife, he needed to die. I had eyes on him, on the both of you, and ordered my men to douse your apartment with gasoline and blow it up the moment you two returned home."

Del stands frozen, his fists balled at his side. He's processing *everything*. He's planning his move. But he's waiting until his father finishes his villain monologue. He wants to hear the rest just as much as I do.

"You had someone following us the night Cillian died, didn't you?" I ask, urging him to keep spilling.

"The night *you* killed Cillian? Yes, I had someone following you and taking pictures. Then I sent Finn the photos after that stunt at the Christmas party. He needed to know the contract killers he hired to kill his loose cannon of a son were also his rivals."

"And then what was your plan? Kill me and poof, your revenge is done?"

He scoffs. "Of course not."

He holds out his hand and Matthew sets a phone in his palm. Percy puts it to his ear.

"Gio Lenetti. I have your daughter."

He hangs up, then types out a text message.

"Your father is on his way. I kill you, then him, then reclaim the QBM and become the most powerful man in this city."

That's when Del makes his move. He lunges for his father, but Matt kicks him, knocking him to the ground. Del is obviously still woozy from whatever they injected into him. How did he not feel being poked? I suppose the adrenaline of the chase could have masked it. It must have happened when Matt had his hand on his shoulder. I found it weird at the time, but I never thought he'd *drug* Del.

Matt stands over him, a gun pointed at his head.

"It's a shame we have to end things like this," Matt says. "I would have taken Noah up on her offer."

An explosion rocks the home above us, and the blast knocks me onto the ground, still tied to the chair.

The pain, the blood loss. It's too much.

I pass out.

Chapter 29

Delancy

Whatever exploded above us sent shards of wood and debris into the basement. Thick smoke fills the air, causing me to cough.

My father's alive?

I crawl on the floor, trying to find Noah, but instead I come across Matthew. He's passed out but alive with a nasty head injury. This asshole. I knew there was a reason I didn't like him. I'll deal with him later. I'm really going to enjoy killing the fucker.

"Noah!" I scream out, but I'm met with silence. Well, not silence. My ears are ringing, and I think I hear angry shouting, gunfire, and people running around above us.

"Son," my father's strained voice calls out.

I ignore him as I keep crawling. The smoke and dust are beginning to thin enough that I can see Noah on the ground.

She's tipped over in the chair, her arms still tied behind her back and ankles secured to the legs. I find a knife on the ground near her and cut her out of the binds.

Blood trickles out of the bullet wound in her shoulder. I check her body for other injuries, but thankfully I don't find any more.

I pat her cheek gently at first, then harder when she doesn't wake. "Noah. Please, come back to me."

I press down on her shoulder to slow the bleeding and her eyes pop open. She gasps for breath.

"There's my rainbow bright," I say, palming her cheek.

"What happened?" she asks, looking around. "Oh, my God. Del, your father. Are you okay?"

"It's fine. We need to get you out of here."

"No. Del, I'm okay. It's through and through. The bleeding has already slowed down. Take care of him."

"Can you stand?"

She nods and holds out her hand. I help her up, and she wobbles a bit before straightening her back and lifting her chin with determination.

Fuck, she's perfect.

I give her a quick kiss on the lips and turn away to find my father. He's on the ground on his back, injured by splintered wood lodged in his stomach. A survivable injury… if we get him to a surgeon soon.

But that won't be happening.

I search the area for a gun and find one next to my father's left hand. He realizes I'm eyeing it and tries to grab it, but he's too injured, too slow.

"Are you going to kill me like you did your mother?"

"Fuck you, old man," I growl. "You know I had no choice."

"You could have let them kill you too."

I aim the gun at his head, and I'm seconds from pulling the trigger.

"Lance," Elias says from the top of the stairs. He carefully walks down, a few steps are gone but for the most part, they're intact. He glances over his shoulder at a woman preparing to follow him. "Stay here, Reine."

Reine? Who is that?

"Sage is here?" Noah asks, panic filling her voice when she spots her best friend.

Ah. Right. Elias knows French.

Reine = Queen.

Sage makes a move to follow, despite Elias's order to stay, then takes in the appearance of the stairs and changes her mind.

"Give me the gun." Elias holds out his hand, and I shake my head. "I need to do it."

"Pathetic," Percy spits out when Elias takes the gun from me. "Have I taught you nothing, Elias? This is not how the QBM Don should lead. I hand my legacy over and you... you share it with the enemy?"

Elias doesn't wait for Percy to go into another villain speech. He pulls the trigger and shoots him in the middle of the forehead.

He stands there, staring down at our dead father.

"Elias," I whisper, and he holds up his hand.

"He doesn't deserve our grief. Not after everything he's done."

"I don't give a fuck about him. I wanted to make sure you're okay. I know that wasn't easy."

Elias turns, his face full of anguish. "He made my life miserable as a kid. Killing him *was* easy because I needed to do it for my own closure. I'm sorry I wasn't there for you that night twenty years ago."

"I thought you always hated me for killing Mom. I thought you wished I had died instead."

Elias's eyes glaze over with tears.

"I never... Lance-a-lot... I hated *myself.*" He rubs his large hand over his face. "I hated that you were the one forced to do it. I was the big brother. I should have been there to protect you. It should have been me, not you."

I walk to Elias and place a hand on his shoulder. "It shouldn't have been either of us."

"I'm sorry I let you believe... I'm sorry. I love you. I always have. I've been punishing myself for that night, and I dragged you into my suffering."

I bring him in for a hug, and he freezes at the move. Neither of us are used to such sentimental gestures. But he relaxes and melts into me after a few seconds.

I hear Noah sniffling behind us, and I pull away from my brother.

"That's so sweet," she sobs.

"What?" Sage screams from the top of the stairs. "What am I missing? Someone fill me in."

Elias and I help Noah walk over debris so we can get the fuck out of here.

"Are all of Percy's guys dead?" Noah asks. "How many people knew he was still alive?"

"And why the fuck did you blow us up? You could have killed us."

Elias scowls at my tone. Always the disapproving big brother.

"We caught a couple of them for questioning. Hopefully, we'll have answers soon," he says. "And we didn't blow you up. This place was rigged with explosives. One went off during the gunfight when we first arrived."

"I can't believe you brought Sage here," Noah scolds my brother. "She could have died."

"Are you kidding me?" Elias scoffs. "You think I had a choice?"

"I can hear you guys talking about me," Sage says at the top of the stairs as we carefully make our way up. "I wasn't letting him leave without me. Literally locked myself inside his car. Besides, I was the one who knew where you were. He had to bring me."

"How *did* you know where to find us?" I ask, suspicious. I don't think Noah could take anyone else betraying her, especially from her best friend.

"Noah and I installed apps on our phones to track each other at all times."

"Right. I forgot we did that."

"Seriously, Noe?"

She shrugs. I hate anything that would make her vulnerable, like apps that could track her location, but she clearly doesn't seem concerned. Sage is her best friend who she inadvertently brought into our world. She wanted assurances that she'd be able to locate her in case of a situation like this. I don't know shit about technology, and I refused to have my hacker friend install anything on her phone, but of course she found a way.

"I texted you about hanging out, but you didn't answer right away, which is normal if you're with Del because you two fuck all the time." I smile, proud of myself for Sage knowing how much I keep Noah's pussy aching. "I had a bad feeling, so I checked your location. You were heading into Queens, which I thought was weird. You never go that deep into Queens. I called, and you didn't answer. I panicked and called Boss, um, Elias."

Oh, they have nicknames for each other now?

"Once Sage gave me the location," Elias says, narrowing his eyes at the woman, "I knew exactly where you were heading. This was our childhood home. A part of me never believed Percy died. Him getting sick and refusing to let us see him on his deathbed always rubbed me the wrong way. Then there was one night a year ago when I swore I saw him. I thought I was losing my mind, seeing ghosts.

"So, when I found out this is where Noah was being taken, I sent in a few soldiers ahead to scope out the place. One of them spotted Percy through the basement window."

"Fuck," I whisper. "At least you were mentally prepared. They drugged me, and I woke up thinking I had died and gone to hell and Percy was the devil."

Noah hugs her best friend once we emerge from the basement. There are QBM soldiers everywhere.

"Are we sure none of these people are traitors?" I carefully scan the men and women in the room, looking for any signs of deceit.

Elias shrugs. "I think they would have made their move by now."

"Are you okay?" Sage asks Noah, noticing her shoulder.

"Yeah, don't worry about me. I've had it worse."

Sage frowns. "I'll always worry about you."

Her eyes trail to Elias.

"Thank you for saving them," she says, tucking her blonde hair behind her ear.

I can see Elias struggling not to go to her. To pull her into his arms. He doesn't though, and I wonder how long this resistance between the two will last.

"Cops are on their way. You two should go," Elias says.

"I'll stay with you," Sage offers, and I almost laugh at my brother's face. I've never seen him shocked. Glad he's found a woman to keep him on his toes.

Well, found, but has yet to convince her to be with him.

"Your father called me after he couldn't get a hold of either of you," Elias says as we all head to the door. "He told me about the strange call and text, which I assume came from Percy?"

"Yeah, he was trying to lure Gio here. I bet that's what the explosives were for," I say. "He was going to level this place with him inside."

Elias nods in agreement, turning his attention back to Noah. "He was in the Bronx, and it was going to take him too long to get here so I told him I was closer, and I'd check it out. You should call him back. He's worried."

Noah turns to me. "Let's head back to the townhouse. I'll tell Gio to meet us there. It's time I finally confront him about all this."

I point my thumb over my shoulder. "There's a guy downstairs. Lenetti's head of security went rogue. He was working with Percy. Save him for us, okay?"

Noah's face lights up at the unspoken promise of my words. I'm sure she wants to kill Matthew as much as I do.

So, we'll do it together.

I wrap my arm around her waist and kiss her temple.

We walk out of my old childhood home, and I turn around to stare at the faded and peeling paint, the vines snaking up the sides, the broken or cracked glass windows. I thought seeing this place again would bring back memories, both good and bad. Instead, a sense of closure washes over me. This home is no longer mine. I've held onto this trauma for far too long. It shaped me, defined my past and present, but as for my future... only one woman matters.

My fake fiancée. Would she want to be my real fiancée? I suppose I don't need a piece of paper or glitzy jewelry to tell me she's mine.

Marriage is outdated and dumb and—Noah would look fantastic in a flowing white dress, her hair up in an intricate style, or falling down her back in curls. What color would she dye it? A stark white to match the dress? Though she'd probably choose a black dress.

Oh... Noah with black hair.

"Del, look!" Noah gasps and points.

A butterfly perches on my shoulder. That's strange. It's winter. We just had snow the other day. Butterflies are dormant during cold months. However, today is warmer. The blue and black wings sparkle in the rays of the setting sun. Did it emerge for me?

"I think your mom sent it to you."

I smile and nudge the butterfly onto my finger. It flaps its wings a few times before flying away.

"Do you think it means joy or change?" Noah asks.

"Change."

"How do you know?"

"Because I've been dying to ask you—"

"Technically, I'm the one who almost died."

I grab Noah by the waist and tug her body against mine. My lips brush over hers. "Will you marry me?"

She smiles against my mouth.

"I thought you'd never ask."

Chapter 30

Noah

It takes us nearly an hour to get to the Lower East Side from Fresh Meadows, Queens. My eyes struggle to stay open. Adrenaline has been pumping through my body for the past few hours and now I'm crashing. I also lost a lot of blood from being shot.

After Del proposed and I said yes, he kissed me until I was nearly out of breath. He only held back from fucking me in the backseat because my wound was still bleeding.

I called my father to tell him I was okay, and I'd explain everything once he meets us back at the townhouse. He was in the Bronx overseeing a large gun shipment with a new supplier when he got Percy's call. He dropped everything to head to Queens but didn't get far because of traffic.

"This is it," I say. "I'm going to confront my father about the Christmas Eve murders and my mother's death."

Del wraps his arm around my shoulders and tugs me to his body before kissing the top of my head.

I have time to shower once we get to my father's. Del joins me and helps me wash my body and hair. He dries me off, then stitches my bullet hole.

He loves taking care of me.

Because he's perfect. I can't believe I'm going to marry him. I never imagined wanting to willingly devote myself to one person, let alone a man.

Del sits on the bed while I change into a t-shirt and leggings. He's holding a book in his hand when I walk out of the closet.

"Oh! My mom's book!"

"*Deadly Deceit*. I was reading the back. It sounds good. Creepy similar to what we just went through though," Del says, handing me the small paperback.

"Right? I was planning on reading it but left it here and forgot."

I flip through the pages and a piece of paper falls out. I crouch down to pick it up.

"It's from my mom's journal... it's her handwriting."

My hands start shaking, my heart hammering against my chest.

"My brilliant star," I begin, reading her words out loud. "I hope you know how much I love you and if you're reading this, then I'm no longer with you. I know how much you wanted to read one of my romance books, so

I'm hoping you find this in time to escape. Your father, as you likely know by now, is the Don of the Empire Mafia. He's led the organization since we moved to New York City fifteen years ago... well before you were born. But he's changed. He's become greedy for power. I overheard him talking about putting hits on the wives and children of his rivals: the Queensboro Mob and the Lords of Staten Island. Innocent women and children. I could not condone this and when I confronted him about it and threatened to take you away and go into hiding, he got angry. I never thought he would harm me, but now I'm not so sure. I told him I'd stay, that I wouldn't take you away. I'm writing this note to let you know that I lied. Our bags are already packed, but if something happens, and we don't make it out, I'm hoping you find this note and you leave... escape this life."

It ends there, and I wonder if she was interrupted or in a hurry and couldn't finish. I remember seeing my bag packed in my room the night she died. I thought it was strange but didn't question it, thinking maybe one of my father's staff had packed it at some point.

"He did it," I say, my voice shaking. "He put out the hits on the other mobs."

"It's true," my father says, appearing in the doorway of my room.

"What the fuck?" Del seethes. "How long have you been there listening to us, Lenetti?"

"A while."

Del takes my arm and moves me slightly behind him. Protecting me, as usual. My father frowns at the move. I expected him to be mad about me finding this out, but instead, he looks sad.

"Why?" I cry out, tears claiming my voice.

"We are the mafia, mio angelo" my father says solemnly. "We kill every day. We leave wives without their husbands, fathers without their sons, children without their parents. It is nothing but business. It's something you will have to do when you take over."

I shake my head. "That's not how I will run this organization. That's not who I am. I would never kill the one I loved."

"I never meant for your mother to die. She found out my plan. She was going to take you away. I panicked, so I called the men I hired to take down the Lords and QBM. They were only supposed to scare her. They weren't supposed to kill her or go after you. They went off orders. I'm sorry, Noah. Those men weren't professionals. I found them through the black market and paid them a lot of money for their furtiveness."

I scoff, crossing my arms over my chest. Tears wet my cheeks, but I don't wipe them away.

"Didn't you think the other mobs would have figured it out? If all the Dons' wives and children were killed but yours wasn't?"

"I was hoping they'd find out. It was a power move. I wanted them to fear me. Show them why the Empire should be the only mafia in New York City."

"All that death and for what? The Empire never gained sole power, and you're certainly not the best. At least, not anymore. Was it worth it?"

He stares at me, not answering for several seconds. "I'm sorry your mother had to die."

That's it? He only regrets that my mother died?

"Did you know those same men forced Lance to slit his mother's throat?"

My father starts at the words.

"Then they chased him, stabbed him, and left him for dead."

"I'm sor—"

"What you did to Del and his family... to me... we will never get over that trauma."

"I know mio angelo."

I turn to Del and hold out my hand. He knows what I'm asking for.

"Let me do it, Noah," Del whispers.

I shake my head. It has to be me.

Del gives me a curt nod and places a gun in my palm.

I raise it, pointing it at my father.

"You're not going to kill me," Gio says, though his face betrays his words. He's not so sure I won't pull the trigger.

"I won't?"

"I know you are Colpa Sicario. But I'm your father. You love me. You won't kill me."

I don't know *how* he figured that out. I was always so careful. I could ask, but that would just delay the inevitable.

"If you know I'm a contract killer, surely that means you know I've killed people for the bad things they've done. And you're amongst the worst."

He closes his eyes and nods.

"You're not going to call your men in here? Stop me from doing this?"

A single tear drips down his cheek and he swallows hard.

"If you're going to hate me for the rest of my life, then no. I couldn't bear it."

The silence in the room is deafening. I at least expected him to fight for his life, but for him to just accept he's going to die? That his daughter will be the one to end him?

It pisses me off.

"Just know," he begins, "I'm proud of you. For never giving up on finding your mother's killer. You're ready to lead the Empire."

"Fuck the Empire," I say and fire the gun.

Chapter 31

Noah

"**A**re you sure you're up for this?"

Del asks, following me to the bathroom as I finish getting ready. I stand in front of the mirror, staring at my puffy red eyes.

"You've barely grieved," he continues, watching me wet my toothbrush and squeeze minty toothpaste on the bristles.

It's been a week since I killed my father. The shock didn't set in until a few hours after once the adrenaline had died down. I cried even though I willed myself not to.

I cried for the memories before I knew my father was a horrible man.

I cried for his victims.

I cried for the man who chose greed and power over his family.

Then I cried for myself because I killed my father.

He deserved a worse death. He deserved to suffer for all the things he did. But I had to be the one to end his life. I wasn't strong enough to torture him. I should have let Del do it. I owed him at least that for all the years he spent seeking vengeance for his mother's death.

When I apologized for Gio's quick death, Del held me and let me disappear into my grief.

He doesn't resent me as I feared. He respects me. He sympathizes with me.

Because now we have something in common.

We've both killed a parent.

"It will get easier. What you're feeling."

My eyes lazily fall to Del as he leans against the doorframe to the bathroom of the Brooklyn loft. He's dressed in black from head to toe, arms crossed, as he stares back at me with concern.

"Guilt, right?"

I give him a terse nod and finish brushing my teeth. Once done, I turn to face him. Del cups the side of my face and swipes his thumb over my cheek. I close my eyes at his touch because he always has a way to make me feel safe and loved and wanted.

"You're stronger than you realize, you know?"

He scoops me up in his arms and kisses me. Soft yet possessive... just enough to have me yearning for more when he pulls away.

"We can let Matthew suffer one more day if you need more time."

I smile and tug at his shirt for another kiss. This time it's devouring. Del's tongue sweeps in and massages my own. His arms wrap around me, squeezing me against his body. I bury my hands in his hair while his hands roam down to my ass. He grabs my cheeks generously, and I moan into his mouth.

"I've been looking forward to this for days. I'm so fucking wet just thinking about it," I whisper against his lips. "Will you fuck me in front of him?"

Del responds by grinding his cock into my stomach.

"I was hoping you'd let me."

With one more peck, Del releases me.

"Let's go fuck him up."

We take Del's motorcycle out to Queens to St. Orion's Cemetery in Fresh Meadows—the cemetery where his mother is buried. The place is nearly condemned, overgrown grass scales the gates surrounding the hallowed ground. Vines wrap around the metal and snake up the bricks of the bordering wall. Inside is just as bad. Gravestones are covered in dirt and grime, many hidden by the tall grass.

Del leads me towards the center of the cemetery to a mausoleum. The gray cement has been stained brown with wear and tear over the years. We pass between two circular columns to a metal door that's covered in rust.

Inside the burial chamber, the ground has caved in and spiderwebs line the corners and the ceiling.

"If I get bitten by a spider and die, I will be pissed."

I hate spiders. They're creepy with their eight legs and a bajillion eyes.

"I'll protect you, Vixen."

He kisses my temple before passing the crypt in the center.

"Goddamn, you smell," Del says to Matthew, who's gagged and tied up in a chair at the back. "Tired of pissing and shitting yourself, traitor?"

Matt narrows his eyes and squirms in the seat.

"You've been busy," I say, scanning Matt from head to toe. He has a black eye, busted lip, and stab wounds all over his chest and arms. He's been here for the past week, allowing Del and Elias to beat and torture him for information about his revenge against my father.

I worried about them being discovered here, but Del assured me he had guards around the clock. He also said no one comes into this part of the cemetery anymore.

"I've been wanting to kill this fucker since the moment he stuck his cock in your mouth."

Speaking of cock... I grab Del's bulge and stand on my toes to kiss him. His dick twitches underneath my hold.

Matt squeals at our teasing, attempting to break free only for the binds securing him in place to tighten around his wrists and ankles.

"Tell me he's been a bad boy so we can punish him," I say, brushing my lips across Del's jaw.

I nibble my way down his neck and bite down. He groans and twirls me around, folding me over the marble of the crypt. There's no body inside, I made sure he chose an empty mausoleum to torture and kill Matt, so as not to disrespect the dead.

"He's been very bad, Rainbow Bright," Del says, pulling down my black pants and panties.

He holds me down by the hair, my face smashed against the cold stone. The head of his cock presses against my pussy, and I suck in a sharp breath.

"He's confessed everything. Now he gets to watch us fuck for his punishment."

I scream when Del thrusts into me, staying seated to the hilt while letting me adjust.

"Eyes open, Matty," Del says and holds my hands behind my back for leverage as he starts pounding into me.

"Fuck, yes, Delancy," I moan, and he picks up speed.

His hand crashes down on my ass, and my pussy chokes his cock in response. He hisses and spanks me again.

"Yeah, sweetheart, you love the pain," he groans, pumping his hips hard enough that the marble digs into my front thighs.

"I need more, please. Choke me and call me a slut," I beg.

He drops his hold on my wrists and wraps his hands around my neck, pulling me up off the marble as he drives into me.

"Pinch your nipples, slut. Show Matthew what a whore you are for my cock."

I do as I'm ordered and slip my hands underneath my shirt and take my aching nipples between my fingers, pinching as hard as I can. Pleasure ripples throughout my body and Del chokes me harder until I struggle to breathe.

He's not holding back, fucking me in a near feral way. A sex starved man despite us having sex last night before bed.

"Touch yourself, Vixen," Del says, his voice wavering as he gets close to his release.

My fingers graze my clit, and I buck at the sensation. When I press down and massage the swollen nerves, I explode into an orgasm.

Del fucks his way through until he's coming too.

It takes a few minutes to catch our breath. Del lays on top of me while I'm sprawled out, chest and stomach flat on the crypt.

When he pulls out of me, his cum leaks out and he swipes it up with his finger.

"Does Matt want a taste?"

Matt shakes his head, his whines muffled by his gag.

"He doesn't deserve it," I say and grab hold of Del's wrist. "Besides, this cum is mine."

I wrap my mouth around his finger and lick it clean.

"Such a good little slut," he whispers and kisses me.

Del helps me pull up my pants then digs in his backpack for our knives. We approach Matt, and his eyes widen. He thrashes in the chair, shrieking again.

"Now that you've seen our sex show," Del begins, "it's time for the encore."

Del tugs down the gag and points the knife at his neck.

"Tell Noah everything."

"Fuck you," Matt growls.

"Now, now," Del tsks. "We've already done that. The faster you confess, the sooner you can die."

"I already told you everything."

"And now you tell Noah."

He's breathing hard, his heart surely pounding against his chest from the adrenaline coursing through his body. He's about to die, after all.

"The moment your father found out you were moving back, he pulled me aside. He wanted to make sure you found a safe place to live since you went against his order to move into the townhouse. I followed you the day you arrived when you were touring apartments. You wanted something under the table, right?"

I nod, crossing my arms and leaning my ass against the crypt where Del just fucked me.

"You stopped inside a coffee shop, and I sent in one of Percy's guys to post a notice on the board inside, do you remember that?"

I gasp. "No way."

Del looks at me, confused.

"It was a rental notice. I stopped the man before he walked out to ask him about it. He told me his tenant broke their lease and moved out and he needed someone to take over ASAP at a discounted rate. I wanted a cheap, low-key place that would let me pay cash and not run my credit. Off the books, you know. And it was in neutral territory, which was even better."

"I guess that explains what happened to my neighbors," Del says. "I thought it was strange they moved out so suddenly."

"Noah's father offered them a lot of money to move out," Matthew explains. "Of course, Gio didn't know I was working with Percy. I needed Noah to move next to you for our plan to work. Easier to track you both."

Del scoffs. "Percy tried to make it sound like I had been the one to put Noah on his radar when it was you the whole time."

Matt shrugs. "And then he watched as you obsessed over her and stalked her. It infuriated him that you fell in love with the enemy's daughter. So, he told me to blow up Noah's apartment."

"You gave those men my keys, didn't you?" I ask.

"Yep."

"Asshole," I say and stab Matt in the stomach. He bends over and wheezes at the pain.

"Fucking bitch!"

Del whips Matt across the face with the back of his knuckles, causing his eyes to roll back into his head.

"Stay awake, fucker." Del slaps his cheeks and Matt flutters his eyes open. "Why did my father fake his own death? Why didn't he just come to us with this plan for vengeance against Lenetti? We could have helped him."

Matt's voice is strained as he struggles with the pain from the stab wound. Still, he answers. He's ready to get this over with and die.

"Because he hated you, Del. For what you did to Imogen."

Del takes a pair of cutting pliers from the backpack and chops off Matt's ring finger.

He screams, tears streaming down his face from the pain. Snot drips out of his nose and spit dribbles down his chin. "Fuck you, man," he wheezes.

"Keep talking, asshole."

"He... he didn't want yours or Elias's help. He wanted to kill Lenetti himself, but he couldn't do that while heading the QBM. He couldn't risk a mafia war. He faked his death so he can plan out his revenge on Lenetti."

"How did you meet up with Percy?" Del growls, grabbing Matt by the hair when his head lulls to the side.

"He found me."

"How?" Del growls.

"I wanted Gio dead too," Matt says, his voice raw and strained. "My father, Lawson, was an Empire soldier until he got sick. Lenetti let him retire as long as I took his place. I was only eighteen. I didn't want to join the fucking mafia. I was pissed that my father agreed to this, but I had to do it or Gio would have killed me and the rest of my family.

"A few months after the Christmas Eve murders, I overheard Lenetti talking about what he'd done. He was proud, the sick bastard. So, I snooped around and eventually found files on the men Gio hired to kill the wives and children of his rivals. At least, I assumed they were the men responsible. It had their pictures and names and their skills listed. Addresses too. That's it. I anonymously sent Percy the files with a note saying Lenetti hired them, hoping he'd investigate and start a mafia war. When nothing happened, I accepted that I was stuck as an Empire soldier for the rest of my life."

"How did you get the files?" Del asks.

Matt's lips form into a lazy smirk. "Did you know my dad taught me how to pick locks and break into safes? Gio's safe was a challenge, but I managed to break in within ten minutes. He had the files in there, like an idiot."

"What about the Lords? Why didn't you send Finn the files too?" I ask.

"I did but either he didn't get them, or he didn't care. Or maybe he thought it was a setup."

Matt coughs up blood, his face turning pale.

"Okay, speed it up. Can't have you dying before you explain the rest. Get to the part about working with Percy."

He wheezes a few times before continuing.

"My father was a lifelong smoker and he had emphysema. That's why he left the Empire. He was too ill to be of any use. After a few months, he became depressed and bored, so he'd spent his days gambling online. He'd go broke then beg Lenetti to lend him enough money to cover rent. He kept borrowing and could never pay it back. Gio had enough. He ordered my sister and mother to be killed as payment. He didn't even care that I was one of his top soldiers. I begged him to let me pay off my father's debt. All that got me was a beating for interfering with his order."

Goddamn it, Gio. Tears well in my eyes. I really do feel sorry for Matt. He didn't deserve all the things that happened to him. He never asked for this life.

"Their deaths were the final straw. I wanted revenge, but I couldn't risk reaching out to Elias and getting caught by Lenetti. One night, I went to this bar on the Lower East Side. I was planning to get wasted and jump off the Brooklyn Bridge. I had nothing else to live for. That's when I met Percy. He'd been keeping tabs on the Empire. He knew what Gio had done to my family.

"We spoke for hours, and I told him Noah was alive. That's when... we formed... our plan..." Crap, Matt's slurring his words. He's about to pass out. "To bring down... the Empire."

And he's out.

"Dead?"

Del feels for a pulse and shakes his head.

"I'm about 99.9% sure Matthew is the one who invited Elias to my father's Christmas party," I say and Del nods.

Elias said he only accepted because the invite stated it was a neutral night of festivities—it wasn't. He'd planned to make connections at the party, try to steal some of my father's powerful contacts for the QBM.

Perhaps that's what Matthew and Percy had also planned. They knew Elias would accept and use the opportunity to help the QBM grow. Elias swears he had no idea.

I bet Matt also sent Finn our photos outing us as Colpa and the Marionette. I wondered how he figured out I was Colpa Sicario. Though, my father figured it out, so maybe that's how Matt knew too.

"Hey!" Del screams into Matthew's face and slaps his cheeks hard enough that Matt's eyes pop back open.

"Is that it?"

Matt nods and tries to close his eyes again.

"Wait," I say and move to stand in front of Matt. I grip his hair to hold his head up. "Are you sorry? For what you did to us?"

"Fuck no. I'd do it again," he wheezes. "Kill me, you bitch."

"Well, that helps my decision," I say.

"What decision?"

"I was considering keeping him alive."

"Seriously?"

"Don't judge me! I was feeling sorry for him. He was screwed over by my father more than once. He reacted like you or I would have. We can't fault him for that."

"Don't pity me, cunt," Matt says and laughs. "I should have killed you myself."

Before I can respond, Del sinks his knife into the side of Matt's head.

"Asshole," Del mumbles. "God, I hated him."

"You were just jealous of him."

"Jealous of what? He wanted you, but you were never going to be his. You're mine. Only mine."

"God, I love you," I say with a laugh.

Del's eyes widen. "I think that's the first time you've said those words to me."

"Officially?" I smile and bite my lip. "Yeah, I guess you're right."

"Say them again."

"I love you, Delancy William Carter."

"You know William isn't my middle name, right?"

"I know! You never told me, so I made one up. What is it?"

"Gene. My mother wanted me to have a middle name similar to Imogen."

Delancy Gene Carter.

I think I like William better. But I know Gene is special to him so, Gene it is.

I scan the mausoleum. Matt's blood leaks into puddles below him and blood splatter covers mine and Del's hands and face.

"Time to clean up?"

"No need. I'm going to bury him in the ground right over there where it's caved in."

"And you're sure no one will find him?"

Del pulls me into an embrace and places a soft kiss on my lips before leaning back to move a piece of hair out of my face.

"I forgot to tell you. I bought the cemetery. I'm going to get it cleaned up and keep the grounds maintained for all the families whose loved ones are buried here."

"You're a good man Delancy Gene Carter."

"How do you feel about burying both of our fathers here in this spot with Matthew?"

"That's smart. Poetic justice of sorts. All the men who caused us pain, who tried to kill us, who died by our hands, buried in one place."

"Exactly. And after I tear down this mausoleum, we'll pour cement on top of their graves and build a monument or statue in honor of our mothers."

"It's a great idea," I say and give Del a quick peck on the lips. "Alright, let's get to work."

I start cutting the zip ties holding Matt to the chair while Del clears out the rocks from the caved ground.

"We should go out for pizza after this. I'm really craving a slice of pineapple and ham."

"That's it. You're dead."

Epilogue:
Delancy

A Few Months Later

The crime world of New York City has changed.

No more Empire. No more Lords. No more QBM.

Three organizations, formed because greedy men desired power, died because of that greed and entitlement.

Noah's father must have known his daughter was going to kill him or maybe he kept his will up-to-date. He left everything to her. His money, which she either donated or handed over to the FBI—to secure herself connections with very powerful people. His townhouse, which she turned into a domestic abuse shelter. His businesses, which she sold for pennies to some of the families Gio wronged.

As for the men who murdered Noah's mother... there were three men that night, not two. Noah only saw two because the third was on the lookout at the door. They were the same men who showed up at my family's home the next night. The same men who I tracked down and killed years later.

The only thing we never figured out is what took Gio away on Christmas day. Noah says he was just being an asshole.

"Are you ready?" she asks, exiting the bathroom in a black sparkling gown to match her black hair. "The traffic into the city is going to be horrible tonight."

We moved into a house with a white picket fence in the suburbs of Westchester County.

Our corgi, Kevin, runs up to Noe, hopping on his short stubby legs, begging to be pet.

"Do we have to go?" I whine, adjusting my tuxedo jacket.

"Yes."

She walks over to where I stand—almost as tall as me in those fuck me heels— and leans in for a kiss. It's too quick, and I consider grabbing her by the waist and holding her hostage in my arms until our mouths are raw from kissing.

My brother is hosting a fundraiser and networking event for his new organization. The Five Boroughs Alliance. FBA. Or just, simply, the Alliance. He considered attaching his name to his crime syndicate calling it the

Cartel Cabal and even the Carter Cartel, but I advised him to keep it neutral, especially after word spread about Percy's resurrection... and his subsequent death.

He was wise to listen to me. Not that I'm his underboss or his consigliere.

Noah and I agreed to take a step back from all crime syndicates. Instead, we're going to travel and focus on us. And our new business venture.

We're pairing up to continue killing assholes who deserve it, but we'll be doing it as a team.

I wonder what we'll be called.

Will our names be merged?

Colpa and the Marionette?

Sicario's Marionette?

Maybe they'll call us Puppet and Master. Or the Puppeteers. No, wait... that sounds like a children's show.

It doesn't matter, because we're finally free to do what we want.

Elias has his new mighty mafia to lead, comprised of soldiers from the Empire and QBM—no Lords since they were all killed or went into hiding.

He's even got the girl... I think. Their relationship is weird, so I don't know.

And I have my rainbow bright.

"What if we skip the event and fuck instead?" I offer, but Noah frowns.

"This is an important night for your brother. Be happy for him. You two are finally mending your relationship."

I hate it when she's right.

"Look, I promise tonight will be worth it," she adds, and I raise an eyebrow.

"What are you up to, Vixen?"

She closes her eyes and hums at the nickname. Her favorite, I've learned.

She adjusts my tie and clutches onto my tux jacket to tug me closer. "I found someone to peg you while you fuck me."

I narrow my eyes at her. As fun as that sounds, I'm quite territorial over Noah. Would she risk bringing in a third party to the bedroom again?

She bursts into laughter.

"I'm just kidding, but it will happen, Delancy Gene Carter. I want to feel your cock inside me while you're getting reamed."

My dick jerks at the words. Fine, I want that too. I want *her* and if this will make her happy, I'll gladly do whatever she asks of me.

"I booked a job for us."

Now that deserves a smile.

"Us? Like, you and me?"

She nods, biting her lip. "It's in London next week. A man running a child trafficking ring out of an orphanage."

My blood boils. Oh, I am going to enjoy killing this man.

"We'll show up as a hopeful couple wanting to adopt, then we'll get the man alone and—"

She runs her thumb across the front of her neck.

Kill him.

"And what about the kids in the orphanage? What happens to them? Or the ones who were sold?"

"I've already lined up adopters for most of them. The ones who were sold are being tracked down now. We're going to spend the next few weeks killing off the buyers. I mean, not all of them are bad, but I'd say the majority of them are."

"You've been busy, Kevin," I say and wrap my arms around her waist, pulling her body against mine.

Kevin, the dog, barks and I roll my eyes. I hate that Noah wanted to name him that because now I can't use it to rile her up. She knew exactly what she was doing.

"After we do this job, we'll spend a couple weeks playing tourist across the UK."

She's finally getting to visit Scotland.

"Now," Noah begins, running her palms up and down my chest, "let's get this over with so we can come back and fuck."

"God, I love you, Vixen."

"I love you more, Puppet."

"Impossible."

"Undeniable."

And with that, she peels herself out of my arms and walks away, glancing over her shoulder to make sure I'm following.

I'll follow her through hell and high water.

My rainbow bright.

The End

Thank You!

Did you enjoy Noah & Delancy's story? Please consider leaving a review!

Goodreads

Amazon

What's next? Sage & Elias's book, Deadly Obsession, is out now.

Acknowledgements

This book was darker than anything I've ever written. It wasn't a dark romance, but there were dark themes. I'm the type of person who is happy and funny, but sometimes life can challenge my silly, goofy mood and I don't always have enough energy to smile or laugh. This book is for people like me who can't always wear a mask.

I am so grateful to be able to continue writing plus-size main characters who are openly sexual. Big bodies deserve to be loved, worshiped, fucked. My male main characters will always love their bodies and appreciate the FMCs for who they are no matter what the cruel world has to say about it. Elias & Sage's story will feature two plus-size main characters, so I really hope this book does well so I can tell their story!

I want to thank my alpha readers Jordan Grant & Xan Garcia. My beta readers Gina Hejtmanek, Candice Hume, and Lexie Eldridge. Your critiques helped bring this story to life and fix all the things I missed.

To my editor, Jenny. Again, sorry about the commas. They are evil. My favorite mistake she caught: I called a toilet a cement throne instead of a porcelain throne.

To Kate Farlow with Y'all That Graphic. Thank you for making a beautiful discreet cover for the paperback!

Also by Settle Myer

Guardians for the Vamp

A Manhattan Monsters Romance

FFM with a Vampire/Sphinx/Gargoyle

The monsters of Manhattan are tired of living in the shadows. The new vampire queen, Layla, is tasked to come up with an unveiling plan, but she finds herself distracted by her new broody gargoyle guard... and the bossy sphinx on the unveiling committee. Find it on Amazon & KU.

Gaga for the Gargoyle

A Fated Mates Monster Romance.

Gaga for the Gargoyle is about 999-year-old gargoyle king, Xander, who has 6 months to find his fated mate before permanently turning to stone. Enter a strange dating app that pairs him with Evangeline, a 40-year-old human. This book is part of the Fated Dates series, a shared world about plus-size MCs meeting their monster mates through a mysterious dating app. Find it on Amazon & KU

A Vow for the Vamp

A Manhattan Monsters Romance.

500-year-old vampire queen, Millie, is ready to face the sun, no longer able to live with the guilt of the monster she's become. When she goes out for one last feed, she meets a 29-year-old golden retriever man named Teddy... who just might be the reason she lives. It's on Amazon & KU

Deadly Deceit

A Rivals to Lovers Mafia Romance (New York City Syndicate Book 1)

Deadly Deceit is the first book in a standalone duet. It's a dark cozy romance meaning the romance is sweet... but the story includes dark themes. Find it on Amazon & KU

The Off Script Series

Beyond the Bright Lights is the first book in the Off Script series of spicy standalone contemporary romances. It features Lana & Mylan's story. Beyond the Fame is book two and features Rebecca & Jensen's story. Beyond the Spotlight is the third and final book and features Savannah & Reynold's story. Find them on Amazon & KU. Beyond the Bright Lights & Beyond the Fame are on Audible

The Trinity Trilogy

If you love action & adventure, badass women with superpowers, diverse characters, found family, and fated mates—check out my sci-fi romance trilogy. Book 1 is a sweet romance with some cursing and violence, but books 2 & 3 have a sprinkle of spice in them. Trinity Found,

Trinity Returns, Trinity Rises. Find them on Amazonand Audible.

Social Media

Check out my website and sign up for my newsletter for updates on new books, discounts, and sneak peeks!

https://www.settlemyerauthor.com/

Join my readers group. Become a Settle Myer Star and be a part of the discussion with other fans. I also posts fun facts about my books, characters, and more!

Follow me on social media

 tiktok.com/@settlemyerauthor

 instagram.com/settlemyerauthor

 facebook.com/settlemyerauthor

 twitter.com/settle_myer

About the Author

Settle Myer lives in New York City with her cats Zombie, Michonne & Birdie. She's currently a TV news writer who hopes to one day leave a world of death, disaster, and politics to write about worlds with plenty of forbidden romance, badass women with superpowers fighting violent villains. She loves all things zombies, cats, karaoke, and tattoos... but not necessarily in that order.